BOOK TWO OF THE BLOOD BORNE SERIES

REPLICA

BOOK TWO OF THE BLOOD BORNE SERIES

REPLICA

NY TIMES AND USA TODAY BESTSELLING AUTHORS

SHANNON MAYER
DENISE GROVER SWANK

CHAPTER 1

LEA

"Get out of my way, you nincompoops." I angled my shoulder to push through the group of gawking, laughing humans. Airports—even I needed a cattle prod to get through the crowds.

Using the points of my elbows, I forced them to make room for me until I was under the large-screen TV that had caught my attention. I looked up at Rachel's face, her mouth moving silently. Her hair was pulled back into a high ponytail, every strand in place. Makeup made her blue eyes look big, innocent and soft. I snorted to myself. That was a crock of shit—the girl was anything but soft, but I understood why they'd done it. To make what she was saying believable. Because the report would be anything but.

Someone cranked the volume as Rachel said the biggest, baddest, most unbelievable word of all.

"Vampires. They are real, they are dangerous, and our government has been using them for bioterrorism." Rachel's baby blues stared into the crowd, begging them to understand.

To believe.

She spoke of her friend Derrick, how he'd died finding the evidence she was now sharing with the world. Then she described the hidden bunker we had destroyed in New York City. Her voice dipped into husky tones as she described the monsters we'd found in the bunker and the terrible experiments that had taken place there. She was telling the truth; I'd been there with her. The explosion of the bunker, which had been front page news everywhere, was only more backing for the words she spoke with such passion.

I dropped my eyes to see how the humans around me were responding to Rachel's report. Their reactions were varied. Disbelief, shock, anger...laughter. The laughter caught on. At first only nervous titters, but it turned into full-on donkey braying. They laughed, but I saw the truth in their eyes.

They believed her.

"My friend, you are damn good," I whispered to myself. There were not too many reporters who could out the existence of a supernatural mythical being without convincing the masses she was handing out bullshit. But, typical of humans, the truth was too scary to deal with. It was easier to laugh it off. Even if they laughed marching to their own gallows.

I sensed the guy before his hand cupped my right ass cheek, making it look like he stopped me in my tracks. "What do you think, beautiful? You think vampires are real?" He squeezed harder; I turned slowly as I extended my fangs. Batting my eyes, I leaned into him, my dark hair sweeping forward to curtain my face.

I flashed him a toothy smile. "What do you think?"

He stumbled back as if I'd shoved him. I wished I had.

The groper was the least of my concerns; I was worried about the human world's reaction to Rachel's announcement.

The laughter continued and people drifted away from the TV. I walked through the terminal as my flight and ID were called again.

"FINAL BOARDING. LEA SMITH. PLEASE REPORT TO GATE 235 IF YOU ARE IN THE BUILD-ING."

Two weeks ago, I would have boarded this plane to go after Stravinsky. As the vampire who'd masterminded the inhumane experiments, the madman behind the terrorism, he needed to be staked. But two weeks ago, I wouldn't have been boarding this plane alone; Calvin would have been with me. Now I was bonded to Rachel—whether she realized it or not. Boarding this plane was a ruse to throw anyone watching off my trail so I could track who went after her, but part of me wanted to board anyway. The desire to kill Stravinsky was almost as strong as the bond I had with Rachel. Even if she didn't know it yet.

However, my allegiance had changed, as hard as that was to accept. I tugged the long gloves further up my arms, pulled my cowl over my head and stepped out of the airport and onto the street. I raised my hand and flagged down a cab.

Madre de Dios, Stravinsky should be my top priority. But seeing Rachel on the screen only confirmed I couldn't leave her alone to face the fallout from her report, which—judging from the reactions of the airport passengers—would be of the nuclear variety. Worse, I felt a tug toward her...like she needed me. I couldn't turn away from that gut instinct.

"Where you off to?" the cabbie asked.

"The Warner News station," I said, keeping my voice low and soothing. He nodded, a smile on his generous lips.

"You see the report on vampires?"

I blinked several times as I tugged the cowl closer around my head. That was fast. If word was already out on the street... "How did you hear about it?"

"Twitter is a wonderful thing. You know, I check everything that's hashtag vampire. I've been hoping something like this would come up." His green eyes swept up to the rearview mirror. "What do you think? You believe in the boogeyman?" He spoke flippantly as he steered the cab into traffic. I sat up so I could see his name badge on the dash.

"Ivan?"

"Yup, that's me. Shitty name, if you don't mind me saying so, but my mother's favorite uncle died young, and well, you get the picture." He smiled, and white, white teeth blinked back at me.

"Russian, isn't it?" I softened my words even more, a niggling suspicion at the back of my neck.

He nodded several times as he steered us through traffic. "Yeah, you good with nationalities?"

I dropped my voice further yet. A whisper of a whisper. "Yes. And where do you think I'm from, Ivan?"

His grin never faltered. "Well, it's hard to say with that dark hoodie on, but your voice has a bit of an accent. Maybe...Italy?"

"Close." I barely breathed the word out.

What kind of game was he playing? Or was I being too fucking jaded, yet again? I leaned back in my seat, but kept my hands at the top of my boots, where my silver stakes resided. They would work on supernaturals other than vampires...including what I suspected was Ivan's particular flavor of monster. His smell was distinct.

Like the smell of fresh snow and maple syrup.

We made it to the TV station without incident. Perhaps it should have told me something that when a simple car ride was quiet, I got...nervous.

I pushed the money through the slot in the plastic barrier, making sure my fingers brushed his. A flicker of energy snapped across our hands and his eyes shot to mine. He was far from harmless, but he wasn't the raving maniac so many of his kind ended up being.

A kid. He was a kid compared to my age.

Rachel wouldn't want me to hurt him, and that was the only thing that kept me from driving my stake through the plastic and into the back of his neck.

I lifted the corner of my mouth so he could clearly see a single fang. "Ivan, not only do I believe the boogeyman is real, I know him quite well. Or should I say, her?"

His mouth dropped open and he spluttered as I slid out of the cab.

Which was why it shouldn't have surprised me when he stepped out of the cab as well. "Wait, I want to talk to you."

I rolled my eyes, but didn't stop. "Go home to your kennel, Ivan."

He let out a snarl and whipped around in front of me.

11

Taller than me, his light green eyes were closer to chartreuse. A tattoo on his left collarbone peeked out from the V in his shirt. The hard edges of his jaw and muscular torso told me all I needed to know. He was an enforcer, good at keeping his people in line. I reached up and tugged his shirt down further. A pack tattoo. A simple maple leaf torn into four pieces with a wolf's tooth between each.

"Russian, indeed. This is a Canadian pack stamp. You running from someone?"

Ivan shrugged and grinned. "Maybe. You want to run with me?" He waggled his eyebrows in a ridiculous up and down movement. I refused to smile.

"Do you have any idea what you're suggesting, you idiot?" I put a hand on his chest and he leaned into it, a chuckle rumbling under my fingers.

He put his hand over mine. "I think so."

The flash of heat between us shocked me. My heart had been tied to Calvin for so long that the idea of being with anyone else...especially someone non-human... I pushed him hard enough to send him back a good ten feet. Which, when pushing his kind around, was saying something.

His grin never faltered. "I want to come with you. Wherever you're going, let me come."

I put two fingers to my forehead. Stubborn-ass werewolves. Once they set their minds on something, that was it. "I could kill you where you stand, drain you down and throw your body in the back of your cab to rot. Without blinking."

Ivan stretched his arms over his head and cracked his knuckles. His eyes never left mine. "You could try. There's a reason I was able to break free of my pack."

I strode past him. "If you follow me, I will kill you."

He fell into stride behind me. "I don't believe you. I think you like me."

I grabbed my stake and spun, aiming for his chest. He caught my forearm, stopping me. "Go away, mutt."

"I've heard it all, sweetheart. Everything and then some. You aren't going to scare me off."

Frustration snapped through me like the flickering of a lightning bolt. Brilliant, hot, and then gone with nothing more than a negative afterimage of what had been there. I did not have time for this shit.

I jerked my hand out of his. Or tried to. I jerked, he pulled and I was suddenly pressed against his chest, those chartreuse eyes staring down at me.

His eyes dipped to my mouth.

"Don't you fucking dare," I bit out, then snapped my teeth at him for good measure. A thread of panic curled over me. He would not kiss me. He wouldn't. He was a... and I was a...

He pulled his head back a few inches, though he didn't let me go. "I don't know your name, or at least not all of it."

That made no sense. I hadn't given him anything, either in the cab or out on the street.

Once more I jerked away from him, breaking free this time, turned my back and strode toward the news station. Rachel. I had to find her and get us both the hell out of here. The certainty that something was coming for her grew more and more. Which meant it was coming for us both.

Behind me, Ivan laughed softly, his footsteps telling me all I needed to know. The dumb-ass mutt wasn't giving up.

"I'm not telling you my name," I said over my shoulder.

He shrugged. "Then I'll call you the only thing I know."

Bitch. Bloodsucker. Vamp tramp. It wouldn't have surprised me for any of those derogatory names to have flowed from his mouth, spilling out into the street between us. What he said, though, could not have shocked me more than if he'd ignored my order and planted his lips to mine.

"I've been waiting to meet you, Cazador."

CHAPTER 2

RACHEL

The camera lights went off and the crew stood around the studio, their mouths open as they stared at me in disbelief. I knew it was a lot to take in. I knew there would be skeptics—how could there not be? If I'd been home watching my report, I would have been skeptical too. I was hardwired that way. But I could tell some of them did believe. They were looking at me with the same expression I'd seen on my boss Don's face when I'd approached him with the story.

Terror.

That was what had convinced him to give me airtime.

Once I'd presented my evidence, he believed me. The issue was making everyone else believe. I had spent forty-eight hours working nearly around the clock with the news team to get the story right.

I was exhausted and proud, but I was also grieving. Derrick had lost his life to bring this story to light. I hoped I'd made him proud. But I had to admit, I was also sad about losing Lea. She'd promised to come back, and while she didn't make promises lightly, she hadn't given me a time frame. For someone who had lived hundreds of years, a few days was nothing. For that matter, I suspected a few months was nothing too.

If only I'd convinced her to let me go with her to get Stravinsky.

But now wasn't the time to think about all that. I had to deal with the fallout of the report first.

One of the stage crew led me off camera as they set up for the next segment in another part of the stage. Kristin Schumacher, the Warner News five p.m. regular anchor, gave me a look that said she thought I'd lost it.

I headed down the hall to the green room, glaring at the people who snickered as I walked past. They wouldn't be laughing when the monsters came for them.

Don waited for me outside the green room, shifting his weight from leg to leg. We hadn't worked together much in person—most of the stories I'd sent him had been email attachments from the Middle East—but it didn't take a genius to see he was pissed.

"This is not going over well."

I walked past him into the green room to get my bag. "We knew we wouldn't convince everyone."

"I look like a fucking joke, Rachel."

I grabbed the strap of my bag and looped it over my

head. "We discussed this ad nauseam. Both of us knew it would be a hard sell. You saw the finished report. You showed it to your boss. You were totally on board. What happened?"

"Sponsors. That's what happened. We've ticked off Hudson Electric and they're a major sponsor."

"And Hudson Electric is a subsidiary of Monroe Industries, which is in bed with Simmons Industries." I shook my head, but I wasn't sure why I was surprised. I'd dug through more of Derrick's research. Simmons Industries had donated money to a *special* government project. "So what do they want?"

"They want us to issue a retraction. They want you to go on camera to admit you made it up."

"You told them to go fuck themselves, right?"

He was ashen, his eyes wide.

I put my hand on my hip. "Oh, my God. You actually want me to issue a statement saying I faked this whole thing."

"My job is on the line."

"And so is mine. We discussed this. We knew we'd face people who wouldn't believe it. You told me you had my back. I guess you forgot to add the caveat that you would only support me until the flames got too hot. Then you'd just throw me into the fire to save yourself."

"Rachel. I'm sorry." He sounded nervous, like he wasn't just worried about his job.

"You want me to do this—to throw away my career— so you can save face? Why on earth would I do that?"

"They'll discredit your father," he said quietly.

I took a step back. "*What?*"

"Your father was involved in an embezzlement case a couple of years before he died in the bank robbery

17

shootout. They'll release a report stating he planted evidence to get the conviction. The guy will walk and your father's memory will be tarnished."

My father had been a detective on the Dayton, Ohio police force—much loved by the community. Hundreds of people had shown up to his funeral, but while it'd helped to know our father was so well regarded, my four brothers and I had still suffered. Our mother had died years before him, so his death meant we were alone in the world.

My reaction had been to run off to college soon after his death, then immediately to Iraq to cover the war, but my eldest brother Michael had dealt with his grief by creating a charity in our father's honor. The program helped match troubled youth with mentors who put them back on the path to becoming productive members of society. If Dad's reputation were smeared, it would destroy everything.

"Those goddamned bastards."

"You have twenty-four hours to issue a statement of your own."

"Let me guess…Kristen is out there in front of the camera discrediting me right now."

He had to decency to look guilty. "I'm sorry."

"Save it for some other idiot who believes you." I shoulder-checked him as I stomped out the door and headed for the elevator bank.

Why was I so surprised? There was big money backing the Asclepius Project. It made sense they would go after me. Whoever was in charge of the mess knew exactly how to get me in line. Had my ex-boyfriend Sean filled them in? He'd always accused me of hero-worshipping my father and trying to live up to his expectations. Sean had always known exactly how to manipulate me like a puppet master with a puppet.

But I wasn't going to do it. Sometimes standing up for

what you believed in meant making sacrifices. This whole mess was a giant powder keg waiting to blow. Stravinsky and the military were nearly ready to unleash a weapon of mass destruction unlike any the world had ever seen. They weren't going to kill people. They were going to turn them into mindless monsters to attack everyone in their path. There was no way I was issuing a retraction when there were thousands of innocent lives on the line.

Standing up for what was right, no matter how much it hurt, was the best way to honor my father's legacy. I couldn't back down.

But my brothers had no idea what was coming, and I had to warn them. While I waited for the elevator, I pulled out my phone and called Michael.

"You've stirred up a big pile of shit," he shouted in my ear as soon as he answered the phone. I heard the hum of voices around him.

"You saw the report?"

"Saw it?" he barked. The background voices quieted. "Everyone came to Vincent's bar to watch. Half the damn neighborhood saw it."

I cringed. At five on a weeknight? The neighborhood where I grew up was full of blue-collar people and über conservative. "So you're catching a lot of flak, huh?"

"You have no idea the shit we're getting."

I pushed out a breath. "Well, it's about to get a whole lot worse." I ran my hand over my head, grabbing my ponytail out of habit. "There's big money behind this whole thing. They want me to denounce my story or they're going after Dad."

"Dad? How can they go after him if he's been dead for years?"

I told him what Don had said. My brother was silent for several seconds.

"Is it true?" he asked quietly. "Are they really doing those experiments?"

I leaned my back against the wall. "Yeah."

"And there really are vampires. You've seen them?"

I'd said that in the report, but I understood his need to hear confirmation from me. "Yeah. I've worked side by side with one. Lea. She helped expose this whole thing."

"Then don't you dare back down, Rachel Sambrook. You stand up and fight like your brothers taught you."

A lump filled my throat. "Thanks, Michael."

"You would have made Dad proud." His voice broke.

I took another breath to steady my voice. "I really wish Dad had told me that. Just once."

He released a soft chuckle. "You think he told any of us kids that to our faces? He worried we'd get swelled heads. But he used to tell everyone who'd listen his Rachel was going to grow up and face the monsters when she became a journalist. She was going to report corruption and save the world. So, no bullshit cover-ups. I'm telling you now, Rach—" his voice lowered, "—go fight those bastards. Your brothers have your back, and I will personally kick the ass of anyone who tries to discredit you."

"I don't know what to say, Michael. Thanks."

I heard someone calling his name. "Gotta go, Rach. When this is all done, don't be a stranger. Come home to visit. And you might want to bring a guy with you to appease Nana. She reminds all of us that you aren't getting any younger."

I laughed, suddenly homesick. "Yeah. I'll see what I can do." I hadn't been home since my college graduation. Maybe it was time.

"Go fight the monsters."

He hung up and the elevator opened a minute later. Thankfully the car was empty. I needed to prepare myself for the stares in the lobby. I was sure everyone was probably talking about my report now. If the investors in the Asclepius Project were this desperate for me to issue a retraction, they must have already set up a campaign to discredit me. And the best way to do that was to make me look like a lunatic.

I'd made it out the lobby and the front doors leading to Rockefeller Center when my phone rang. I checked caller ID, wondering if it was one of my other brothers, but the ID had been blocked.

I considered ignoring it, but worried it might be Lea. She should have been on the plane, about to take off, but what if something had happened? I wasn't taking chances.

"Hello?"

"Ms. Sambrook?"

My back stiffened. "Yes."

"I saw your report tonight. The one about the vampires and the monsters."

I steeled myself, ready to be insulted or threatened. "And?"

He chuckled softly. "I'm about to become your best friend."

CHAPTER 3

LEA

I van grinned down at me. "That *is* your title, isn't it?"

"How the hell do you know about Cazadors?" I wanted to take a step toward him, using my body as a threat. But really, getting close to the big wolf was not a good idea.

He shrugged and gave me a wink. "I have my sources."

I took a few steps back. Obviously he wasn't going to tell me what I wanted to know. I'd wasted enough time with him. I spun and strode toward the front doors of the TV station. I leaned against the bar in the middle of the glass door. Locked. Sitting at a desk directly across from me, a secretary filed her nails and chewed gum like she was working on her cud.

With the flat of my hand, I smacked the glass. "Open it."

"You know," Ivan breathed behind me, far too close to my ear, "if you ask nicely, they're more likely to do what you want. Humans are all about manners."

I inhaled slowly to steady myself, to keep my hands on the glass. Better than wrapping them around his neck. He leaned against the door beside me and knocked with one knuckle as he grinned at the secretary.

"That's not going to work—"

Before I could even finish getting the words out, the door to the left of me pushed open and the secretary peered out. "Is she with you?" She flicked her head my way while batting her eyes at Ivan.

A grin slowly spread across that mouth of his as he looked at me over her head. "I'm not sure."

Heat flushed through my body, which only pissed me off more. I grabbed the edge of the door and yanked it open. The secretary squeaked as I shoved past her and made my way into the station. I took a long slow breath and picked up Rachel's unique scent. Even under her perfume, the smell of gun oil lingered.

I couldn't help but smile. Good girl. Keep you friends close and your weapons closer.

"You can't go in there!" the secretary yelled after me. I kept moving, following Rachel's smell deeper into the station without looking back. I pushed through a pair of double doors onto a live set. There was a red light blinking like mad overhead, flashing the words *On Air* like we wouldn't otherwise notice the bright red neon.

No one even looked at me.

The anchorwoman smiled into the camera. "Again,

we apologize for the previous report. Rachel Sambrook is known for her pranks; we just had no idea our station would be center stage in her biggest stunt to date." Her eyes tightened, but the smile stayed plastered to her face. "Our station does not condone her choice of jokes, nor do we endorse her lies."

I couldn't help myself. I closed the distance between the anchor and me until I was just behind the camera. Her eyes flicked to me, away, and back again.

I grinned at her, wide enough that I knew my fangs were clearly visible. The woman paled and her hand went to her throat as she stuttered a strangled squawk. I turned and ran for the door, spanning the distance in less than a second.

She let out a screech. To her, it must have looked like I'd disappeared into thin air.

"Take that, dumb ass," I muttered to myself as I slipped out the door.

"You didn't like what she had to say?" Ivan was again, rather annoyingly, right there as I started down the hall. I spared him a glance and tried not to notice the curve of his biceps under his shirt. Too tight. His clothes were too tight.

"No."

"Why? You had to know they would discredit her."

It took all I had not to hunch my shoulders. I *had* known. And I'd let Rachel go into it anyway. In fact, I'd encouraged her to do this report.

"Holy shit, you're using her to flush them out, aren't you?"

Fuck, if he'd figured it out, Rachel would too. I had to get to her fast and explain.

"Our only way of reaching those who know about Stravinsky and want to help was to go wide. Rachel had

25

that reach. And they had to think I'd left her or they never would have approached her."

"If this is how you treat your friends, remind me not to get on your bitchy side."

We turned a corner. At the end of the hall a portly man with thinning hair was pacing and muttering under his breath.

"Rachel, you're a goddamn idiot. I should never have listened to you."

That was it, I'd heard enough Rachel-bashing for the day. I strode toward him, thumping my feet into the carpet hard enough for him to hear me coming.

He frowned and pointed at me. "Hey, you don't belong in here."

"Don't I? Didn't you just do a piece on vampires?"

"Ah, fuck me. Get out of here, you loony tunes. Vampires aren't real. The piece was a farce. A...political statement clearly hidden under..."

I snarled at him as my fangs descended. "What was that about vampires not being real?"

"Oh. Fuck," he whispered as he spun. I was on him in a second, yanking him with me down the hall as he squealed like a pig.

Ivan laughed and I glared at him. "What?"

"You really have a way with people, don't you?"

"Go the hell away, wolf."

"Not a chance. This is far too interesting." He followed me as I pushed the human into a tiny room. I flicked on a light and picked up the portly man, pinning him against the wall.

"Rachel isn't here," I said.

"No, no, she left. Please don't kill me," he whimpered.

I tightened my grip on him and leaned closer. "I haven't fed today."

"She's not here. I swear it!"

He kicked his legs feebly, then let out a groan. The sharp scent of urine wafted up between us. I glanced down at the wet spot on the front of his slacks.

Ivan let out a roar of laughter and slapped his hands on his thighs. "Really, this is how you get information? My beautiful creature of the night, you need lessons."

Ignoring him, I pulled the man off the wall and slammed him against it once, hard enough to rattle him.

"Where is she?"

"I don't..." His eyes flicked to mine, then he swallowed hard and shook his head. "No, you'll kill her."

Heaven help what was left of my soul. "I'm her friend, dumb fuck. The one who helped her gather the evidence. You're the one who hung her out to dry, aren't you?"

The words were as much for me as they were for him. I'd known what would happen, and I'd encouraged her anyway. All on the slim chance it would open the doors we needed to find Stravinsky. I should have come clean with her.

"The Hilton Hotel. On First," he breathed out. His eyes rolled back and he drooped in my hands. I let him fall to the ground in a puddle of his own piss.

"Good thing your cabbie stuck close, huh?" Ivan held the door open for me. Like we were on a date.

I would *not* smile at him. But my traitorous lips twitched as I walked past him, and maybe my hips swayed more than they should have. Damn him.

As we passed the receptionist's desk, the secretary glanced up and held a fluttering piece of paper out to Ivan. "I'm free on Saturday."

I snatched the paper and tore it in half. "He's not."

If Ivan had laughed right then, I would have cut his balls off and roasted them over an open flame. Our eyes met and his smile fell. "Shit, you're from zero to sixty in less time than it takes to shape shift."

"The cab." I pointed and he held the front door for me. And again when we reached the cab. I slid into the back-seat and put a hand over my eyes. The early evening sun wouldn't kill me, but it hurt like a motherfucker, and the longer I was in it, the more of my energy it drained.

"Why did you really take the paper from her? I know I intrigue you—it's all over your scent. But that's it, no lust even, and I must say it kinda hurts my feelings that I don't turn you on when I'm working so hard to make you notice me."

My jaw tightened. Thank God he hadn't noticed, or smelled, that I indeed had felt a spark of attraction.

"Because the less humans we interact with, the better. How do you think monsters are created? By accident?"

"No, but—"

"No buts. If you're going to come with me, you play by my rules. We don't play with the humans unless they are working with us and understand the stakes. The woman back there didn't. She thought she was going to get a din-ner, movie, and maybe some time between the sheets. She wasn't signing up to learn how to howl at the moon." I opened one eye to peer at him.

Ivan clenched the wheel, and the edge of his jaw ticked. "I'm not sloppy. I wouldn't have turned her."

"Everyone fucks up."

"Even you?"

I snorted. "Except me."

A few minutes later, we pulled onto the street opposite the entrance to the Hilton. Ivan put a hand to the door.

"Stop," I said. I leaned forward and watched the vehi-cles parked around the hotel. Three were of a color and style I recognized all too well. Government black. Men in dark suits and glasses sat in those three cars.

"She's being watched. Which means they probably have a description of me."

"And you don't exactly blend in, with your leathers and cowl."

I grimaced. He was right, and we both knew it.

"I have an idea." He slipped out of the cab and was gone before I could say a word.

I closed my eyes and tried to rest, but my mind wouldn't relax. To say Rachel would be pissed when she figured out the manipulation I'd pulled was an understatement. And seeing as she was one of my few friends, I couldn't afford to hurt her.

Not to mention the tiny fact I'd bonded her to me without her knowing.

The cab door jerked open. Ivan slid back in and handed a plastic bag back to me. "Here, get changed."

I peeked into the bag. Red crinoline and sparkles, along with a pair of stiletto heels. "What the hell is this?"

"A disguise. We'll leave your gear here in the cab, and we can go in as a couple. They aren't looking for me. They'll still notice you in that dress, but for the wrong reasons."

A part of me hated that he was right. But at my age, I'd learned to let pride go, from time to time. I slid out of my clothes and pulled on the dress. Fire-engine red and strapless, the dress was snug around my bust, and the skirt flared out to mid thigh. The crinoline pushed it out further. Like a Barbie doll outfit. I put on the heels and stared down at my bare legs.

"You got sunglasses?" I held a hand out to Ivan. He gave me his. They were large and round, far too big for my face, but they would have to work. I let my hair down, fluffing it.

"This isn't a beauty contest."

I lowered the glasses to glare at him. "I need as much skin coverage as possible, wolf."

"Shit. I forgot about that."

"Kind of an integral part of my life," I muttered. "We're going to do this fast. I can handle the sun for only a few minutes before I start to blister." Just my luck the setting sun was positioned just right between the buildings to shine on the entrance.

"Ready?" He had his hand on the door. I nodded and did the same.

Ready as I was going to get.

CHAPTER 4

RACHEL

"Who is this?" I stepped closer to the building to get out of the flow of people.

"Someone you want to know."

I sighed and rubbed my hand against my aching temple. "If you don't cut the bullshit and get to the chase, I'm hanging up."

He released a smug laugh. "I have information that can help you."

"Like what?"

"I know about the suicide pills."

Now he had my attention. My investigation of a series of serial killer crime scenes was what had landed me in this rabbit hole. All the victims had met with death by vampire. I hadn't mentioned it in my report, but I'd found a vampire suicide pill outside one of the scenes. My on-air time had been limited, and other information had taken priority. What was the point of mentioning something like that when there were far bigger issues to discuss, like the bioterrorism weapon that turned humans into crazed monsters? Or the vampire blood that cured diseases but created others? Why would someone give a shit about vampire suicide pills if they didn't even believe in vampires? "How do you know about them?"

"Rachel, you're a reporter," he said in a mocking tone. "Why are you asking the wrong questions?"

His voice set me on edge. He sounded like a patient serial killer, toying with his victim before he got to work. Yet I couldn't hang up. "Okay," I said, stalling to come up with a plan. I needed to play his game. Based on his egotistical tone, he wanted to make this about him. Time to suck it up. "You must be someone of importance if you know about the pills. From what I've gathered, only a few strategic people know about their existence."

"Very good, Rachel." Pride infused his voice. "You're catching on."

"Did you work in the Rikers Island facility? Before it was destroyed?"

"I was assigned there at one time, but I've since moved on. I'm part of the Aglaea division. Do you know what that is?"

"Sounds Greek to me," slipped out of my mouth before I could help myself. It was probably a wrong move. It sounded like this guy got off on an obedient subject.

Being flippant would either leave me out in the cold or possibly hunted and killed.

To my surprise, he laughed. "Clever girl, aren't you?"

"I like to think so."

"Aglaea was the goddess of beauty and magnificence. Can you guess what I worked on?"

"The vampires." Which explained how he knew about the pills.

I heard a grin in his voice. "You *are* a clever girl." I also heard a hint of a British accent. He sounded like he was in his thirties, maybe early forties.

"Do you still work in the Aglaea division?"

"I want to help you, Rachel. Will you let me?"

The sudden change of subject made me shudder. This guy was giving me a serious case of the creeps. "I can use all the help I can get…" My voice trailed off. "You know my name, but I don't know yours. What should I call you?"

He chuckled. "Call me Hades."

"Death?" When he didn't respond, I added, "Now *you're* the clever one. Hades controlled the underworld. Why do I think you're someone of importance in the Aglaea division?"

"Oh, Rachel, I knew you were the one…" His words trailed off, almost like he was getting off on the connection I'd made.

Jesus. How badly did I need this guy? Unfortunately, I already knew the answer. "Why did you call *me*, Hades?" I felt ridiculous calling him that, but I'd call him the messiah if he helped me stop these people.

"I want to share something with you."

"Does it pertain to the Aglaea division?"

He laughed. "Yes. Meet me at midnight."

I looked around. "I'm free now. I'm at Rockefeller Center. How about I meet you for cheesecake at Junior's? My treat."

"No. Not until later. Midnight, the Financial District. It's quiet then."

Quiet in New York City was a relative term. But the Financial District would be a ghost town at midnight. The fact that he wanted as few people around as possible worried me. He knew I wasn't working with any authorities, so he couldn't be concerned about entrapment. And if someone followed me, a legitimate possibility, it would be easier to ditch the tail in a crowd.

Of course, there was the possibility he was a vampire himself.

"They call it the witching hour. The perfect time to discuss Aglaea."

Way to ease my concerns, ass wipe. Witching hour was three in the morning, not midnight like everyone assumed, but for all I cared, he could repeat that mistake on his next cryptic phone call.

"I'm not sure I want to meet Hades at the witching hour."

"Don't make me sorry I called you, Rachel. I've already told you more than I should."

I read his implied threat loud and clear.

"As a sign of my good faith," he continued, "I will give you information that will prove I have knowledge of the inner workings of Aglaea."

"I'm listening."

"I know you found a suicide pill, and I know you had it analyzed." He paused. "I'm sure the technician looked for toxins. He found VX, but you need to ask him if he looked for specific inert elements."

"And what should he have looked for?"

"Blood cells. Ask him the unusual aspect he found and

then tell me tonight at midnight. I'll explain the significance."

"How do I know you're not working for the military?"

"No, my precious ewe. I'm the one trying to save you from your slaughter."

A chill ran down my spine. "*Am* I about to be slaughtered?"

"One could say you've already been slaughtered metaphorically. But perhaps you're being offered up as a sacrifice by someone else."

"Who?"

"I'll tell you when I see you at the address I'll text to you." Then he hung up.

Shit. I needed to get back to the hotel to see if I could dig up any information on anything he'd told me. And I needed to call Tom, my contact in the coroner's department, on the way. He'd arranged for the pill to be tested.

I pulled up Tom's number in a hurry, and to my relief, he answered right away. "Rachel? I'm surprised you're calling me. *Now.*"

"You saw my report."

"I can't believe you did it."

"You don't believe me, either?"

"I didn't say that. I just can't believe you put yourself out there like that. It was a brave thing to do." He laughed. "Stupid, but brave."

I shook my head. "Thanks. I think. But there's a reason for my call."

"I figured as much."

Ouch. But Tom had a point. I only called him when I needed something. Every time I swore to myself that the next time I called him it would be just to chat. But it still hadn't happened. I knew I needed to treat Tom with more care, if only because I did need him.

As a forensic scientist in New York City, he had access to the kinds of information that could help me with my own investigations. I couldn't officially use it in my reports, but it often either pointed me in the right direction or confirmed facts I'd already uncovered. I'd been in New York for a year and I'd known Tom for ten months. Truth be told, he was probably my best friend in town.

Other than Lea. But who knew when I'd ever see *her* again.

I definitely needed to treat him better. "I'm sorry. I'm a shitty friend. I'll make it up to you."

"You already owe me, remember? The wedding?"

"Of course." I'd agreed to go to his co-worker's wedding with him in exchange for his help with the pill.

"Are you gonna have time to go with everything else going on?"

"Of course." I hoped.

"So what do you need?"

Now I really felt like shit. "I guess it pertains to the favor that got me the wedding invitation in the first place."

"The fingerprint?"

"No, the pill."

"Crap. That's what I was afraid of. What about it?"

"I need to know about the inert compounds in the pill, specifically whether your friend found any blood cells. And anything specific regarding them."

"Rachel, they test for specific things they're interested in finding. But he found organic compounds, so he checked further."

"Wait, you're telling me the tech knew to look for VX when he ran the tests?" I asked in disbelief. "A nerve toxin that was supposedly completely destroyed in the 1950s?"

"Okay, so I told him to look for the unusual." He

paused. "Do you have any idea what else you're looking for?"

"I don't know. Something unusual about the blood cells. If I can tell him what it is, he'll explain the significance."

"Him, who?"

I sighed, rubbing my forehead. "I don't know who he is. But he knows things, Tom. I think he can help."

"Help you do *what?*"

"Stop the evil people who are behind this whole scheme. If everyone refuses to listen to me, I'll have to bring these guys down myself."

"Rachel. That's crazy."

"When did *that* ever stop me? They pissed off the wrong person, Tom."

"I'm going to regret this, but how soon do you need it?"

"Not to worry, you have a few hours. Midnight."

He cursed under his breath. "Then I've got work to do."

And so did I, if I was going to be ready to meet the guardian of the underworld.

CHAPTER 5

LEA

"Hold my hand, Cazador." Ivan reached for me. I plopped my hand in his and bore down, my nerves getting the better of me. He grunted. "Okay, maybe that was a bad idea."

My eyes were glued on the front door of the hotel. Four lanes of traffic and the sun shining onto the entrance like a veritable hammer. If I thought we could have waited a half hour, I would have done it. "Hurry."

I'll give him credit—he didn't hesitate. With a jerk, he all but dragged me into the road as I struggled along in the high heels. The sun cut into my bare arms and legs, slicing into me like a dull, rusted razor blade.

The blare of a horn, screech of tires and the screams of someone royally pissed off could barely be heard above the thumping of my heart. A hiss slipped out of me.

And it hurt like a motherfucker. "Hurry," I repeated.

Ivan scooped me into his arms and I curled into his neck to protect my face. "Talk to me, it'll help block the pain. What's your name?"

"Lea." I drew a breath, my body shuddering as I fought to keep my focus. "Are they looking?"

"Yes."

"Fuck."

I tightened my grip on him. It was a piss-poor plan, why had I gone along with it? I knew better than to go out without weapons, without being covered. Yet Ivan had thrown this ridiculous outfit at me and I'd jumped into it like he was the one in charge.

We burst through the doors and the shadows and overhead lighting of the hotel lobby were a soothing balm on my exposed skin. I let out a sigh and Ivan lowered me to the ground. He kept an arm around my back. "They were watching, but not like they knew you."

I took a swift look, peering over the top of his shoulder. The closest black sedan could be seen through the glass doors. Ivan was right; the men weren't even looking at the hotel anymore.

"How are we going to find her? They probably have her room flagged, too." Ivan steered me toward the front desk.

I glanced up at him. "What makes you an expert?"

"I was an enforcer. It's what I would do."

I stepped up to the desk. The matronly concierge smiled brightly at me. Her eyes all but twinkled when they landed on Ivan. "Welcome to the Hilton. How can I help you?"

Her eyes were blue, so pale they were almost gray. Staring into them, I reached out and touched her nametag. "Mary," I said in a soft, lulling voice, "I need to know what room a friend is in. And I want you to forget I asked as soon as you tell me."

Her smile slipped at the edges, and her eyes lost focus. "Of course."

I leaned forward, keeping eye contact with her. "Rachel Sambrook. I need a key card to her room."

Her fingers flew over the keyboard. "Seventh floor, room 710." She slipped a key card into the card reader. When it buzzed and clicked, she pulled it out and handed it to me. I took it and tucked it into my cleavage.

"Damn, that's smooth." Ivan squeezed my side and I flinched. Not because it hurt, but because it already felt far too natural to have him by my side.

I was not in the market for a pet. Certainly not one his size.

I backed up, my stilettos clicking on the tile. "Forget me, Mary."

"Who are you?" She frowned and put a hand to her forehead.

I said nothing as we backed away.

"Seriously," Ivan said as we turned our backs to the desk and Mary, "that was damn slick. Does it work on werewolves?"

When we reached the elevator bank, I paused and stared at the doors. The last time I'd been in an elevator, things hadn't gone so well. "Stairs."

I led the way to the discreet door in the corner of the lobby.

Ivan took several big strides to make it there before me,

then held the door open. I glared at him, but he didn't seem to notice. "You didn't answer my question."

"I've never tried. Werewolves are stubborn."

"Ah, so you've noticed." He grinned at me from a few steps above. I didn't grin back.

At the seventh floor, Ivan peered out the door and took a long slow breath. "Just humans, nothing nasty waiting."

I grunted softly. "For the moment." I pushed past him and caught a glimpse of myself in a mirror at the far end of the hall. Bright red dress, raven black hair, stilettos that gave me an additional three inches but still didn't make me as tall as Ivan. My reddened skin was already repairing itself.

"Stop staring at yourself; you look good."

My eyes popped wide, but I refused to give him the satisfaction of seeing me shocked. I kept my back to him and strode down the hall. But the damn heels weren't working with me. They sunk into the soft carpet and seriously impeded my movement. I stopped and pulled them off, then walked the rest of the way to Rachel's room barefoot.

I knocked, not expecting an answer. Her scent was faint, suggesting she hadn't been here for hours. I paused, thinking the scenario through. If the men below were going to take Rachel, they'd want to do it quietly. They'd wait until she'd been back in her room for a while, wait for her to relax. Which meant this was where I would wait on her.

The key card blinked a steady green when I put it in the slot. I opened the door a few inches with one toe, then put my face to the opening and breathed in. Nothing but Rachel.

A sigh of relief slid out of me as I stepped into the room.

Ivan of course followed. He stretched as he paced through the room, then flopped down onto the bed. "Nice. Maybe we could come back here sometime."

Time to set him straight. "Ivan, let me be crystal-fuck-ing-clear. You and I are not an item. I'm tolerating you only because you did help me get in here."

"And I helped you get into the TV station," he pointed out with a far-too-innocent look in his eyes.

I glared at him. "Rachel is going to show up in a very short time and you will leave when she does. Understand?"

He shrugged. "I do what I want. And I know stuff."

I rolled my eyes. "Please, you think that is going to work on me?"

"Hoping."

I paced the room while we waited, and Ivan was smart enough to keep his mouth shut. Rachel should already be here.

I was about to go looking for her when the doorknob rattled. I raised a palm to Ivan, keeping him where he was. Just in case.

The door whooshed open and Rachel stepped in. Her eyes were on me in a flash and her hand went to the small of her back. I grinned. "Like the new clothes?"

"Holy fuck, Lea. You scared the shit out of me." Her eyes flicked to Ivan. "Who's that?"

"Ivan, meet Rachel," I said.

He stood and held a hand out to her. I batted it down. "No, you are not making friends. Time to go home like a good doggy."

"You're going to need me again." He swatted my ass as he went past, then slid out the door without another word.

"What the fuck was that?" Rachel shook her head. "I feel like I just walked into one of those weird dreams after eating too much spicy food at the market."

"Long story."

Rachel moved further into the room and slumped into

a chair. "Okay, I know this goes without saying, but obviously you aren't on a plane."

"Obviously."

"Why not? And what's with the dress?"

I sat on the edge of the bed, letting the crinoline skirt bunch up. Feeling exposed in more ways than one. "I couldn't leave you here to face the fallout on your own. Not when I was the one who pushed you to do it. And the dress is courtesy of the suits downstairs."

"You didn't make me do anything, Lea. And I saw the suits. Waved a finger at them." Rachel grabbed her ponytail and absently tugged on it. "I will admit this is probably one of the worse days I've had in a long time."

"Worse than last week?" I raised an eyebrow.

She laughed, but it was forced. "Okay, the worst *normal* bad day I've had in a long time."

We sat in silence for a minute before I sucked it up. "I knew the fallout was going to be bad."

"Yeah, so did I."

I rubbed a hand over my face, wincing at a couple of burned patches on my skin. "No, I knew it was going to go south... I..."

"Spit it out, vamp," Rachel snapped.

I stood up. "Fuck, Rachel. I used you as bait. How many people saw the report? Someone who knows about Stravinsky's work will reach out to you. I was banking on it."

Her blue eyes flicked downward. Just a heartbeat, but there it was.

"Someone already has, haven't they?"

She stood, putting us nose to nose. "You threw me under the bus?"

"Yes."

"You bitch."

I grinned. "Isn't that why we work so well together?" Ivan really was a bad influence on me.

Her mouth dropped open and she burst out laughing. "Shit. I want to hate you, I really do. But I would have done the report even if you'd told me I was being baited."

I couldn't help but heave a sigh of relief. A soft knock turned us toward the door. I took a sniff and frowned. "Ivan, go away!"

"I have your clothes and I think you're going to need them."

Rachel went to the door and grinned over her shoulder at me. "He's cute. I like him."

"He's a werewolf," I said as she opened the door. Ivan strolled in like he owned the place and handed me my clothes all rolled up. I grabbed the edge of my dress and yanked it over my head as soon as Rachel shut the door.

Ivan spun his back to me. "Give a guy some warning, would you?"

"Don't expect me to be shy—" I whipped on my top and pants and bent at the waist to pull on my boots. The position put me eye level with the window.

Three sets of eyes stared back in at me. I moved with care. "Rachel, you remember those things that attacked us outside of the bakery?"

"Yeah, why?"

"Don't move, but we've got the same monsters." I finished dressing, put my weapons in their places, and pulled the cowl over my head.

Ivan let out a low growl. "What the hell are those things?"

"Personally," Rachel said, "I like the name demon dogs. They climb walls, have no fur, and are generally a pain in the ass."

Her calm delivery was a cover for the stress that spiked

in the room. "The door, Ivan." I stepped back as the dogs started to claw at the glass, shattering it within seconds.

Ivan yanked the door open, and I grabbed Rachel and leapt into the hallway. Ivan tried to wrestle the door shut, but the demon dogs' pale legs jutted out around the edges, digging into the wood. "They've got their claws between the door and frame. I can't shut it."

I yanked a silver stake from my boot. Lunging forward, I slashed down and cut three of the legs off. Howls rent the air and Ivan was able to slam the door shut.

"That won't hold them long," Rachel said as we strode toward the elevator. The light above it binged and the metal doors slid open.

Eight men in dark suits, guns out, spilled onto the floor.

"You've got to be fucking kidding me," Rachel breathed out.

I had to agree. "This way." I pulled her toward the stairs just as another four men poured out of the stairwell doorway.

"You see, Ivan? Bad idea following me around." I moved toward the smaller group of men. The stairwell would be easier to defend if it came to that.

"Oh, I knew what I was getting into." He flexed his back and a low growl trickled out of him that curled down my spine. I shivered and focused on the task at hand.

"Lea, we can't kill them. It'll only convince them we're dangerous and they'll send more men next time," Rachel said. I wanted to let out a sigh of frustration, but the first bullet zipped by.

"They don't seem to have the same concern."

I grabbed her and zigzagged down the hall. Ivan was ahead of us. He grabbed the first man just as his gun went off. The werewolf's only reaction to the direct hit was to jerk and let out a snarl. The bullet popped back out of his bulky bicep and dropped to the floor as Ivan hefted his attacker into the air. Unless he was wounded with something silver or by another supernatural, he'd heal faster than me.

"Holy shit, we should keep the puppy," Rachel said.

That's what I was afraid of. That the puppy would be at our heels.

He threw the man into the other agents like he was rolling a bowling ball. They went down in a clatter, several guns going off at once.

Ivan stepped over them and held the door open. His eyes met mine. "Ladies first."

Indeed.

Chapter 6

RACHEL

"I've been with you less than ten minutes and we've already fought off demon dogs and government agents," I said as we ran down the steps.

"Never a dull moment," Lea grunted, obviously frustrated by my human pace. Even the werewolf behind me was getting impatient if the way he was crowding my heels was any indication.

"It would have been great if I'd had time to change into more appropriate on-the-lam clothes." At least I had on decent shoes. It had taken me less than a week to figure out that only the most practical walking shoes would work in a city this big.

"Are you really discussing your outfit at time like this?" the werewolf snapped as I took the last steps the ground floor. "Typical blonde."

We needed to stop and assess the surveillance in the lobby, so I had no qualms about whipping around and hooking my foot around the back of his ankle. I caught him off balance and shoved him against the wall with my forearm across his Adam's apple, not an easy task considering he was so much taller than me. But he'd bent his knees when he fell, putting off his center of balance. "Don't *ever* make a statement about my hair color in conjunction with my intelligence or ability again," I forced out through gritted teeth. "Got it?"

A slow grin spread across his face. "You have an interesting friend, Cazador."

Lea grunted as she cracked open the door to peer outside.

The werewolf looked completely amused. "You do realize I could rip your head off? I could flick you away like a fly."

"How many *blondes* have caught you off guard like I just did? One stumble and I could have easily shoved a silver stake into your heart." I poked the left side of his chest to make my point, then dropped my forearm. "Do *not* underestimate me."

My comment about the silver stake had wiped the grin off his face and he stood to his full height, glaring at me.

"If you two children are done, can we go?" Lea asked, glancing back at us. "I only see four men by the exits, but who knows how soon the others will be down."

I shifted my messenger bag, thankful I hadn't taken it off in the room. "Let's do this."

"Maybe we can find a side exit and get out undetected."

Given our lousy luck, that seemed unlikely, but I let Lea lead the way. We stuck close to the wall and headed toward a hall to our left. To my surprise, we almost made it, but one of the guards caught a glimpse of Lea and alerted his friends.

I took off in a sprint. "Run!"

Lea pushed me ahead of her. "Go, I'm right behind you!"

I sprinted around the corner, skidding to a halt when a man in a suit stepped in front of the glass door leading to the street. Despite the half dozen people in the lobby, he lifted his gun to shoot. Lea jumped in front of me as the sound of a gunshot filled the hall. Ivan released a low snarl and bolted for the shooter. The man's eyes widened as he lifted his gun toward Ivan, but Lea reached him before he could pull the trigger again. She struck his arm, sending his gun skittering across the floor, and Ivan shoved him against the wall. His head hit the marble with the sound of an overripe melon.

The agent sank to the floor. His head flopped over like a rag doll's, but his chest still rose and fell with his breath. "Wait," I said as I squatted beside him.

Leah growled, "We don't have time to wait."

But I'd already pulled out his earpiece and microphone. I switched the microphone off and inserted it into my own ear. "Now we'll know what they're up to." The other agents' voices filled my ear.

Ivan gave me a grudging look of approval as we took off for the street, Lea in lead.

As soon as I hit the sidewalk, I saw the men headed toward us. "Shit."

Lea bolted into traffic, and cars screeched to a halt to

avoid hitting her. Ivan and I followed her path, but the agents crossed behind us, so we didn't gain much ground.

Ivan grabbed the corner of a newsstand as soon as we reached the sidewalk, the worker restacking a rack of magazines. He pressed his shoulder into the edge and the entire stand lifted off the ground and crashed onto the sidewalk. Merchandise spilled into their path, creating a bottleneck of shouting pedestrians and raging newsstand owner.

We took advantage of the diversion to race south, agents still pursuing. I began to get winded after two blocks of that grueling pace. The agents were losing ground fast, and after another two blocks, I could see neither hide nor hair of them.

"We need to find a subway," I panted.

"Where's the nearest station?" Lea asked.

Ivan ran beside me, barely looking winded. Asshole. "The Rockefeller, but we'll be too easy to find. We need to head to Grand Central. We can lose them in the tunnels."

"There's no one to lose," I snapped. "We've lost the guys behind us."

"But now we have fresh pursuers," Lea said, pointing to a tight group of men headed straight for us.

"They're directly in our path to Grand Central, not to mention it's at least six more blocks," I said. "We need to hide."

Lea shot me a nasty look and pulled her cowl down around her face. Then she grabbed me, flung me onto her back, and took off at an even faster sprint in the opposite direction of our new pursuers. My only consolation was that Ivan struggled to keep up with her.

She slid around the corner, turning east, and I clung to her for fear of being flung off. The men behind us had little chance of keeping up, but we still weren't in a position to lose them yet. Ivan steered us down Madison.

"There's an entrance close," he said. "A couple blocks."

People gave us odd looks—an inhumanely fast person with a woman on his or her back was bound to draw attention, but it was New York City. For all they knew, it was a scene from an action movie. Hopefully they wouldn't figure out there weren't any cameras rolling.

We'd made it several more blocks, and I knew we were close when I heard something over the earpiece. "They're sending more backup," I shouted. "They're two blocks behind us."

"They're close," Ivan said, looking over his shoulder. "But I think we can make it."

Lea pushed forward with a new burst of speed, only slowing when we reached the entrance. I slid off her back and the three of us entered the station. With any luck, we'd get lost in the crowd, but that seemed unlikely considering my companions were a big beefy guy and a woman in leather and a cowl. I had a better chance of getting lost on my own, but there was no way that was going to happen. I pulled my subway pass out of my bag as well as a spare I kept in case I lost my other.

"Lea, lower your cowl."

"What? Why?"

"We have to blend in. Or try to."

I led the way to the turnstiles, then ran my other pass over the card reader and motioned her through.

"Are you shitting me?" she asked in disbelief. "Always the rule-follower. Even in a foot chase."

"See that guard over there?" I gave a flick of my finger toward a man who was standing with his back to the wall, keeping a watchful eye on the turnstiles. "He sees us jump the stiles and he's going to call for backup."

"Ladies," Ivan said, already through the stiles, "let's continue this discussion on the train."

Lea stalked through the gate behind me.

"Which line?"

"The one with the closest platform." I was starting toward the first tunnel when Lea tensed.

"They found us."

"Shit." We bolted down the steps as a train pulled into the station. "Hurry!" I shouted. "I think we can make it."

The men in black suits were right behind us as we reached the bottom of the stairs. The passengers were already loading, which was a bad sign. We were still far enough away that we might not make it.

Seeming to sense my concern, Lea grabbed my wrist and rushed toward the train, pulling me so quickly my feet barely touched the tile floor. We squeaked past the closing doors just before they sealed.

I grabbed a pole, hanging over while I tried to catch my breath. It was only as the train pulled away from the platform that I realized Ivan was still on the other side of the door. And the men in suits were only feet behind him.

Oh, shit.

CHAPTER 7

LEA

"Damn, I thought he'd be faster than that," Rachel said.

I watched through the window as the men in suits reached for Ivan, only to find him already gone, climbing over the people on the platform to evade capture.

"He has a thing about opening doors for women," I muttered as I turned.

Rachel was already doing a sweep of the car, moving quickly. Checking the far end to see if any suits had made it onto the adjoining car.

Without any training on my part, she was already a better partner than Calvin. He'd been such a mess at first, focused only on revenge.

"You're hunting the monsters who did this?" He pointed at the two bodies on the floor of his apartment. Wife and child, throats savaged, very little blood to be found. I nodded and kept my mouth shut. The last thing he needed to know was that he'd be working with a monster to catch the monsters.

He ran a hand over his dirty blond hair, making it stick up in every direction. His blue eyes hardened as he nodded. "I'm in."

"I'm the boss. You will do what I say. When I say it." I spoke evenly, putting only the slightest bit of pressure behind my words.

"Fine. But we'll get to kill them?"

"Yes."

He held out his hand to me. "I'd sell my soul to the devil to find the monster who did this. To make him pay."

I gripped his hand. "Well, Calvin, you may have done just that."

I blinked, looking for Rachel. "Ivan will catch up—"

Over Rachel's right shoulder at the far end of the subway car stood an impossible sight. Tall, dirty blond hair, blue eyes, one eyebrow raised as he shook his head. It was as if he'd stepped out of my memory. "Calvin?"

Rachel spun around, but I was already moving. I pushed past her and bolted to the end of the car. People, there were too many damn people, no matter how hard I shoved them. Less than ten seconds passed and I was standing where I'd seen him. The space was empty. I rubbed a hand over my face. Was I seeing things?

"What the hell? Did you say *Calvin?*" Rachel caught up to me.

I nodded. "Maybe. Fucked if I know."

"There isn't a person over fifty on this car, Lea," Rachel pointed out, her hands on her hips.

I drew in a breath, scenting the air on the back of my tongue. There was nothing that smelled like Calvin. Just a subway car full of poorly washed bodies. "No, he looked like he did...when he was younger."

"Not possible."

I let out a breath. "I know we left him behind, Rachel. Yes, he was dead. Yes, the facility blew up. But—"

"Lea. Even you know it isn't possible. Not this time." Her voice softened enough that I knew she understood. I wanted Calvin not to be dead. I wanted to know my old friend was still alive and out there somewhere.

The subway car slowed to a stop and the light over the door blinked. I didn't look where we were getting off, just stepped onto the platform and started out of the tunnel. Rachel jogged to catch up. "Hey. It's normal to see people you care about after they're dead. I went through it with my buddies in Iraq. Three of them, actually."

I said nothing simply because I wasn't sure how I felt. The only way Calvin could be alive was as a vampire. That was the only answer.

And I didn't want that for him. I'd stake him myself before I let this world make him the thing he hated most.

Without having to say anything, we both knew the suits would come for us at one of the subway line's drop-off points. It would be nice for things to work out like they did in the movies, but we weren't stupid. This wouldn't be a clean getaway.

We moved with serious speed. At the top of the stairs, I tugged my cowl tighter around my face, more out of habit than anything else, since the street was swathed with shadows from the nearly set sun, and did a visual sweep of the area. So far, so good. The apartment building across the street caught my eye. "We need to get to higher ground so we can see them coming."

"Agreed." Rachel pointed. "That apartment building work?"

Again, she showed just how much she trumped Calvin as a helper. I tapped her on the arm. "Keep close," and we were off, sliding through the grid of cars that might as well have been a parking lot rather than a street. As I scanned the area, a feeling I hadn't experienced in a long time pressed in around me.

Being hunted was a shitty sensation. I much preferred to be the hunter.

I led the way around the side of the building. A fire escape ladder hung a good twenty feet in the air in a dark narrow alley.

"You can reach that, right?" Rachel asked me, like it was no problem.

"Who do you think I am? The Jolly Green Giant in disguise?" I grinned, though, and ran at the wall. I leapt straight up as I reached the building, scrabbling with my hands and boots to propel me the last few feet. Dangling from the ladder, I jerked my body and the mechanism let loose and dropped to the ground with a grinding screech.

Rachel winced. "I hope none of those fucking dog things are around to hear that."

"Other things make noise besides us, Rach."

She lifted both hands as she put a foot on the ladder. "Really? I'm beginning to think they could hear us fart if we let one rip."

The laugh that burst out of me caught me by surprise. And apparently Rachel too, because she stared at me like I'd sprouted a second head.

"Sorry."

"No, it's good. Just...shocked the shit out of me."

My lips twitched. "Please don't go there."

She grinned and started up the stairs. I followed, then pulled the ladder up from the first landing. A single screech, and it was locked back in place. We were at the third floor before we found an unlocked window.

Sliding through, it was easy to see why.

"Rich people always think nothing bad is going to happen to them. Like their money somehow protects them." Rachel ran a hand through the silk curtains. The place was solid white: floors, ceilings, walls, artwork, curtains, and furniture.

Perhaps it was a bad sign that my first thought was we were probably going to get blood on everything and the cleaning bill was going to be a real bitch.

The thought of blood made my throat tighten. "I need to feed soon after all that exposure to the sun. So let's hash this shit out."

Rachel nodded as she moved to the wet bar across the room and poured herself a big glass of water. She downed it, then pulled out a half full bottle of something else. Whiskey aged in oak barrels, judging by the smell.

"Not a word. I need it after the day I've had," she said as she tipped a generous amount into her glass with the last of her water.

I drew the scent in and let it coat my saliva glands. What I wouldn't give for the burn of a shot of whiskey. Unfortunately, my taste buds wouldn't pick up the nuances and the alcohol would make me sick.

I moved around the side of the brilliantly white leather couch and sat, leaning into the overstuffed cushions.

"Something bad is coming." I rubbed a hand across the

back of my neck as if to scrub away the sensation of being hunted.

"No shit—" Rachel paused and stared at me over the rim of her glass, "—Sherlock."

I rolled my eyes. "We've pissed off enough people; there's no way to know what direction the blow will come from. Men in suits today. Vampires tonight. Demon dogs in the morning. Something new by mid-afternoon."

"You don't know that." She put her glass down.

"Just a guess. Who contacted you after the report?"

Her eyes flickered down to her glass and back up. "A creepy-ass scientist. I'm meeting him tonight."

I raised both eyebrows. "Really? Let me guess, midnight?"

She grunted. "Not real subtle, is it?"

I rubbed a hand over my face. "No. You feel okay about going on your own?"

"Why? What are you going to do?"

The slightest shuffle of cloth at the window had me on my feet and spinning toward it. Ivan grinned at me, already half in through the opening.

"Never going to sneak up on you, am I?"

"How the hell did we not hear the ladder?" Rachel snapped. "Seriously, did you fly your ass in here?"

He grinned at her, but his charm didn't work on Rachel. She glared back. He let out a sigh. "I jumped. Those ladders are always squeaky."

Rachel flicked her eyes my way, as if to confirm it was, indeed, possible for him to do that. I gave her the barest of nods.

"Fuck. I'm surrounded by X-Men." She slugged back her whiskey.

"Is she always this touchy?" He looked at her, then back to me.

Time to lay the ground rules. "You're going to keep following me, aren't you?"

"You don't know it yet—" he stepped through the window and leaned against the frame, "—but you're going to need me. This goes deeper than vampires, Lea. And to answer you, yes. I'm going to keep following you. Besides, the view is nice."

"What the fuck is that supposed to mean?" Rachel moved out from behind the wet bar.

"It means I'd like to get to know her on a more personal basis. She has a nice ass." He winked at me and Rachel threw her glass at him. He ducked and came up with a frown etched on his mouth. There it was—the look of an enforcer.

Rachel gave him a long hard look before she said, "Why do you think we need you?"

He shook his head, and I pulled one silver stake out of the top of my boot and pointed it at him.

"Let me be crystal-fucking-clear. Rachel comes first. We get in trouble, I'm getting her out before I do anything else. You come with us, you better understand that. If she asks a question, answer it, wolf."

Rachel's surprise was a palpable sensation in the air, but I ignored it and kept my focus on Ivan.

His green-yellow eyes locked on mine. "You think vampires are the only ones with blood that has power? Werewolves age slowly. We don't get sick. We heal faster than you vamps because we aren't dead."

"Fucking fantastic." Rachel slapped the wall beside her with the flat of her hand. I tucked the stake back into the top of my boot.

"You going to listen to me, Ivan?" I asked.

"I'm going to help," he countered.

That would have to be good enough.

"I'm going to hunt me up a vampire. It'll be best to get the information straight from the horse's mouth," I said.

Rachel didn't seem convinced. "That didn't go so well last time."

I grimaced. "Caine was an old vampire. They're always a pain. I'll look for someone younger."

Her eyes met mine and I forced myself to hold her gaze. I had convinced a young vamp, Louis, to follow me back to Rachel's now-destroyed apartment a few days ago. I'd hoped to chat him up, get some useful info. He really hadn't been a lot of help other than to spill the beans about a vampire council I'd had no knowledge of. Rachel had asked me not to kill him. I'd promised I wouldn't.

And then Calvin, whose vendetta against vampires had never faded, took the choice from me, killing Louis before I could stop him.

"That won't happen again," I said. "Calvin isn't here. Ivan isn't going to rip heads off unless we let him off his leash, right?"

I swung my gaze to the werewolf. He'd moved closer without me realizing it. While that should have worried me, a very small part was rather turned on. How long had it been since a man could match me for stealth, agility... stamina?

I took three quick steps back as my mind wandered to places I dared not go. "Ivan. You follow Rachel. I don't trust the scientist she's meeting later, and she might need backup." I headed to the window, paused, and looked over my shoulder. "Remember where we met Sean and his buddies?"

She nodded.

"Meet there right after the meeting."

I slipped out the window, the silk curtains billowing around me. I climbed up to the roof and then sprinted across to jump the gap to the next building. Time to find a vampire.

Chapter 8

RACHEL

I groaned as I watched Lea jump out the window. "For the record," I said, turning to Ivan, "I don't need a babysitter."

He sat on the leather sofa and leaned back, extending his arm along the back and crossing his ankle over his knee. "You've proved that."

I poured myself more whiskey in a new glass, then walked to the dining room table and pulled my laptop out of my bag. "So why aren't you chasing after Lea?"

He shrugged and grabbed a remote, flicking on a large-screen TV attached to the wall. "She thinks you need someone to watch your back."

"Keep your eyes off my *ass* and this might work." I studied him as he cast a side-glance out the window. Hmmm…it would seem he was only interested in one ass—and it wasn't mine. More relief than I'd expected accompanied that realization. I had enough to do—the last thing I needed was some beefcake making advances on me.

But from the look in Lea's eyes, she enjoyed his attention.

Good for her. She was welcome to him.

I cast a nervous glance toward the door, wondering if maybe we should go someplace where we'd be less likely to be arrested for breaking and entering.

"I'll hear someone coming," Ivan said good-naturedly, keeping his eyes on the television screen. "We'll have plenty of time to get out the window."

Since I didn't really want to find someplace else, I decided to trust him. I opened my browser using my hotspot and plugged in the address Hades had texted. A twenty-four-hour diner in the heart of the Financial District. I opened Google Earth to check out the surrounding businesses. Mostly office buildings and Starbucks. A dry cleaners. A jewelry store. Nothing else that would be open around that time. It would be a wasteland, all right.

The sound of cheering filled the room, and I looked up to see a baseball game on the screen. "Mind turning that down?"

"Yeah," he said, keeping his gaze on the screen. "I do mind."

"One of us is trying to work here."

"You're wasting your time. You're not going to find what you're looking for on the computer."

I sat back in my chair. "Oh? And I suppose you know the answers?"

He turned to look at me, his face expressionless. "No. That's why I'm here."

"Yeah. Let's address *that*." I scooted my chair around to face him. "You just appear out of nowhere and suddenly you're stuck to Lea like a leech to a coon dog. Why?"

He pushed out a breath and leaned over his legs. "I don't blame you for not trusting me. In fact, I'd be suspicious of you if you did. But I'm here to help. This thing runs deep, and it affects my species as well as yours and Lea's."

"Species?"

"Isn't that what we are? Altered genetics." He shook his head slightly. "I've been looking for her since I heard about those serial murders the vampires committed. I knew they were trying to draw her out to destroy her. I was hoping I would find her before they did."

"They?"

"The people behind the monsters."

I lifted my eyebrows, waiting for more of an explanation, but when I realized none was coming, I scowled. "I know she's a big bad vampire, but she's *my* big bad vampire. If you so much as put a nick in her with one of those canines, I'll kick your ass back up to Canada." When he looked surprised, I rolled my eyes. "Please, your accent."

"We need to work together on this. We're on the same team."

I'd been told that before by more men than I could count. One of them had tried to kill me. I'd discovered Sean, my ex, near the last of the serial vamps' crime scenes. Him and his military enforcers. He'd been hot on the ass of my best friend Derrick. Sean had ultimately killed Derrick to keep his story quiet, and Lea had, in turn, killed Sean.

I felt no remorse about letting her do it—Sean had killed one of the few men I'd ever trusted.

And now I was left with no one.

My gaze shifted to the still-open window, the cool night air blowing the silk curtains.

Maybe not no one.

I glanced back at Ivan. "You think you're the first pretty face attached to a beef stack of muscles to tell me that? *Please…* You have to earn my respect and trust, and I've been burned so many times, I suspect you'll *never* make the cut."

He shrugged, looking unconcerned. "I can live with that."

I caught his barely-there glance at the window. He could live with my animosity just fine. It was Lea's approval he was after. Maybe we could use it to our advantage.

I pulled out my headphones and spent the next hour tuning out the ballgame on the screen while I searched Derrick's files for anything that hinted at the Aglaea division or Hades, but as I suspected, there was nothing. While Derrick had found plenty of signs hinting at the U.S. government's involvement, he'd known very little about the inner workings of the project.

I texted Tom about five times, probably annoying the hell out of him with my endless requests for updates. Finally, about ten minutes before I needed to leave, he sent what I'd been waiting for.

The contents of the pill are as follows:

VX 10%

Magnesium stearate 85%

Red blood cells 5%

Blood cells are off the chart with electrical impulses though. Never seen anything like it.

I pushed out a sigh of relief. Now I could meet that bastard Hades. And while I hadn't paid a lot of attention in my anatomy and physiology class in college, I was pretty damn sure blood cells didn't give off electrical pulses. Interesting.

I pulled out my headphones and shut down my laptop. Ivan looked up, but returned his attention to the TV when I walked down the hall to use the bathroom. After I finished, I dug through the bedroom closet to see if I could find anything useful to help hide me. Unfortunately, the uptight woman who lived here only had designer clothes, and the man who shared a small sliver of her closet was only allowed space for his suits and dress shirts.

I opened several dresser drawers before I found the two relegated to him. The hooded sweatshirt buried in the back was exactly what I'd hoped to find. Light gray too, to make me less suspicious. I found a Mets baseball cap and stuck it on top of my head.

I slung my bag over my shoulder. "Time to go."

He flicked off the TV as I moved toward the window. "I don't think we should be seen together," I said. "You know they're probably still watching for us. I can blend in more easily than you." I looked up at him. How tall *was* he?

"I've played this game before. I know what I'm doing."

"Good." I gave him the list of subway lines I planned to take, then waited for some kind of comment, but he just gave me a devilish grin. "After you."

We made it the subway and to the coffee shop without incident. I could see him lurking twenty feet away, blending in as well as someone his size was capable of blending. I hated to admit I was glad he was there. That I could text him an SOS if I needed backup. The two-block walk to the diner had me on edge. Humans, I could handle, but there were so many unknowns in this new world I'd stumbled into. And now I was on my way to meet a man—or a vamp,

REPLICA | THE BLOOD BORNE SERIES BOOK 2

werewolf, or monster—with an ego large enough to fill an underworld.

He was easy to spot, the only customer at a table in a diner with only three other people—a couple in the midst of an argument, and a old man hunched over his bowl of soup.

I stood next to the table, my hands in the jacket pockets. "Hades?"

A slow grin spread across his face. "You came."

If I had run into this guy on the street, I wouldn't have given him the time of day. He looked to be in his forties with a slight receding hairline. His pasty complexion suggested he spent the majority of his time inside, probably in the underground lab Lea and I had destroyed only days ago.

He was dressed up—trousers, a blue button-down shirt, and a blue and white striped tie. He wore eyeglasses, possibly to hide the mad gleam in his eyes.

The hair on the back of my neck stood on end, but I gave him a sly grin as I slid into the booth seat across from him. "After an offer like yours, how could I refuse?"

"Did you get the results?"

"Not so fast." I'd activated the microphone app on my phone before entering the diner. "How do I even know you have any information about the Asclepius Project? Maybe you're someone who saw my report and decided to try to get inside info." One look into his eyes had told me he was the real deal. And that he was at least slightly unbalanced. Still, it would be stupid not to vet him first.

He sighed, sounding irritated, then slid a finger up and down on the sweating glass of water in front of him. "I thought I'd proved myself during our call."

I tilted my head. "How do I know you're the man I talked to on the phone?"

"Rachel, I only have a short time before I must catch a flight. You need to ask the right questions." He sounded exasperated.

His response made me pause. "You're supposed to give me information."

"And I will. But first you must ask the questions. You have five. Then we are done." He slid a pile of sugar packets in front of him, next to the glass, arranging them into a neat line. Five.

Well, fuck. I hadn't planned for something like this, which was plain stupid on my part. His whole phone conversation had been a game of questions and answers.

I took a breath, clasping my hands in front of me. "What does the Aglaea division work on?"

A grin spread across his face as he picked up a sugar packet and ripped it open. "You were correct during our previous conversation. The Aglaea division worked with vampires." He poured the packet into the water and watched the sugar granules float to the bottom of the glass.

"Worked? Past tense?"

He picked up two packets, ripped them open, and dumped them on the table, looking into my eyes as they spilled everywhere. "One thing you must know about me, Rachel—I am a very literal man. You have just wasted two questions."

Shit. I tried to quell my panic. He hadn't given me any answers at all. Not really.

"Where exactly should we look next?"

He picked up a sugar packet and ripped off the top, holding it over the table for a moment before pouring it into his water.

I resisted pushing out a breath of relief.

"You need to go to Iraq. To the Lelantos facility. They

71

are planning to conduct a field test. You'll find answers you're looking for there."

Which meant I had one more question left.

"Hades, are you my enemy or my friend?"

He picked up the remaining packet of sugar and poured it into the glass, then picked up the glass and drained it dry before he smiled. "I am only one of many boogeymen in your worst nightmare."

My breath caught in my throat. Staring into his cold dark eyes, I believed he was just as bad as the rest of them.

"What about the pill?"

He grinned. "You're out of questions."

My back tensed. "You said you would address the blood cells."

"All in good time. I will give you more answers when I think you need them, but know that for now we are allies in this quest." He got up and moved beside me, leaning over to whisper in my ear. "There is no black or white in this world, Rachel. Only shades of gray.

Then he placed an envelope on the table and walked away.

CHAPTER 9

LEA

Clouds rolled in, darkening the evening sky. Fine by me. I pulled the cowl back and breathed in the night air, rolling it across my tongue. Finding a vampire was no easy task. Even when I was actively hunting them, I would sometimes go weeks, even months between sightings.

Now I had to find one in a matter of hours.

"Scene of the crime," I said softly. Vamps were creatures of habit, and I knew of a place more than a few of them frequented.

Amore Sangre. The restaurant had been owned by my

patron, Victor, whom I'd killed for lying to me and trying to entrap me. "Ass fuck."

I made my way to the restaurant, staying on foot wherever possible. The city no longer felt like a bustling human metropolis. More like a potential crypt with the door slowly shutting in my face.

I shook my head and pushed back the analogies.

The restaurant loomed in front of me in no time. Ten stories high, the actual eatery was on the top floor. As I slipped into the building, I faced a decision. Elevator or stairs?

My hesitation was minuscule. Stairs. Again, easier to maneuver. As I climbed, I went over in my head what we needed. The place Stravinsky had fucked off to. What he was doing. Who else was involved.

"Simple," I breathed out.

At the top of the building, I paused and peered back the way I'd come. No sound of footsteps behind me, no scent of anyone following. But I couldn't throw the feeling I was being watched. Swiveling around, I panned the walls for a camera. Nothing.

I pushed through the door that led out of the stairwell. The front of the restaurant was done up in lovely wood paneling and the doors were shut. I walked up to them and tried the handle.

The knob twisted in my hand and I stepped into the semi-darkness. From the right, a sharp wind blew through the windows I'd busted out the week before. Glass still glittered on the floor, and there had been no obvious attempt at cleaning up.

But the scent of cooking beef and fresh vegetables teased my nose, so someone was home and busy cooking. I headed toward the kitchen, following the smells.

A few pots clanged together, then nothing but a low muttering no one but me would have heard.

"I hate you, you bastard."

Interesting.

Curiosity and the need for answers pulled me forward even though I knew things didn't add up. The restaurant was obviously closed, yet someone was cooking. I paused at the swinging doors and listened.

"Damn you, Victor. I was a rising star." The bang of a knife in a cutting board, the thunk of something being cut into. It probably said something for the state of my mind that my first thought was that the cook was probably dismembering the sous chef.

I put a hand on the door and stepped into the kitchen. The chef had his back to me, and there were only vegetables on the board, no sous chef.

"What did Victor do to you?"

The chef spun around, his knife raised. "Oh my God. Don't *do* that to me. I could have cut you in half!"

"I doubt that." I took a few more steps into the room, trailing a hand along the stainless steel appliances. I hardened my voice. "Answer me. What did Victor do to you?"

He pointed the knife at me. "You can't be in here."

I slammed the flat of my hand into the refrigerator, concaving the outer shell. "I'm losing patience, boy."

His face paled at a rapid rate. "Oh, shit me out on a piece of toast. You're one of the blood drinkers."

"Answer me." I was close enough that he could have stabbed me. But he seemed smarter than that.

"He ruined me. I..." Light brown eyes flicked up to mine and then away as he slumped against the counter. "I was the talk of NYC. But when he disappeared, someone leaked documents claiming I'd been using tainted meat. That people were getting Hep A from eating here."

I frowned. "Why would he do that?"

"Because he's an asshole? I don't know."

There had to be a better reason. Victor was an asshole, on that I agreed. But he had never ruined someone without reason.

"What happens when a kitchen gets condemned like this?"

He waved his knife around. "In our case, the FDA came in with the CDC hot on their tails."

"For Hep A?" My eyes widened. "Seems like overkill, don't you think?"

He grunted. "Not for a restaurant like this one. Lots of patrons with lots of money. Money greases wheels, if you haven't noticed."

Whatever had been hidden here was probably long gone, but I drew in a deep breath and held the air, tasting it. "Let me see the freezers."

"They've been shut off. They aren't cold."

"So?"

"They were cleaned, but they still smell funky."

Now that was interesting. "Take me."

Chef boy led the way further into the kitchen. I had to hand it to Victor. Even his cooking staff knew how to obey orders.

"Here." He pointed at a pair of large steel doors propped open. I grabbed his arm and shoved him ahead of me. "Hey, don't!"

"Little late for that," I said. I didn't even have to take a deep breath when I stepped into the doorway of the freezer. The smell of blood permeated every crevice. I tightened my hold on chef boy. "How long ago did they clean it up?"

"A few days," he whispered.

"Where are all the vamps?"

He shook his head. "Gone. They disappeared when Victor did."

So before the CDC came in, someone had professionally cleaned out all the blood Victor used to keep in here. His head chef had taken the blame, and no one would be the wiser about what had really gone on at *Amore Sangre*.

The ding of a timer going off whipped me around. A heavy billow of gas rolled over me. "The lines have slipped...can you fix this?" I asked.

I dragged him with me, hoping he could do something. He started to blubber. "I can't live without my cooking."

Oh. Fuck.

I dropped his arm and sprinted through the kitchen as the fumes spread. One glance at the stove and the blue flames licking at the bottom of the four pots he had going told me all I needed to know.

Time was not on my side. The fumes caught the blue flames and a brilliant flash popped up behind me.

The hiss of flames nipped at my heels, the heat spurring me forward. I was out the main doors by the time the first boom rocked the building. The elevator door opened on my left, beckoning me, as three demon dogs burst out of the stairwell to my right. They carried a scent I knew as well as my own.

Calvin.

I had no time to consider what it meant.

Elevator it was. I stepped in and hit the button to close the doors repeatedly. They closed, but not before one of the demon dogs leapt through them. It hit me in the back, scrabbling and clawing at my side, then reaching down and clawing through my pants and into the flesh of my thigh. I twisted, then flipped us over so I was positioned over it, sitting on it, then yanked a silver stake from the top of my boot and slammed it through the dog's left eye socket. It whimpered, gave a full body twitch and went still.

A second boom rocked the building and the elevator shuddered. I jumped up and pushed the escape hatch open over my head. Above me, the world was nothing but flames two floors above me. The elevator lurched to a stop, swaying in place.

"Seriously?" What was it with these particular death traps and me lately?

A chunk of burning metal dropped toward me. I jerked back into the elevator as it bounced off the top of the tiny hanging box, and the whole contraption groaned. I pulled myself up through the hatch. There was only one choice—I had to get to another floor and work my way down. The cables above me groaned, and two of them snapped, slicing through the air. I leapt to the side and hooked my fingers onto the doorway above my head as the remaining cables gave way and the elevator plummeted down the shaft.

I pulled myself up to the edge of the doors and pried them open. The racket was almost unbearable to my sensitive ears—sirens blared in the distance, and there were continued smaller booms from above. Which was my only excuse for not seeing him until I was all the way through the door.

Calvin stared down at me. "Are you okay?"

I put my hand in his and blinked several times. No. Not Calvin, but a young human who could have passed for his brother. The same hair color, eyes, and build. I tightened my grip on his hand as hunger surged through me.

Had he been left here to toy with my emotions?

"Come with me." I tugged him and he followed, falling under my thrall so swiftly I knew he'd been used before. Most people fought the urge to obey. He just got in line and did as I commanded.

We worked our way to the stairs and started the long climb down, conspicuously free of demon dogs. The fire-fighters had just arrived by the time we reached the bottom floor. I paused and put a hand on the lead man. "Don't go up yet. Let it burn."

His eyes fogged. "Don't go up yet."

"No. Stay here."

It was the only thing I could do to keep the humans safe not only from the fire, but from the demon dogs up there. They couldn't handle doors on their own, which meant someone had helped them. Rachel would have wanted me to at least try to keep the men safe.

I walked away, my new pet trailing behind me. After a while, he jogged to catch up to my side. "Where are we going?"

I didn't answer, not wanting to know him for anything other than what he was. Food.

Three blocks down, I stopped and ducked into an alley. The Calvin lookalike smiled at me and tipped his head to the side. I took the invitation and yanked him to me, burying my fangs deeply into his neck. He moaned and wrapped his arms around my waist. The hair, the smell of Calvin still buried deeply in my mind, the intense need for blood, the sensations Ivan had aroused.

I couldn't control myself, but to be honest, I wasn't even sure I tried. I drank the lookalike all the way down. His death was a heady rush, the final beats of his heart the strongest, the last of his blood the richest and most vital. I ripped my mouth from his neck and tipped my head back, breathing hard.

My entire body was sensitized to the world, the humans around me, the feel of the wind along the back of my neck. I breathed out as the new vampire in my arms stirred.

"Thank you, I've wanted this for so long. I thought I would never be turned after the other vampires left."

He tightened his hold on me, as if to pull me into a hug.

I hadn't given him my own blood, which meant he'd had vamp blood before. I'd found him in Victor's club, so that shouldn't have been a surprise. Instead it was a disappointment.

I pulled my silver stake out and rammed it into his heart. "You're welcome."

CHAPTER 10

RACHEL

I opened the envelope and dumped the contents onto the table. Several photos and a piece of paper. The photos were of a nondescript building in what appeared to be a desert.

One focused on an entrance with two armed soldiers standing guard. It was hard to see their faces, but the uniforms looked U.S. Army. On the back of one photo were numbers. 30.5 N 47.816 E. Latitude and longitude coordinates. I suspected Hades had just confirmed that the facility in Derrick's notes was indeed where we needed to go. I opened the folded paper next and read a cryptic phrase.

What you found will not be what it was.

What the hell did that mean?

There wasn't time to think about it, though. I needed to follow Hades and find out where he went.

I burst out the front door, searching the shadows across the street where Ivan was supposed to be hiding. My phone vibrated in my jeans pocket, and I pulled it out to read the screen.

I'm following the mad scientist. Meet back up with you later.

Should I leave Ivan to it? It wasn't like I had much choice, not that I was happy about it. Hades had practically disappeared into the shadows. Sure, I had an initial fifty-fifty chance of going in the right direction to start, but he could have turned down any number of alleyways. And yet…how did Ivan know where to meet us later? Lea had told me to meet her where we'd met Sean the other night. Why would Ivan know where that was?

I didn't trust the werewolf. That was probably grounded in the fact I no longer trusted men in general, but the timing of his appearance was a little too suspect. Even if he arranged for us to meet with the werewolves, it could be a trap. And for a brief moment, I wondered if Lea's judgment of him could be trusted. I'd seen how he affected her. I knew firsthand how a man could make a woman behave like an idiot.

Never again.

I headed back to the subway station, pulling the jacket hood over my head. A light drizzle began to fall, which helped hide my face. I doubted anyone was looking for me here—I hadn't been followed by anyone resembling the government drones who'd chased us in Midtown—but it couldn't hurt to be too careful.

I headed down the steps to the station, my mind reeling with the Rubik's cube of how to get into Iraq. We couldn't just hop on a plane from New York to Baghdad. Even if flights were available, we'd never get an official visa. We'd have to take a more indirect route, and Turkey was probably our best bet.

We could fly into Istanbul, take a smaller flight to Diyarbakir, and then take a taxi across the border into Zakho, Iraq. I'd made that trip several times in my last years as a war reporter. I just needed to make sure it was still a viable route. And I'd have to reach out to my contacts to get under-the-table visas. There were a lot of variables in play, but we needed to get to that facility. I'd tunnel underground if it came to it.

The subway platform was quiet, making it simultaneously easy to notice if someone was following me and creepy as hell when a man descended the stairs from the opposite end of the platform. He waited at the other end, keeping his attention on the tunnel. He wore jeans, boots, and a leather jacket. His hair was in need of a trim, but his beard was very close cut. In fact, it looked more like a five o'clock shadow had been given a few days to grow. There was something about him that set me on edge, but I couldn't figure out what. Was he human?

I had to laugh at that one. Until a couple of weeks ago, I only would have asked that question while drunk.

The train pulled in and no one got off, so I headed toward a middle car, keeping my eye on the man as he boarded toward the front, not even giving me a glance.

I really was paranoid.

Paranoid enough that I didn't sit in a seat even though there were several empty ones around me. I hung onto the pole instead, keeping my gaze on the doors while casting furtive sideways glances. The only thing of interest was a couple in the throes of a hot and heavy makeout session to my left. That was good. The few people around them looked uncomfortable, which gave me a good excuse for standing out of their PDA zone.

I had to change trains to get to the vacant hotel. The next three stops were uneventful, so I started to let my guard down when I boarded the next train, ready for a longer trip.

I was still too edgy to sit, so I was standing and staring at the doors when something caught my attention out of the corner of my eye. The man from the first platform was several feet in front of me, a purposeful look in his eye. I turned to run, but he grabbed my hand and pulled me to his chest. "There you are, baby. I told you the front car," he said loud enough for everyone to hear, then lowered his mouth to my ear. "You're being tailed."

"No shit. You're proof enough of that," I snarled, my hands on his chest, prepared to push him away. Two things stopped me: One, he was holding me in a vise grip with his arm, and two, if he was right, I didn't want to draw any more attention to myself. But now I was worried. Had these supposed tails seen me meet Hades?

"I don't think they saw you meet your contact at the diner. You seemed to pick them up here in the station."

I gasped as I looked up at him. Did this asshole have mind-reading abilities?

He gave me a cocky grin, but his eyes were full of warning. "I know more about you than you think."

"Just what every girl wants to hear."

He chuckled softly, then leaned in closer, his tone turning serious. "You're playing a dangerous game here, Rachel."

He knew my name. Shit. But then again, I'd been on TV earlier that evening. A report like that was bound to set all the crazies loose. "I'm a big girl. I know how to take care of myself."

"Are you trusting the right people?"

That gave me pause. What exactly did he know? "Is there someone I shouldn't be trusting?"

His breath blew warm against my ear, sending a chill down my back. "The supernatural world is not to be trusted. They don't like to be outed. I hope you have a plan."

My heart skipped a beat. "Is that who's following me right now? Someone from the supernatural world?" Shit. I needed to get some silver stakes pronto. I could handle humans, but I was no physical match for vampires. While Lea had said there weren't many of them, it made sense they might try to eliminate me for speaking out about their world.

"Keep your friends close and your enemies closer. You're right to stay with her for now, but don't trust her for a minute."

He knew about Lea, and he believed in the supernatural world. Which meant he saw me as a pawn in this game. If he was warning me, that meant I was currently serving some purpose for him. "What's your stake in this?"

"I don't think you're adequately prepared to handle the mess you've created."

"You think I should back off?" I asked in belligerence.

"No, you're exactly where you need to be, but you aren't ready to defend yourself."

He was right and it pissed me off. But there hadn't exactly been time for a visit to the anti-supernatural protection store. If there even was one.

His hand cupped my cheek and tilted my head up to face him. I sucked in a breath as I stared into his intense brown eyes, my hold on his jacket beginning to loosen in anticipation.

I felt something several inches long and most likely made of leather slip into the back waistband of my jeans.

I stiffened, but before I could jerk away, his arm tightened. He whispered, still staring into my eyes, "I need you to stay alive, Rachel Sambrook. Can you do that for me?" The intensity in his gaze almost made me believe he gave a shit about me.

Almost.

I pushed on his chest, but his hold didn't slip an inch. "Why the fuck should I believe you care about me?"

The train was slowing down, and the speaker overhead announced the next station.

He grinned, but it wasn't the cocky expression I halfway expected. It was just the barest lift of the corners of his mouth. The intensity in his dark brown irises mesmerized me. Pinned in his gaze, I didn't put up a protest as his face lowered, his lips lightly skimming mine.

I froze as his warm breath fanned across my cheek, his kiss growing bolder. My fingers dug into his jacket in an effort to remain upright as the train came to a stop.

The doors opened and I felt movement to my side as someone boarded the train, but this man's mouth had me spellbound, blocking out everything and everyone around me except for him.

His head lifted and determination filled his eyes, before they softened. "Don't worry, pet. You will see me soon enough."

Then he shoved me hard, throwing me out of the train car. I landed on my side as the doors shut.

I saw him through the car windows, knife in his hand, facing two men. As the train pulled away, they rushed him, and the way he defended himself led me to believe he could hold his own.

Something poked the top of my ass cheek. I reached

back and pulled out a six-inch-long leather case with a sil-ver handle sticking out the top. I pulled it free, gasping at the sleek silver blade. There was no doubt it was designed for killing supernatural creatures. The question was, why had he really given it to me?

CHAPTER 11

LEA

I crouched in the second floor window of the broken-down hotel. This was where we'd met Sean, where he'd done his damnedest to convince Rachel I was the bad guy and he could be trusted. Turned out he was wrong, a mistake that had cost him his life.

Rachel was below me, pacing from one end of the blown-out room to the other. She hadn't seen me yet, and I'd decided to watch her to see if anyone followed her into the abandoned hotel.

Her hands went to her lower back, paused, then fluttered up to her lips.

"Son of a bitch," she muttered, never slowing her steps.

Interesting. An image of Ivan kissing her sent a shot of pure adrenaline through my system that shocked the shit out of me. There was no way she would have let him kiss her. But then, where was he? I'd told him to watch over her.

I waited another full minute. Though I told myself it was to make sure we were safe, the real reason was that I was pissed at Ivan for being missing.

And more pissed at the thought of him kissing Rachel. I drew in a slow breath. No, I was not going there. Ivan was a werewolf—lecherous, dangerous and unpredictable. I had no reason to be surprised he hadn't followed through with my command.

I pushed off the window ledge and dropped to the floor, deliberately landing on a stack of wood. It clattered away from me and Rachel spun around, whipping out a six-inch silver stake. I couldn't help my eyes from widening. There was no way Ivan had given her that.

"Good reflexes."

The stake was a replica of mine, right down to the length of the handle. A Cazador's weapon. Even more interesting. I didn't ask her about it, I didn't need to. There were very few people who would have access to silver stakes.

I walked toward her as she tucked the stake away. "Who kissed you?" The question popped out of me before I thought better of it.

Her mouth dropped open, but she snapped it shut so fast her teeth clicked. Her face flamed an interesting shade of pink visible to me even in the dim light. "No one."

A lie so thick it all but hung in the air between us. "Where's Ivan?"

"He followed my contact." She seemed to pull herself together. "How is he going to find us?"

I shrugged and Rachel narrowed her eyes. A few

beats of silence passed between us, and then she smiled a slow-growing grin I didn't like.

"Oh my God. You think Ivan kissed me? Girl, he is so not my type. Irritating as hell is about all he is to me."

My jaw ticked, but I struggled to keep eye contact with her. I finally put a hand to my forehead. "*Madre de Dios*, what wrong with me? Hundreds of years and I've never been affected like this."

"Not even with Calvin?" Ever the journalist, she asked the one question that cut to the heart of it.

"No. Not even with him. That was...slow." I shook my head, remembering all too vividly the scent I'd picked up right before the restaurant had blown up. Time to change the subject, and I'd have to do it rapidly to avoid the girl talk we were falling into. "I don't think Calvin is dead. I caught wind of him and then it disappeared just as quickly right before I ran into trouble."

Rachel crossed her arms, her blue eyes hard as ice in the dead of winter. "What kind of trouble?"

"The usual. Explosions, demon dogs, and monstrous flames. No way out."

She swallowed hard, her throat bobbing. "If he's a vamp, would he really turn on you?"

I closed my eyes and searched my heart well and truly for the first time, letting myself see Calvin for all his flaws as well as his strengths. "He will hate me for not killing him, with the passion only a true zealot can have. So, yes. He could turn on us." I opened my eyes and let out a long breath. "He knows my ways, knows how I do things. Calvin would be the perfect vampire for them to set on us."

"Well, that's just fucking great, isn't it?" Rachel spat out as she began to pace again.

I leaned back against one of the broken pillars. "Who gave you the stake?"

"Some guy." She raised her left hand to her lips again—an unconscious gesture. So. The man who'd given her the stake had also kissed her. Her face pinked up again, but I didn't pursue that line of questioning. There had to be some give and take in the trust department, on both sides, for our partnership to work.

"Where's the vampire you were going to bring back for questioning?" Rachel half turned toward me.

"They've all fled the city. Except for Calvin, and I have little hope of finding him until he's ready to be found. Since Ivan is following the contact, I assume that means you got nothing."

Rachel dug into the bag hanging at her side and pulled out an envelope. "Not nothing. But not everything I'd hoped for, either."

I took it from her and flipped through the contents. A couple of pictures, one of them with coordinates written on the back, and a phrase that meant nothing to me.

"This is where we'll find Stravinsky." I tapped the back of the picture, holding it with the coordinates. "This just confirms that we're on the right path."

"That would make the most sense. It almost feels too easy, though. Like a trap."

I snorted softly, memorizing the coordinates and the phrase before I tucked the documents back into the envelope and handed it to Rachel. "Life is a trap, my friend. It's how you handle the snap of the killing blow that determines if you are the prey or the predator."

"Lea," the way she said my name should have tipped me off, "why do you hate vampires so much? Not that I'm against going after them, but I met Louis. He wasn't a bad guy. And while you're a crazy-ass bitch when it comes to fighting, you don't go around killing vamps left and right. They can't all be bad."

"No? Do you know that for the first fifty years of a vampire's life, the blood lust is nearly uncontrollable? They'll feed on anyone without thought unless controlled by a master vampire. Louis was only as polite as he was because whoever made him had a tight hold on the reins. One slip, and he would have been on you and Calvin in an instant."

"Then why didn't you kill him?" she asked.

"Because I gave you my word!" I snapped. "You ask questions because it's in your blood. And I kill vampires because it is in mine. They took everything from me. They drained my older sister, making her one of them."

I closed my eyes and tried to breathe through the memory. "They left me and my parents tied to three chairs, cuts in our necks so the blood dripped freely." I could taste the fear on my tongue, the salt of my tears as I cried for Anna to wake up. Her dark hair just like mine spread about her face as if she were sleeping. Rachel said something, but I didn't hear it as the words poured from me.

"She did wake up. Anna drained our mother first. My father screamed for her to stop, begged her. Called on God to stop her. His cries drew her to him next. Whether he meant to or not, my father bought me the time I needed."

"Lea. You don't have to—"

"I worked my hands out of the bonds before she made it to me, and she was so intent on her feeding, she didn't notice I was free. I took a silver candlestick and rammed it through her heart as she drained my father. Her screams echoed through the night, and the Cazadors found me sobbing in a puddle of my sister's blood. They told me my parents would rise as monsters if I didn't drive stakes through them too. But that was a test to see how strong I was. I later learned they wouldn't have turned without drinking vampire blood."

I stared hard at Rachel, seeing the fear in her eyes. "I am not angry you asked. But it is not something I like to remember."

"I'm sorry."

"So am I," Ivan said from the shadows. Rachel and I had our stakes out, one right after the other.

I glared at Ivan, unreasonably angry that he had heard my story. Even more so that he'd snuck up on us.

Again.

"Stop doing that," Rachel snapped. "Make some fucking noise, would you?"

He grinned at her. "Bet you don't yell at Lea for being quiet."

"She's on my side."

"So am I."

"Stop it," I said. "Both of you. Did you catch up with her contact?"

His grin faltered and he shook his head. "No. I have no idea how the hell he slipped me, but from one street to the next his scent was completely gone. Maybe even from one step to the next."

Rachel looked at me. "Like Calvin? Could they be using something to mask their scent?"

I nodded, already on that same line of thought. "He's a scientist and he's worked with Stravinsky from what we know; it's plausible they've come up with a way to keep us from tracking them."

The numbers on Rachel's papers swirled in my head. I wanted to find that bastard Stravinsky so I could dig him out and roast him on an open fire.

"That grin, Lea. It's disturbing." Rachel wrinkled up her nose at me.

I laughed. "Thinking about what I'm going to do to Stravinsky when we find him."

A wicked glimmer lit her eyes. "I assume I get to help with that part."

"Bring the lighter fluid."

Ivan looked from me to Rachel and back again. "You two are scary together."

"Do as you're told, and we'll get along just fine," I said, then paused and waved my hand forward. "Ready to hunt him down?"

Rachel nodded. "Let's do this."

Chapter 12

RACHEL

G reat. The giant pain in the ass was coming. "Do you even have a passport?" I asked him, my hands on my hips, my voice echoing off the walls of the vacant hotel.

His eyebrows lifted in amusement. "I have several. Which country of origin do you think I should go for?"

Asshole. He annoyed the hell out of me, mostly because he seemed to take Lea slightly off her game. And ordinarily I'd tell her to chase a piece of ass, but in this situation, I needed her all there. Not distracted by an oversized asshat. "United States will do. Less suspicious that way."

"Harvey Warhol. Louisville, Kentucky."

It was my turn to lift my eyebrows. "You think you can pull that off? You don't have even the slightest hint of a southern accent."

"I'm a paper salesman who was transferred last year from Boston."

I pushed out a breath. He seemed to have the story down. "You need to book your own tickets. We all do. We can't travel together or we'll draw attention. I'll travel under an alias. At least to London. Too many people might recognize me on a flight originating from the U.S. I'll pull out my Turkish alias and passport later."

Ivan burst out laughing. "You expect to pass for Turkish? Are you counting on Lea's power of persuasion to pull that off?"

"You really are an idiot, aren't you? Turkey has one of the most ethnically diverse populations in the world. Have you heard of the Adyghe people? No?" I asked when his grin fell. "Russians driven south. No, they're not typically blond, but a wig will take care of that. I've used that ID before without incident."

I turned to Lea, already done with him, and explained the travel plan I'd cobbled together on the way over—London to Turkey to Iraq. "I think we should use different aliases for the flight from London to Istanbul. The problem is getting visas for you two, but I think I can arrange something. I have a border guard contact who can be persuaded to help."

"And by persuaded, you mean bribed," Lea said dryly.

"Exactly."

I pulled out my phone and tried to open my email app. "I need your aliases to make it happen. And we've got to go somewhere with Wi-Fi. I'll use my VPN to hide our tracks."

"VPN?" Ivan asked.

"Virtual Private Network. It hides my location and makes it harder for the bad guys to track us."

Appreciation filled Lea's eyes. "Smart."

I shrugged. "I've done this a time or two. But we need to throw them off. So when I book tickets, I'm booking them through to Germany." I glanced over my shoulder. "Ivan, you need to go to Zimbabwe."

"Why Germany?" Lea asked.

"The Nazis were famous for their medical and genetic experimentation. And with the name Stravinsky...we'll lead them on a wild goose chase. Make them think we're off track. Traveling separately will strengthen our deception. Then we'll disappear in Heathrow and fly to Turkey— separately again."

"*Very* smart."

I performed a quick search on my travel app, then looked up. "It's 1:30 a.m. How quickly can you be ready to go?"

Ivan's eyes widened. "An hour."

Lea nodded. "The same."

"Then let's take the four a.m. train from Penn Station to Philadelphia and catch the ten a.m. flight to London."

"Why Philadelphia?" Ivan asked.

"To throw them off. They'll be watching the airports in New York."

Lea's mouth curved into a predatory smile, making me once again glad we were on the same side. "I like it."

"I need to get Derrick's bag and a Wi-Fi hot spot. I say we all meet at Penn Station in two hours."

Lea gave me a pointed look and frowned. "No, we stick together from now on."

I put a hand on my hip. "You don't trust me?"

"I don't trust the creatures you plan to use that stake on."

She was lying—I could feel it as clearly as if she were in my head. She wanted to know where I'd gotten the stake, but I wasn't ready to divulge yet. She was keeping secrets from me. I knew she'd encountered more than the usual mayhem and madness while she was gone.

She'd been evasive about finding a vampire to question, which made me wary. Was the man on the subway right? Should I be careful whom I trusted? Perhaps Lea considered this a temporary alliance. But we were both out to achieve the same goal—stop Stravinsky and the Asclepius Project. That had to be good enough for the moment.

"Fine. Derrick's bag is in Penn Station, so I only have to find a twenty-four-hour diner with Internet to book our tickets and get in touch with our contact."

"There's Wi-Fi where I'm headed." She looked past me to Ivan. "Can you meet us in two hours?"

"Of course. And I'll grab your bag from my abandoned cab. Which is probably impounded."

"Is that a problem?" Lea asked.

He grinned. "Not at all."

I shot him a derisive look. "Remember, you need to book your own flight to London. With your alias. It's United Flight 2980. Then onto Zimbabwe."

He smirked. "Trying to ditch me?"

I shot him a sneer.

Lea sighed, clearly exasperated with our bickering. "Ivan, book your ticket. It's better this way. Rachel, let's go."

We took the subway to Victor's bunker. After acting as

her benefactor for years, Victor had turned on her. It was hard to imagine Lea having a benefactor, but since killing vampires was her actual job, she had to be paid somehow.

Victor had been an interesting man. While his father had wanted to purge the world of vampires, Victor had wanted to become one—a gift Lea had repeatedly refused to give him. It had been his undoing in the end. After his death, Lea had taken over his secret bunker and all that was in it. Which included multiple specially-developed weapons to fight supernatural creatures.

"It's a shame we can't take these with us."

I pulled my laptop out of my bag and booted it up. "I suppose we might have gotten away with hiding a few things in a checked bag, but our bags will go straight to Berlin…and we won't. Too bad we can't hire a private jet."

Lea glanced up at me.

Did Victor have that much money lying around? "No, we need to stick to this plan. They know I'm going to do something to prove my story is true. If I just disappear without a trace, they'll start actively looking for me in Iraq. We need to buy all the time we can get. But *you* could take a private jet."

Some emotion flashed in her eyes. "No. We stick together."

I nodded. I preferred it that way too. I wanted her in my sights as much as she wanted me in hers.

She grabbed a stack of cash from a safe and several passport books. "I have several nationalities to choose from when we fly into Turkey. My Spanish passport might serve us best."

"Sounds good." I bought the tickets separately, using Victor's credit card. "I'll purchase the tickets to Turkey on the train," I said. "I don't want them to be bought so closely together."

"Good idea."

We reached Penn Station with time to spare. Derrick's bag was in a weekly rental locker. I grabbed his laptop and papers and stuffed them into my bag and slung it over my shoulder. "Let's go."

We purchased our train tickets separately too. Lea stood about twenty feet away while I took a seat in a plastic chair, my nerves a ball of unbridled energy. I'd never been good at sitting around, waiting for life to happen to me. And while I knew we were taking the offensive, I still had an uneasy feeling. The bearded stranger's words hung in my head.

The train pulled in and the few passengers disembarked. I climbed aboard and took a seat by a window looking out on the platform. There was still no sign of Ivan, but Lea was standing in the same place. Though she was trying to look like she didn't care, I could see worry in the slight curve of her shoulder. I watched her as she pretended to talk on her cell phone—or was it real? She hung up and waited another minute. When the overhead speaker announced the train was about to depart from the station, she climbed aboard the car behind mine without a sideways glance.

Had Ivan gotten held up somewhere or had he gotten what he wanted? Lea had to be disappointed, even if she would likely act otherwise, but I couldn't pretend I wasn't happy. After my encounter with the man on the train, I didn't trust Ivan.

The doors closed and the train was about to pull out of the station when a man burst through the turnstiles, racing for the train at superhuman speed. He pushed the doors open and slipped through them just as the train began to pull away.

For better or worse, it was the three of us. Whether I liked it or not.

CHAPTER 13

LEA

I van tumbled into the train, falling to his knees right at my feet. He lifted his head and his eyes met mine, but it was the gash down the side of his face and the smell of blood that captured my attention. I grabbed his arm and hauled him further into the train.

"What happened?"

"They were waiting for me at the cab."

Which meant they knew we were working together. Fuck. I found a private car and shoved him in. "Sit. Stay." I pointed for good measure.

Rachel was right behind me when I turned around. "How bad is it?"

"He'll heal. We just need to make sure we aren't noticed."

"Then maybe you should get in there with him, Miss Leather and Hooded Cowl," Rachel said with more than a touch of sarcasm. I grimaced.

"I have other clothes in the bag Ivan brought me. I'll change."

I ducked into the small space with Ivan. He was flat out on his back, or as flat out as he could be in the tiny bed space allotted to each stateroom. Thank God this wasn't some subway train with standing room only.

His long legs hung off one end, his arms off the other. My leather bag was clutched in one hand.

"Where's your bag?" I took my bag from him and opened it on the floor. A pair of jeans and a long-sleeved shirt with a hoodie attached would do the trick. I peeled off my leathers and bundled them up, quickly yanking on the more mundane clothes. Ivan's gaze was heavy on my skin, but I refused to acknowledge it.

"Didn't have time to get mine."

"Well, you need one. No one will think you're flying to London for fun if you don't even have a carry-on."

I stood and shoved my bag under the bench bed. "Who attacked you?"

Rachel opened the door and stepped in, a snarl on her lips. "You idiot, you were tailed."

Ivan sat up with a grimace. "No, I wasn't."

"Then who the fuck is asking for us *by name* while they search the train?" she whispered. "They have pictures too. These aren't tourists looking for an autograph."

"Could they have traced your phone while you made the reservations?" I asked her.

"You're going to side with *him*?"

I shook my head. "No. I'm not siding with him." *Madre de Dios*, it was like dealing with two squabbling children, both wanting my approval. "If Ivan led them to us, that's a problem. If the phone led them to us, that's a bigger problem. We need to know which it is, so I'm going to find out."

I pushed past her and out into hall. I pulled my hair into a twist and tucked it down the back of my shirt, hiding the length. My one nod to vanity, I didn't have the heart to cut it off even after all these years.

My steps took me into the main car of the train. Two men dressed in jeans and polo shirts were walking in my direction, talking to the passengers. Government, or someone else? One had a light windbreaker on that rustled as he walked. Here and there, I could see the outline of a gun through the thin material.

I was betting *someone else* based on the shape of the gun alone. It was far from government issue.

I leaned against the back wall and listened to their spiel.

"Sorry to bother you, we're looking for our two sisters. Our mother is dying and they left for a trip today. We just want to find them so they can say goodbye."

I couldn't help the arch of my eyebrow as it rose to my hairline. The passengers seemed largely sympathetic. Many just shook their heads, but a few whispered words that were far too kind.

Mr. Windbreaker reached me first. "Miss, can you take a look at this picture? It's my sister Rachel."

I had to fight a sharp intake of breath as I took the picture from him. It had been taken outside Victor's safe house a few hours ago.

"You know, I think I did see her. She was sitting this way." I didn't make eye contact with him, only turned with the picture in my hand. Mr. Windbreaker let out an exaggerated sigh of relief. "Oh, that's great. We've been looking for her everywhere."

"I'll bet," I said softly, glancing back at him. His buddy followed along, and I inadvertently caught his eye. He glanced at the picture in his hand and then back at me as he moved through the passage between the cars.

"Fuck. It's the vamp."

I kicked backward, driving my foot into Mr. Windbreaker's solar plexus, which sent him flying into his little friend. Hard enough to hurt, but not enough to kill. We needed answers and they were going to give them up.

As they tumbled to the floor in a heap, I headed back to the room where I'd left Rachel and Ivan. I opened the door and poked my head in. "Company. Be ready."

Rachel nodded and Ivan sat up. I looked back the way I'd come and then ducked into the room just as the two men came into view. All they would see of me was a glimmer of movement disappearing through the doorway.

I stood behind the door, Rachel to my right, Ivan still on the bed. He touched my leg. "They're at the door."

Fuck, his hearing was even better than mine. I jerked the door open and the two men tumbled in. I grabbed Mr. Windbreaker and lifted him over my head by his throat, flashing my fangs for good measure. Rachel grabbed his buddy and yanked him around so his neck was in a perfect lock of her arms. In seconds, he was out cold from the chokehold and she dropped him to the floor.

Mr. Windbreaker whimpered, "Don't kill me."

I slowly lowered him to the floor, but didn't let go. Neither had gone for their guns. They hadn't even made an attempt.

"Who are you?"

"Evan Smith. That's Marvin Eckles."

Ivan laughed. "Awe-inspiring names if I ever heard them. And I have heard them before."

Evan looked past me to Ivan and his face paled to a faint green. "Oh God. Please don't let him near me."

"Shut your mouth before I shut it for you, Evan." Ivan's voice had none of the humor I'd come to expect from him.

Rachel's brow furrowed as she watched Ivan. I wanted to look back at him too, but we all had our secrets, and I didn't have time to dig into Ivan's.

"The wolf listens to me," I said. "So you'd better start talking unless you want me to give him a new chew toy."

Teeth chattering, Evan nodded. "The guns are empty. We...we aren't here to try and hurt you."

"Try is the word," Rachel muttered. I had to agree.

"Then why are you following us?"

"We broke clean from the facility. They don't know we're still alive. We know what they're planning, and we want to help you."

A chill climbed my spine, like a tiny row of spiders skittering along my skin. "Talk."

He quivered from head to toe. "You don't have much time. They're going to start testing on large numbers of people. Villages. Then cities. Turning innocent people into weapons." His eyes flicked from me to Ivan, then to Rachel. "I don't know if you three can stop them. But you should know they're on to you. They know you're coming."

Rachel stepped closer to him, her blue eyes flashing. "How?"

He swallowed hard, his throat bobbing as if he couldn't get enough saliva down. "One of you has a tracer on them. I don't know which one, I only know it's one of you three. If you don't find it, you're royally fucked."

Rachel's eyes shot to Ivan. "You fucking idiot. You've got a tracer on you!"

"I don't. I'd feel it," he said, calm as a summer's day. "The low current of electricity would be enough to drive me insane in a matter of days. Which means it's one of you two ladies. If Evan is telling the truth, that is...he could be messing with us. Shits and giggles and all that."

"Well, how the fuck are we going to find the tracer then?"

The train slowed, the brakes letting out a heavy screech.

Evan whimpered, "They're here, we have to go. If Hades shows up, don't trust him. He'll lead you on a merry chase and then slit your throat once he's finished with his fun." He stepped out of the room, dragging his buddy with him.

"How much time do you think we have?" Rachel asked. "Maybe we can get on the roof of the train, make a jump when it slows down more."

"If one of you is being traced, they'll still find us," Ivan said.

"Then we'll split up," she said. "See which one of us gets followed."

I lifted a hand, stopping them. "I think it's me. The demon dog slashed me up badly. We weren't being followed until then. Not like this. It could have been fitted into its teeth or claws as an injectable."

Rachel's eyes widened. "Fuck."

"My thoughts exactly." I yanked off my shirt and slid down my jeans. "Ivan, could you pick up the vibration in your hands? You said you'd be able to tell if the tracer was in you."

He grinned. "You want me to feel you up?"

"Do it, wolf, and do it now. We're running out of time," I snapped. I didn't do vulnerable well and this was as about as exposed as it got. Nothing but underwear, no weapons, asking a man I was intrigued by to run his hands over my body while the bad guys were hot on our tails.

I pointed to where the demon dog had hit me. "Side, thigh, lower back."

Ivan started on my back, his big hands super-heated on my cooler than normal skin. I let out a low hiss.

"Don't you two get kinky on me," Rachel said. I glanced at her, horrified at the thought. And realized she'd said it to break the growing tension.

"Nothing," Ivan said as he moved to my side, cupping my waist. "Not here either." Down to my thigh he went, all but caressing my skin. I closed my eyes, knowing already—

"Got it. Rachel, hand me a knife."

I kept my eyes closed as he pressed the blade to the meat of my thigh. "Do it. I won't flinch."

"Of that, I have no doubt," he murmured. The knife cut in with a quick flick. His fingers slipped in and I grimaced as they pulled on me, tearing at the edges of the cut.

"Rachel, my hands are too big." Ivan held my thigh open. I looked back at her. Blue eyes narrowed.

"I did not sign up for this shit," she said, but she was already at my side, her hand sliding into my open wound. The train continued to slow as the seconds ticked past. Time was almost up.

"Got it!" she yelled as she yanked the red blinking, small button-sized device from my flesh. Ivan grabbed his shirt and ripped off a piece to wrap around my leg. I pushed him away. "Leave it. I'll heal."

"You know that reopening the demon-dog wound will probably slow the healing—make it human-slow."

He was right, of course. The bioengineering makes their saliva and claws the perfect weapon against supernaturals.

Already the burn of the injury was spreading up my leg

to my hip. Why hadn't I already thought of that? Fuck, I was slipping up. I jerked my leather pants out of my bag and pulled them on. They would hold the wound tightly. Hoodie shirt back on, I strapped on my weapons in seconds.

Scooping up the tracer device, I nodded at the window. "Rachel, I like your idea. High ground has always worked for us before. You ready?"

She grinned. "You bet your red panties, I am."

I rolled my eyes but still laughed. "They were on sale."

"Sure, sure."

Ivan opened the window and glanced back. "Since when do panties go on sale?"

We pushed him out first, and he hung off the roof, holding a hand out to us. Rachel's eyes met mine, serious once more. "Do you trust him?" she whispered.

"Not like I trust you."

She jerked in surprise. "You trust me?"

"With my life."

Why was she surprised? And then it hit me. Whoever had given her the silver stake had warned her against me.

Fucking hell, I did not have time for her to get nervous. She went out the window first, and Ivan hauled her to the roof. Before I could clamber out after her, the door behind me burst open and several guns were pointed at me.

"Put your hands up!"

I lifted my hands, a grin sliding over my face. "If you say so."

CHAPTER 14

RACHEL

My mind was already spinning as Ivan hauled me to the top of the train. If we jumped off, we'd be seriously behind schedule to catch our flight in Philadelphia. But at the moment, I was more concerned with surviving.

I glanced behind me. "Where's Lea?"

"She's still in the room." His brow lowered as he leaned further over the edge.

"Be careful," I said. "You're going to fall off."

He shot me a grin, but I could see the worry in his eyes. "Aww…you care about me."

"No, but Lea seems to. I'd hate to have to explain why I let you fall off the damn train." He looked back over the edge again, and I said, "You really care about her, don't you."

His head jerked up. "She's important."

"That's such a bullshit answer."

Rather than respond, he leaned over and hauled Lea up with him this time. She had several fresh blood splatters on her hoodie.

"Run!" she shouted, already racing toward the roof of the next train car.

Ivan took off after her and I followed. The crack of a gunshot behind me gave me a new burst of energy. The source seemed to come from several cars down, thankfully, which meant they had a better chance of missing us, or more specifically me. I was the most fragile of all of us.

That thought must have occurred to Lea too, because she slowed and reached for me when she got to the end of a car. "Get down and head to the dining car. I'll meet you there."

"I think that's a bad idea. For so many reasons."

"If we get separated, meet me at the airport in Philadelphia."

"Are you *kidding* me?"

"No. Go." She turned to Ivan. "Wolf, stay with me."

A grin spread across his face.

I rolled my eyes and squatted next to the metal ladder leading down to a door. How the hell was I going to get down there while the train was still moving?

I wasn't. Fuck with doing what I was told. I'd gotten where I was today by disobeying orders. Why mess with what worked? But I started down the ladder anyway. This wasn't the time for an argument.

Lea had already lost interest in what I was doing and

headed back to the middle of the roof, where she stopped, probably waiting for the gunman. Seconds later, I heard grunts and the sound of gunfire.

The train's brakes squealed, drowning out the sounds above me. If we were slowing down even more, then it would probably be a good time to jump. But I had no idea what was going on overhead and I wasn't about to leave Lea behind.

Looping my arm through the ladder, I pulled the gun I'd taken from Vincent's bunker out of the back of my jeans and scrambled back up. Lea and Ivan were surrounded by six men. They seemed to be holding their own, even though Ivan wasn't in great shape. Not that it stopped him from beating the crap out of the guy in front of him.

The train vibrated as it continued to slow, but I braced my arm and aimed at one of the men on the periphery. I squeezed the trigger and he fell in a heap, but I'd already pointed the gun at the man next to him, aiming at his head. He fell too.

Four left.

One was so tangled up with Ivan, I couldn't get a clear shot. The other three were blocked by the werewolf. Dammit. I was going to have to climb higher. Just as I started to pull myself up, Ivan tossed the man he was fighting over the side and moved on to one of the others, clearing my view.

I squeezed the trigger and brought down another of our attackers. Lea suddenly grabbed the man she was hitting, and lowered her face to his neck. The man fell to his knees, but she went with him. She had to be draining him, probably to get answers. The vamps had a nifty little trick— they could absorb a person's—or creature's—memories if they were drained enough. But she'd drawn Ivan's attention away from his opponent. The man pulled out a knife, the blade gleaming in the moonlight. Silver. He jabbed forward, but not fast enough. I shot him twice in the chest, throwing him backward.

Ivan shoved the man over the side with his heel. Seconds later, Lea lifted her head and pushed the man over the side. She turned to me, anger in her eyes.

"I told you to wait in the dining car."

I climbed to a squat, then stood. "You're welcome. Now, what did you see?"

"He didn't know shit. All he knew was that he was supposed to kill Ivan and me, then take you to someone. He didn't know who."

"Government? Vampire council? Hades?"

"Vamps would have sent their own to deal with me," she snarled. "And who the fuck is Hades anyway?"

"The contact I met earlier. But I doubt it's him. He went out of his way to give me information about the lab in Iraq. He wants me to go there."

"Evan said we can't trust him."

"No shit, but we still need to get to that facility. Trap or not."

"So that leaves the government. Which means they'll be watching for you at the airport."

I ran my hand over my head, smoothing back the stray hairs that had escaped my ponytail. "Fuck. Let me think." I looked up at her. "How much of Victor's money do you have access to? Enough to hire a private jet?"

"How much are you talking?"

I sucked in a breath. "For all three of us? I don't know, maybe fifty thousand. That's just to London. And more if we want to keep it quiet."

She gave a quick nod. "I have a way. First we have to get off this train."

"You better check on your wolf. He's not looking so

good." Ivan had dropped to one knee and his shirt was covered with blood.

"I'm fine," he grunted.

"You're a fucking bullet pin cushion," Lea grunted. "We have to get them out."

"First we have to get off." I scanned the track ahead, spotting a curve. "We can jump off there," I said, pointing. "We find a car, then hide in a motel while we nurse Ivan's wounds and figure out the new flight arrangements to London."

Nodding, Lea pulled Ivan's arm around her shoulder and tucked her bag under her arm.

"We're not holing up anywhere," Ivan forced out, his voice shaky with pain. "I'm fine. I'm a damned werewolf."

"Who just got shot with silver bullets," Lea said, climbing to her feet and pulling him with her. "I just told you they intended to kill us."

"Play Hercules after we get off this train," I said, moving over to the edge. Damn, this was going to hurt like a motherfucker. "There's a field up here. It's our place." I was relieved to see several houses a few hundred feet away. We wouldn't be in the middle of nowhere.

Lea and Ivan got into position beside me as the train turned the corner.

Tuck and roll.

I moved my bag around to my abdomen, then leapt, landing on my upper back with a jarring pain and continuing to roll. When I finally stopped, I lay on my back, staring at the stars in the clear sky. Pain shot through my shoulder and I sighed, my breath escaping in a white, wispy cloud.

"Rachel? You all right?" Lea asked to my left.

I pushed up to a sitting position, clutching my arm to my chest. Pain radiated through my upper body with enough intensity that tiny bright stars flashed across in my vision. "I think I dislocated my shoulder and maybe broke my collar bone."

"Fuck."

"I'm fine. Let's go." I got to my feet and opened my bag, feeling inside my padded computer case to make sure it had survived the fall. I couldn't be positive it still worked, but at least it wasn't in pieces.

"*Rachel.*"

I turned to face her, immediately regretting the rapid movement. "We have two hours tops until the sun rises. We need to get somewhere where we can hide and figure things out."

She gestured to Ivan, who was lumbering to his feet. "He needs help. Can he make it to one of those houses?"

"I can make it," he growled.

If I weren't hurting so much, I would have laughed.

I started walking, counting each step as it sent a jolt of pain through my body. We slipped between two houses and onto the street.

"There," I said, pointing to an older car parked in a driveway. "I can hotwire that car and we can take it."

"No," Lea said. "You and Ivan both need to rest and we'll have trouble getting a motel room this early in the morning. That house at the end of the street…the one with the For Sale sign. It looks empty. We can hide out there today and rest, then take off tonight."

"Fine," I said.

A privacy fence surrounded the overgrown backyard of said house. When we reached the back door, Ivan held up a hand and pressed the side of his head to the door.

"It's empty."

I lifted an eyebrow.

"I was listening for heartbeats."

I groaned. "Of course you were."

Lea forced the door open and we walked into a kitchen and closed the door behind us. Ivan went straight to the refrigerator and opened the door.

"It's fucking empty."

"Then the house really is vacant," Lea said. "We need to find the basement."

I opened a door, revealing a set of stairs leading down into darkness, the pit of hell for all I knew. "Found it. Let's just hope they don't have any showings today."

"Surely we're about to get a break," Ivan said as he started down the stairs.

With our luck, I wasn't betting on it.

CHAPTER 15

LEA

Rachel clutched her injured arm to her chest. She was playing it off well, but the hammering of her heart revealed the extent of her injuries. The truth of it was, both she and Ivan were a hell of a lot more than bruised up.

"There's a way to speed your healing, Ivan," I said as I followed him down the stairs.

"I heal plenty fast."

I stepped off the last stair and into the unfinished basement. Apparently the upstairs was empty because they'd shoved all their belongings into the basement. Everything from piles of clothes, carefully stacked framed pictures, a box labeled "Canned Food," and a random pile of mismatched mattresses. Perfect. I grabbed the first mattress and pulled it away from the wall. "Ivan, lie down."

With a pained grin, he went to his knees. "Not exactly soft and sweet, but I'll take it."

I pointed at him. "Stay."

He would go along with what I was planning. Rachel, though...I wasn't sure she'd like it. I took a breath. "Rachel, I need to put your shoulder back in and that's going to be nearly impossible with a broken collar bone."

She closed her eyes and sagged against the bottom of the stairs. "Why am I not surprised?"

"There's a way around this." I forged ahead before she could ask questions. "A small amount of my blood will help you heal faster. It'll make it so we can set the bones without pain—"

"No fucking way. Don't take this wrong, but I do not want to end up with fangs and a hankering for blood." Rachel took a step back, moving up the stairs.

"I'm not going to force you." I twisted my lips. "*Mierda,* a little blood won't turn you into a vampire. We'd have to exchange blood at least a couple of times, and then you'd have to be drained by me or another vampire." I put a hand on Ivan's shoulder. "Same for you, wolf. Except I'm not giving you a choice."

He wrapped his hand around my calf. "What about the bullets?"

I shook him off my leg, but not because it didn't feel good—on the contrary, it felt way too damn nice. "I'm going to dig them out first."

Ivan grunted. "I always hate this part." He pulled his shirt over his head, every inch of his upper body flexing like he was one giant muscle. Werewolves, God love them. They were built like brick shithouses for a reason.

The tanks of the supernatural world, they were as dangerous as any vampire, but had less trouble fitting in with the human populace seeing as how they had no light or food restrictions. He stretched out on the mattress. I let my eyes rove his body, looking for bullet holes.

Right.

"How many times were you hit?" Rachel asked. "And where? I'm not sure Lea can find them."

A frown curved my lips as I turned to face her. "Why would you say that?"

"You've been staring at him for a good minute and don't seem inclined to start. I figured they must be hidden well. You know, since he has no shirt on."

I whipped around and dropped to my knees, horrified at my own behavior. Time to get this under control in more ways than one.

"I need a knife that isn't silver."

Ivan reached around under him, wiggling his hips to get to his knife. He pulled it out and handed it to me. Only a small pocketknife, but it would do. I flicked it open, then looked over my shoulder at Rachel. "I'm giving you until I finish with Ivan to decide. A small amount of my blood and healed in less than an hour, or I heal Ivan and he takes you to the nearest hospital, where you stand a chance of being picked up by very bad men, thereby putting all three of us in unnecessary jeopardy yet again."

I turned my back to her as she sucked in a sharp breath and then let out a pain-filled groan. "I think I hate you right now."

I shrugged. "Ivan's going to join you in that."

"I doubt it," he muttered.

I put the knife tip to the first bullet hole. "Let me know if that changes when we're in the middle of this." I pushed the blade in, ignoring the quiver of his muscles around it and the way his heart rate picked up. I treated him like I would a vamp I was interrogating. No emotion, no slowing of the knife. A job to be done and done efficiently.

The first bullet popped out in good time. Then the second and third. Blood smeared everywhere, and it was a good thing I'd fed on the train or the smell would have undone me. On the fourth and final bullet hole, he put a hand on mine, stopping me as I put the blade to the edge of the wound.

"Give me a minute. I need to breathe."

"No."

"Lea, a minute won't cost us." Rachel put a hand on my shoulder, and for the first time I really looked at the scene and allowed it to sink in. Ivan was bleeding profusely despite my tidy work and his skin had turned as white as the mattress below him. Or as white as the parts not covered in blood. My hoodie sleeves were saturated in it. Ivan's eyes were closed and his breath came in ragged gulps. "Maybe I hate you a little."

I snorted. "We aren't done, and the last bullet is deep."

"Do it. Get it done," he whispered, his whole body tensing. I put a hand on the left side of his chest and eyed the last wound. It was going to be a bitch; there was no way around it. I dug in, moving quickly—at least I could spare him a little pain by acting quickly.

The bullet popped out with a ting on the floor. He groaned and passed out.

I pulled my hoodie over my head and tossed it aside. I'd changed my mind about giving Rachel a choice. It was going to piss her off, but it would be easier on her in the end. If she was "forced" into taking my blood, the blame was mine. Not hers. I could do that much for her.

"Rachel, I'm going to give him blood. You're next."

"You can't fucking make me drink your blood."

I found the pulse in my wrist and pierced through to the vein with the tiny knife. The cut welled up and I pressed it to Ivan's mouth. "I'm not letting you put all three of us in jeopardy because you suddenly want to be a squeamish princess diva."

"I'm not a fucking princess!" she snapped.

A thud from upstairs whipped my head around before I glanced back at Rachel. Fear and anger warred in her eyes. Calvin would have died before taking blood from me, so I understood her reluctance.

Rachel moved to my side and went to her knees. She took a knife from her belt and jerked my free arm to her. Not a word was said as she jabbed me with the point of her knife. I looked away before she put her mouth to my skin.

Another thump from upstairs, not as loud as the first but closer. *Madre de Dios.*

I took my hand from Ivan and he sat up, his wounds healed over and his eyes brightened with energy. He grinned and winked at me. Then he pointed at Rachel and laughed silently. She jerked her head up and glared at him.

I grabbed her, spun her around, and put a hand over her mouth. Time for the shoulder. Ivan scooted between us. "I've done this lots," he whispered as he took her arm and jammed it back into place with a quick twist. "Besides, shouldn't she get to hate us both?"

Rachel lurched to her feet, but I could already see the color improving in her face. She took a step, touched her arm and collarbone and then looked at me. I gave her a quick nod, grabbed a new hoodie from a stack of clothes, and pulled it on. Tight it might be, but I would need it if we were caught in the sun.

Laying a hand on Ivan's arm, I brought his attention back to me and spoke in a low whisper. "Look for a window. It won't be big considering how little light there is down here."

I moved to Rachel's side and she shrunk from me. Only a little, but it was there. I fought not to let that bother me.

Upstairs doors were being opened and closed in rapid succession. "We don't have much time. What is the dog doing?" she bit out.

"Smelling for a fresh air source," I said. I had a great sense of smell, but it was to Ivan's as mine was to Rachel's.

He reappeared from around a stack of boxes and crooked a finger. Somewhere in the piles of random shit, he'd found a new shirt, I noticed. Bright yellow with white stripes—hardly incognito. More surprising was that it fit him.

Rachel and I hurried toward him. He flicked the window open. "Ladies first." He put his hands on my waist and swung me up to the ground-level window. I grabbed the ledge and pulled myself through. Rachel was right behind me. Ivan had to twist to get his broad shoulders through, but he managed. Crouching, we hurried across the front lawn and down the road. "Run," I said.

Ivan took off, and so did Rachel. I bolted after them, hard pressed to keep up. Of course, they were both tweaked out on my blood, while I had been weakened by my donation.

It was nice not to have to carry anyone for a change. I ran beside Rachel, keeping time with her. She glanced at me once, and her eyes widened as she seemed to realize the significance of what was happening. "Holy shit, I'm keeping up with you."

"'Bout fucking time," I threw back. She grinned, her eyes a little wild. That would ease as my blood faded in her.

We ran for another hour before the sun began its inevitable rise. I slowed them down with a wave of my hand. "Let's arrange for that private jet. I think we can manage to do it without using all our money. Ivan, can you act like an asshole? I need you to pretend to be Victor once we board the flight."

Rachel snorted. "He's a man. It's not an act."

"Bitter much?" He tipped his head to one side, looking for all the world like a dog begging for a treat.

"Stop it. I can get someone to pick us up and take us to a private airstrip. I can't make them see someone who isn't there, but I can make them believe you are Victor."

They both turned to me and Rachel frowned. "I'm not sure I like it."

My turn to frown. "It's Victor's. And I'm not entirely certain which of his people know I'm the one who killed him. Or if they even know he's dead."

Ivan laughed softly. "Well, let's see if it works."

I pulled out my phone and dialed the emergency number I had for Victor's right-hand man. "Who is this guy you're calling?" Rachel asked.

"He handles all of Victor's non-business ventures. An assistant of sorts," I said as I waited for the other end to be picked up.

"So he's Victor's Alfred?" Rachel asked. I frowned at her. What the hell was she talking about? And how did she know his name?

Ivan grinned. "That's totally what it sounds like."

"Doesn't look like—"

I turned my back on them.

"Good morning. Is that you, Lea?"

"Alfred. Yes, it's me."

My companions burst into laughter that I couldn't understand. I shook my head. Must be still giddy on my blood.

"What can I do for you, Lea?"

"Alfred—" another burst of giggles I ignored, "—I need a car to pick me up at my current location, then take me and two associates to the airstrip. Victor has asked me to travel with him on his next excursion." With any luck, he wouldn't know Victor's traveling days were over.

"Oh, thank God! You know where he is? You've spoken with him?"

"Only by text. He asked me to meet him at the airstrip." I paused. "I can give him a message if you'd like."

Alfred was quiet a moment. "No. No, don't bother. I doubt I'll be working for him much longer. Give me your address and I'll send a car 'round for you. We have a new driver, pay him no mind; he's a bit mouthy from time to time."

I gave Alfred the address, or more accurately the intersection where we were standing, then handed the phone back to Ivan. He shoved it into his pocket and grinned at me.

"What?"

"Alfred? You really don't know who that is?"

I shrugged. "Do I care? No, no, I don't."

Ivan and Rachel bantered back and forth about Alfred and someone named Batman. They were getting along better than they ever had.

They took blood from you at the same time, you idiot. They bonded through you. The thought hit me like a hammer blow and I took a few steps back. How long would it last? I couldn't remember. I'd learned the ropes on my own, and this wasn't the sort of situation I'd found myself in before. I squeezed my eyes shut.

Ten minutes passed in a weird silence. Weird because Rachel and Ivan kept sneaking glances at me, then at each other, then their lips would twist in smiles they suppressed.

Like a couple of kids.

I rolled my eyes as a long black limo pulled up.

A swarthy man in a limo driver's suit stepped out and tipped his hat at us. Dark eyes and hair. He was handsome in a way that reminded me of home. As in Spain.

He smiled at me, but his eyes never left Rachel.

And hers never left his.

Well, this was interesting.

CHAPTER 16

RACHEL

What the actual fuck?

Should I acknowledge I knew him and tell Lea I'd seen him on the subway? That he was the one who'd given me the silver blade at the small of my back? That he had warned me not to trust her?

But he took the lead, shifting his gaze to Lea. "I'm Antonio and I'll be your driver today. Per Alfred's request, the car is suited to your needs."

Lea gave him a curt nod as he opened the back door and waited for us to get in.

Ivan gave Antonio a quick once-over before sliding into the back. Lea slid in next, cutting in front of me.

As I looked up at Antonio—if that was even his real name—he put his finger in front of his lips, then lowered it slowly, mouthing, "Trust me."

The sight of his lips sent my pulse into overdrive. What was this hold he had on me? It reminded me I should quiz Lea about other beings in the supernatural world—specifically if any of them could control humans like vampires could. Maybe he was a vampire who had mind-controlled me, but I quickly marked that off the list. His lips and body had been far too warm.

Don't go there.

He stepped closer, as though to usher me into the car, and the musky scent of his shampoo filled my nose, flavored with a scent I knew had to be his alone. Lea's blood had kicked my sense of smell into overdrive and my body flushed, liking what it was picking up. The thought of screwing him right there and then flooded my brain, and it took everything in me to control myself.

This was not me. My reaction to him was ten times stronger than it had been in the subway the night before.

He studied my eyes, his gaze darkening as it flicked into the car and back. He leaned into my ear and whispered so quietly I shouldn't have been able to hear him. "The blood will pass out of your system soon enough, and I will be there to watch over you."

I pulled back and gaped at him in surprise. How did he know I'd taken Lea's blood? But the thought of screwing him was overwhelming, especially with him so close, and I took a step toward him, fully intending to shove him up against the car.

His fierce gaze turned to agony as he gave me a soft push toward the open car door. There were two seats facing one another. Lea and Ivan sat next to each other in the seat facing the front. I climbed in and reluctantly sat in the rear-facing seat, hating that I was in such close proximity to Antonio. Even before I was seated, I knew Lea sensed something was up. She didn't look at me, but a slight tensing of her shoulders gave her away.

I took several deep breaths, trying to control my raging libido, smelling my own freaking pheromones.

Ivan must have picked up on them too, because his gaze honed in on me.

"It's the vampire blood," Lea said, sounding irritated. "I'd let you do him to get it out of your system faster, but I suspect you would hate me for it later. I've heard it would be the best sex of your life, so it would ruin you forever."

"I'd be willing to give it a go," Ivan said with a wicked grin.

"I'll give you a pillow to hump instead," Lea grumbled.

Antonio soon had us on our way. The small window separating the front and back was cracked open. His smell seeped through, making me want to dive into the front seat, so I reached behind me to shut it. I gripped the leather beneath me as I took several deep breaths through my nose and out my mouth.

"I want to know more about the supernatural world," I said, after a minute.

"What brings this up?" Lea asked, her dark eyes penetrating mine.

"I've been thrown into the middle of this shit, so I want to understand what I'm facing. Like what vampire blood does to me."

"Besides its healing powers, vampire blood increases your senses, makes you more sensitive. The reason you're so horny is you can smell him, much more so than usual."

Her mouth quirked up into a sardonic grin. "And I must say he smells quite good."

"Hey!" Ivan protested.

"How long will it take before I'm back to normal?" I asked, my face burning with embarrassment. I'd have to be dying before I ever consented to drink vampire blood again.

Lea paused, but Ivan answered for her. "It depends on how much you drank. I would guess you had enough to last two to three hours."

"Great," I mumbled. "Just fucking great."

"Does werewolf blood have the same effect? Or any at all?"

Lea laughed, but it wasn't friendly. "No."

"How the hell would I know?" I asked hatefully. "It wasn't like I asked for any of this."

"Are you sure about that?" she asked, her gaze penetrating mine.

"It would take a bite for our magic to have an effect on you," Ivan said, sounding guarded. "That saliva that entered your bloodstream would do it. But it would make you one of us." He paused. "You're right. You do need to understand the supernatural world. Lea should have told you more by now."

"Shut up, wolf." She didn't bother to spare him a glance. "We haven't exactly had time."

He leaned forward, his forearms resting on his thighs. "There are three species of supernatural creatures. Two are made and one is born."

"The made are vampires and werewolves," I said. "Are the ones who are born into it witches?"

"Yes," Lea said, shooting Ivan a glare before turning back to me. "Witches are not to be trusted."

"Because vampires are?" I asked dryly.

Lea scowled. "*None* of them are to be trusted."

"Hey," Ivan said good-naturedly. "Speak for your own species."

"So werewolves can be trusted?" I asked, turning my attention to him.

"Just like everything, it depends." He sat upright and stretched his arm along the back of the seat, behind Lea, and I found it interesting she didn't break his arm off. She definitely had it bad for him. I suspected she needed a good lay herself, but I still worried he would distract her from our task.

Right now I had other men to worry about. Particularly the mystery man sitting behind me and my reaction to him.

"So what does it depend on?" I prodded.

"Wolves are territorial. Pack creatures. Everyone has his or her place. As long as you stay in yours, you are not only safe, but protected."

"So werewolves can trust each other as long as they follow the rules?" I asked. "What happens if you don't follow the rules?"

"Following the rules is expected. Those who don't are punished. The punishment fits the crime, so to speak."

"So why did *you* run?" Lea asked dryly, slowly turning her head to face him. "You're not with your pack. In fact, you're hundreds if not thousands of miles away. Get too cold for you? Or did it get too hot?"

He kept his gaze on hers, the heat between them palpable. "Some of us aren't born to follow."

"So you're a lone wolf? That makes you dangerous. You need the pack to keep you emotionally in check."

He gave her a lazy shrug. "Maybe, maybe not. I seem to be just fine on my own."

"Trying to start your own pack?" Lea asked.

A slow grin spread across his face. His eyes never leaving hers, he said, "Are you volunteering?"

"Good God," I groaned. "Do I need to sit up front and give you two some privacy?"

Ivan's eyes darkened. "My reasons for being on my own are a lesson for another time."

"I want to know more about witches," I said. "What can they do?"

"They harness the energy of the earth," Ivan said. "They have specialties—water, air, earth. Most are weak. They've diluted their lines and haven't passed their ways down for generations. There are a few powerful witches, but they typically avoid vampires and werewolves."

"And vampires avoid werewolves, and vice versa."

"Typically."

I cocked my head. "Why do I hear a *but* in there?"

"Things are changing. The magical world is being threatened. We'll all have to work together to save ourselves as well as the humans." His entire body tensed and the air in the car felt electrically charged.

"Because of Stravinsky?" I asked.

"The vampires are not the only species he has experimented on." His voice was hard and tight, and I suddenly realized Ivan wasn't here just because of Lea. He had a stake in this deadly game. "He's a monster that must be stopped or the whole world is at risk."

"Finally something we all agree on," Lea said, not sounding very happy about it.

I had more questions to ask, but I couldn't stop wondering what Ivan had seen. If he'd lost people he loved. But the murderous expression on Lea's face stopped me from asking more.

We arrived at the private airstrip in no time, and Antonio hustled us out of the car, through the small airport terminal, and onto a waiting jet.

I suspected the vampire blood was beginning to leave my system because my energy seemed to fade with every step. I climbed the steps to the plane, which turned out to be a luxury jet. Score one for Lea. I found a seat and collapsed, shocked to see that Antonio had followed us aboard.

Lea gave him a glare, but he ignored her. "Alfred has instructed me to make sure you all are comfortable. The jet is stocked with food and drink." His gaze landed on her. "Including refreshments to suit your own special needs."

"Thanks," Lea growled. "Now, get out."

A slight grin lifted his lips, but he turned around and exited the plane.

"Jesus, Lea," I forced out. "You could have been nicer."

"I'm saving your ass."

"What's that supposed to mean?"

"Nothing. Go to sleep."

I looked a question at her.

"*Madre de Dio*. Anyone can see you're crashing from the blood."

I sat up in my seat. "Don't treat me like I'm a fucking drug addict," I snarled. "You know it wasn't my first choice."

"Ladies, ladies," Ivan said. His words were friendly, but the tensed cords of his neck betrayed him. "I think we're all a bit strung out right now. Let's just get this metal box off the ground and regroup in a few hours."

Lea gave him a strange look, but remained silent.

My eyelids felt like weights were attached to them, and I dozed off a little, trying to stay awake until after we were in the air, but that was a useless battle. I was about to let myself fall asleep when I opened my eyes, shocked to see Antonio standing in the doorway to the back of the plane.

His gaze drifted around the plane and then he squatted next to me and whispered, "I told you I would watch over you. Sleep."

Panic surged through me, but my body was too depleted to stay awake. I crashed and fell into a deep slumber, wondering if he'd be alive when I awoke.

Because I had a feeling Lea was going to kill him.

CHAPTER 17

LEA

The captain of the private jet, Johnson by his tag, gave me a nod. "Getting into Turkey won't be a problem. Are you sure that's where you want to go?" His eyes flicked to Ivan, whom he believed to be Victor.

The werewolf nodded. I kept a hand on the captain's shoulder. "He's sure. And he pays your bills, so off we go like a good little fly boy."

Captain Johnson's face went slack for a split second under my compulsion and Ivan poked me in the back. "You want him to be able to fly, don't you? Ease off."

"I think I know what I'm doing." I bit the words out, but I let go of Johnson's mind. He shook himself once, nodded, and twisted in his seat. His hands worked over the dials and levers at a rapid pace.

"If you two will buckle up, I'll get my co-pilot in here and we can take off. We'll stop over in London for a fuel up, then head directly to Istanbul."

I didn't want to tell him yet that we were only pit-stopping in Istanbul. From there, we would do another quick fuel up and fly straight to Baghdad.

I stepped out of the cockpit and into the main body of the jet. It seated only twelve, but the seats were so big even Ivan would fit with room to spare. Rachel was where I'd left her, passed out in the mid-section of the plane.

The supposed limo driver was bent over her.

"What the fuck do you think you're doing? Did I not just tell you to get the fuck off this plane?" I strode toward Antonio, fully expecting him to cower.

He smiled, but it didn't reach his eyes. "Alfred instructed me to stay with you three and make sure you were well cared for on your flight."

We were almost nose-to-nose. "We don't need your help."

The jet lurched forward and Antonio stumbled, grabbing the back of Rachel's seat for balance. "I am here to do a job. You are not the one who calls the shots."

Ivan put a hand on my waist and pushed me sideways into the seat next to Rachel. "Sit, we're about to take off."

I glared up at him, even though I knew he was right. *Mierde*. When the werewolf was right, I was obviously in trouble.

Rachel's breathing was deep and even, and I leaned close enough to smell the air escaping her. My blood had faded in her. There was only the barest hint of it in her system now, a whisper that would be gone by the time she awoke.

The jet engines roared, rumbling through the cabin, and I breathed through the anxiety that rolled across my chest. There was a reason Calvin and I had driven everywhere for the last fifty years.

"Don't tell me you're afraid to fly," Ivan whispered across the aisle to me.

I kept my eyes closed. "It goes against God and nature. A large metal box soaring through the air defying gravity is not something I consider safe."

"You'd survive a crash." His words made my teeth clench and he sucked in a breath. "Shit, have you survived a plane crash?"

The tremor started in my hands and I clenched the armrests. "Twice."

"Damn, you are a badass. I'd still like to spank you, though."

I sucked in another sharp breath and whipped my head around to glare at him. "You did not say that."

His yellow-green eyes sparkled. "I did. And it's the truth. You've got a great ass, all but made for spanking. And I did peek when you changed in my cab. The rest of you isn't half bad either."

"Wolf, do you have a death wish?"

"Nope." He grinned and I stared at his mouth, my mind racing with all sorts of thoughts. Naked bodies and biting mouths, hands tracing muscles, and the softness of lips meeting in ecstasy. I shook my head.

Ivan didn't look away from me, but let out a wide yawn. "I'm going to have good dreams, I think. Those panties fit you perfectly, just this side of too small."

He closed his eyes and tipped his head back, exposing his throat, which did all sorts of bad things to my libido. I pressed my body back into my seat, but didn't dare close my eyes. The images were too strong.

And then I realized what he'd done.

"You sneaky bastard."

"You're welcome," he murmured sleepily.

His distraction had kept the anxiety at bay long enough to get us in the air without me flipping out. My lips twitched and I let out a long breath. The cabin was small enough I could hear everyone's heartbeat. Rachel and Ivan slept deeply, their bodies healing from the wounds and trauma they'd experienced.

The captain and his co-pilot were wide awake, but calm, thank God. Antonio, though...the steady beat of his heart told me that not only was he awake, but he was hyper focused. I unbuckled my lap belt and stood. Antonio was sitting at the back of the plane, his eyes closed and his head leaned back.

I walked down the aisle, my skin prickling. Limo driver, my spankable ass. I crouched beside him, breathing in the different scents he had swirling around him. Peeling back the layers, I picked up on the faintest whisper of oak. The hair along the back of my neck rose and my skin prickled. Every Cazador took an oath in a grove of oaks, and the scent stayed with them for years, the oath seeming to burn it deep into their very beings.

"¿Por qué estás fingiendo dormir?" Why are you pretending to sleep? The question was simple, and I knew he'd heard me. But he rolled his back to me even as his heart picked up pace.

I stood and backed away. My seat cushioned me as I slid into it, but I took no comfort in the plush seat. There were times even I needed more than superficial comfort.

I reached over and put my fingertips on Rachel's wrist,

feeling her pulse bounce under my skin. I tipped my head back and let her heart rate slow my own.

My dreams caught hold of me as I slept.

The smell of oak on Antonio had stirred up the darkness of my past, dredging up memories I had avoided—no, run from.

The dark of the night caressed my skin; I hated it. Hated that I had become the very thing I'd fought for so long to destroy. I went to the only place I could find respite, the haven that had taken me in after my family had been shattered.

The Cazadors held their secrets tightly, and their places of safety even closer. The crumbling castle didn't look like much, but it was in the hidden passageways that led downward that I finally felt my fear slip from me. Death was not something I ran from, no. I would be with those I loved.

With those who had loved me.

The passageways were silent as always, but the smell rolling up through them caught me off guard. Blood.

Far too much blood for a sanctuary.

I ran toward the smell, feeling it on my skin like a band that strangled me as it grew stronger.

In the last few steps, I stumbled and fell to my knees. The scene was straight out of my nightmares.

The bodies strewn about, the blood on the walls, viscera coating the floor.

"No, no!" I screamed the word over and over again, my head flung back.

We were the last band of Cazadors, the last of those who hunted the night.

"I found them through your memories."

I was on my feet in a split second, facing the direction I thought the voice had come from. "I will find you and spit you over an open fire!"

"And laugh while I scream? Rather melodramatic, don't you think?"

"I will kill you." I spun again, the voice seemingly behind me now.

"I doubt it. You are weak. You want only death, but you are death, Cazador. That is your calling now, to prey on the weak. To feed from them."

"NEVER!" The word ripped out of me and I ran from the place I'd called home and into the dying night. Never. I would never prey on the weak. I would hunt down the one who'd made me.

The one who'd taken my second family from me.

I jerked awake as the jet gave a shudder. Captain Johnson's disembodied voice crackled over the speaker. "We're getting ready to land at Heathrow in about an hour. Shouldn't be more than another one-hour delay. Everyone stay on the plane."

"Lea, you okay?" Rachel asked.

I turned to her, realizing only then that I still had my fingers on her wrist. I pulled back.

"Yes."

"Nightmares?"

That she'd guessed so easily should have upset me. But it was a relief to share even a small part of myself with her.

"Yes."

"Bad."

I nodded. "I'm going to chat with the captain. Make sure the compulsion is still on him."

Rachel's blue eyes softened—only a little, but I saw it. "You want to talk?"

"Not yet. Maybe later." I stood and walked away from my first friend in a long time.

I paused mid-stride and couldn't help but glance at Ivan. He slept still, snoring softly. Maybe two friends in a long time.

What in the world was happening to me? If I wasn't careful, I'd end up going soft.

And soft wasn't something I could afford to be.

CHAPTER 18

RACHEL

Lea disappeared into the cockpit and I turned in my seat. Antonio sat in the last row, on a front-facing seat across from a back-facing one. He flashed me a grin that pissed me off six ways to Sunday. I had no idea what he was up to, but I sure as hell was going to find out.

I unbuckled my seatbelt and moved to the back of the plane, sitting in the chair across from his. "I don't believe we've been formally introduced," I said sarcastically.

His grin spread and he sat upright in his seat. He gave off an air of nonchalance, though he was anything but.

As his sharp eyes watched me, his fists slightly tensed. "I believe I introduced myself when you got into the car." He shifted, then held out his hand. "Antonio Valdez."

I sat back in the seat and crossed my arms. "Rachel Sambrook, but you already know that, don't you?"

He winked.

I stifled a groan. One of those assholes who thought he could get a woman to do whatever he wanted. "You work for Victor?"

"Everyone needs a job, no matter how unsavory." A non-answer. His gaze flicked to the front of the plane. He was talking about Lea, but I wasn't sure in what context.

"So where do you fit into the whole supernatural hierarchy?"

He shifted, resting his arm on the armrest, but his grin never wavered. "I'm on the outside looking in. Courtesy of my job, of course."

"Oh, really? Did your job have you working on the subway last night? Where I just *happened* to run into you. And you just happened to be carrying an extra silver blade. You need to renegotiate your contract if you're really working 24/7."

Aggravation filled his eyes, and he leaned forward. "There are some things we shouldn't discuss here." His gaze darted forward again.

I looked behind me. Ivan was still sleeping—although I wouldn't put it past him to be faking—and Leah was still up in the cockpit. I swung back around, lightly resting my hands on the armrests. "I don't like secrets. Why are you really here?"

He chuckled. "A reporter who doesn't like secrets? Next you'll be telling me there's no Easter Bunny."

"I ferret out secrets, and right now, I wish I had a giant backhoe to dig into you. You obviously don't want Lea to know what you're up to, and yet you expect me to trust you at your word."

His grin faded and he grew serious. "I have your best interests in mind."

"Ha!" I snorted. "If I had a dollar for every time a man told me he knows better than I do..." I leaned forward. "Try again, dick weed, because I'm pretty damn sure Lea can rip you to pieces. And I mean that quite literally."

His eyes darkened. "She can try."

Time to take a new tactic. I pushed out a breath and gave him a sexy smile. "You think you can take her?"

"I know I can."

I leaned forward and lowered my voice into a husky whisper. "So you're strong?"

He looked wary. "I can take a vampire."

"One as old as Lea?"

"Of course. I've killed many."

"I suppose it's wrong to tell you that totally turns me on."

One corner of his mouth tipped up. "Not as far as I'm concerned."

I moved toward him, settling myself sideways onto his lap, facing the window.

Of course, Lea came down the aisle just then, and her expression turned ugly when she saw me. "Rachel."

I lifted my eyebrows and gave her a smirk. "I'm not high on vampire blood. I've just always wanted to join the mile high club." I turned to Antonio. "Is there somewhere more private we can go...play?"

Antonio wrapped his arm around my back, digging into my hip. Oh, the cocky bastard. "I know just the spot."

Lea looked like she was about to rip my head off, but I stood and let Antonio take my hand and pull me to the back into a small hallway and shut a curtain.

"Standing up?" I asked. "Could be tricky if there's turbulence."

"Nah...I want to savor this." He showed me to the seats behind a barrier in the back, presumably for flight attendants.

I gave his chest a hard push, and he stumbled backward, landing in one of the seats. I straddled him and slid a hand down his neck. "I should hate you, you know," I whispered.

"There's a fine line between lust and hate, *mi amor*. I'm just surprised you're so assertive."

"I'm about to pull off the craziest stunt of my life. There's a strong likelihood I won't survive this. It's been too long since I've had sex." I pressed my mouth against his warm neck and slid down toward his collarbone. Definitely not vampire. "We're two consenting adults here."

"*Si, mi amor*, we are." He grabbed the back of my head and kissed me.

Had I not been so determined to see this through, I might have been detoured from my plan. There was no denying the chemistry between us, so there was no *pretending* to enjoy it. He wasn't the first bastard to try to use my body against me, though, and the stupid fool couldn't see he was being played.

He pulled my shirt over my head, exposing my black bra, and I let him. Then I tugged his off too. He looked up at me with lust-filled eyes and I grinned down at him. He was almost where I wanted him.

He grabbed my head again, bringing our lips together in a hard kiss I enjoyed a little too much. At least I wasn't faking my reaction to him. "Lea can hear us."

He grinned. "I don't care."

"I do. I'm not into voyeurism."

He gave me an exasperated look. "Do you want me to

toss her off the plane?" He looked a little to eager to follow through.

"There's no need for something so extreme." I pulled out my phone and opened my music app, picking something with a strong beat and turning it up loud. I wanted answers, and I wanted to run them through my own filter before handing them to Lea. I had no idea if this would actually drown out our conversation for a vampire and a werewolf, but it was worth a try.

I tossed it onto the seat next to him and gave him my best fuck-me smile. Admittedly it was a bit rusty from lack of use, but he seemed to get the meaning.

"I like how you think, *mi amor.*"

I pushed him back and took in the sight of his chest. What a waste of a gorgeous man, but I'd learned long ago that the prettier they were, the more they thought women were stupefied by their charm. But unfortunately for him, I was a reformed addict. I lowered my mouth to his, less than an inch away. "I'm more than just a pretty face, Antonio."

"I agree, you have a body to match."

I'd considered letting this go a bit further to catch him off guard, but that statement just pissed me off. I bit his lip a little harder than playful and he jolted, only settling back after I licked it.

"You like it rough, *mi amor?*" he asked, sounding even more turned on.

"Oh, you have no idea." I leaned forward, kissing him hard as I reached into my boot and withdrew the silver blade, then quickly brought it up to his jugular. Barely lifting my lips, I whispered, "Just how rough, *Diablo?*"

His body slumped slightly, but there was no anger in his eyes. "I am not your enemy, Rachel." I was grateful he kept his voice low. He must have quickly jumped onto the same page as me, although that could be to my disadvantage.

"You're sure as hell not my friend."

His cocky grin returned. "I disagree. We were pretty friendly a moment ago." He lifted his hips, pressing against my open legs to show me just how friendly he still wanted to be.

"What's your part in this?"

"I told you, I work for—"

I pressed the knife harder, drawing a drop of blood to the surface of his skin. "Try again."

"If Lea worked for Victor, why couldn't I?"

"Because you're not a vampire."

"And do you even know what she did for him? What he paid her to do?"

"He was her benefactor."

"But what does that mean, *mi amor*?"

"I'm not your love, so save the bullshit for someone who falls for it."

"You evaded my question. Maybe you don't want to believe your friend can't be trusted."

"Okay, asshole, tell me why I can't trust her."

"She's a vampire, and vampires by definition are selfish, soulless creatures with one purpose."

"And that is?"

He grinned. "Okay, maybe two. Fucking and eating."

"So?"

"They are parasites that must be scourged from the face of the earth. They prey on humans and take without asking."

"Their blood."

"Among other things."

I cocked my head. "Look, maybe the vague bullshit routine works for you with all the other pretty faces you screw, but I have a headache the size of Cleveland, which is making me a little twitchy, if you know what I mean." I twisted the blade slightly to make my point. "So how about we cut all the bullshit out of this dog and pony show and you just tell me the facts."

His eyes filled with appreciation, along with a hint of respect. "I worked for Victor so I could keep an eye on the underworld. He had a fascination with vampires and anything supernatural, and he drew them to him. It made my job easier."

"Why would you want to keep an eye on them? What are you? The underworld police?"

"In a way. Each species has their own enforcers." He cast his eyes sideways. "The werewolf with your friend was one for his pack."

That didn't surprise me. I'd already figured that out from Lea and the werewolves on the train. "If each species has its own enforcers, why are you needed?"

"Everything and everyone needs supervision, *mi guerrera*. Especially the supernatural world."

"Who appointed you?"

"A secret society, but your friend knows of them."

"Why are you interested in Lea?"

"I'm curious about her motives. I'm certain she killed her benefactor, which makes her unpredictable."

Did he really know Victor was dead or was he fishing? "I know what she's up to."

"She's told you she wants to destroy Stravinsky and bring light to what he's doing. To protect humankind."

"Among other things." I sure as hell wasn't going to spill her secrets. "So you're just here to watch Lea?"

He shifted underneath me, showing me he hadn't forgotten our original plan. "I've enjoyed watching other things as well."

I dug the knife a little deeper, until a trickle of blood

trailed down his neck. "I warned you about bullshitting me."

"If we only had me hooked up to a lie detector, you would see that wasn't a lie, *mi bella*. Although I am fairly sure this is a lie detector of its own."

"Okay, other than watching my ass, what are doing with us?"

"Protecting you."

His answer surprised me. I thought he might be lying, but something in his eyes told me it was at least partially truth.

A ghost of a smile skated across his lips. "Why are *you* doing this? You yourself declared this a suicide mission. I suspect you are right. So why go through with it?"

"Because it's the right thing to do."

His eyes twinkled. "No. There's more."

"And what do you think that is?"

"Unlike you, I love a good mystery, *mi tesora*. I will enjoy uncovering your secrets, layer by layer." His fingers skimmed up my side a few inches.

I started to jab him with my blade, but he grabbed my wrist and pushed my hand from his neck, trying to turn me on his lap.

I let him think he had the upper hand, then pushed my knee into his crotch, putting as much weight into it as I could.

He released his hold on me, gasping for breath as I got to my feet.

"Don't underestimate me again, Antonio. It could· be the last thing you ever do." I squatted to pick up my shirt and grab my phone off the seat, then turned off the music. He watched me with darkened eyes, still recovering as I squatted and tucked my blade into my boot. Then I flung the curtain open, my shirt still in my hand. Lea's angry eyes instantly landed on me.

"I hope that was as good for you as it was for me," I called over my shoulder.

Ivan was watching me, barely containing his amusement. His gaze landed on my chest.

"They're called breasts, Ivan," I said. "Although I haven't seen them for myself, I suspect Lea's are quite lovely. Once Antonio recovers from our workout, maybe you'd like to take Lea back there and check them out for yourself."

Ivan burst into laughter as I plopped down in a different seat, looking at the clouds outside the window, mulling over everything I'd just learned.

Antonio was a pawn. A foot soldier for some group that wanted something from me. Were they trying to find out what I knew about the facility? My connection to Lea? Or something else entirely? It had to have something to do with Lea since he'd worked for Victor in some capacity. What exactly did he expect Lea to do? Was I was missing something?

I nearly gasped as a new thought hit me. What if I was wrong about him being a pawn? What if he was the other Cazador? But surely Lea would have known. Surely she would have told me.

One thing was certain—once we were on the ground, Antonio had to go.

CHAPTER 19

LEA

I dropped into the seat beside Rachel as she tugged her shirt over her head.

"What, no lecture about sleeping with the enemy?" she asked as her head popped through the opening.

"Is he an enemy? I thought he was just a limo driver." I kept my words even. I leaned back in my seat and closed my eyes. "Buckle up, we're going to land."

She grunted and did as I'd suggested, but her movements were jerky and full of irritation. "I think he's a pawn."

My lips twitched. "You threw yourself at him to get information?"

Across the way, Ivan chuckled. "I wish you'd try to get information from me that way."

I leaned forward to glare at him, but my words were for Rachel. "What did you learn?"

"Nothing."

Lie number one. I'd heard Victor's name tossed around between the thumping beats of the techno music on her phone.

The jet shuddered as the landing gear lowered and I gripped the edge of the seat. We were silent as the plane dipped to land on the runway.

"Lea, tell me you aren't afraid to fly." Rachel's words were a perfect echo of Ivan's.

I gritted my teeth and took shallow, quick breaths. "No, I'm breathing like this because I'm so turned on by Ivan's dog smell."

Rachel laughed. "Now that I'd believe." She turned to look out the window, lost in her thoughts.

I was buried with my own. The plane refueled and we walked around the cabin until the pilot told us we were ready to take off again.

Rachel seemed less anxious, and she'd had time to sift through her thoughts. It was definitely time to try again.

I sat in the seat next to her and slowly turned to look at her, needing to focus on something other than my fear. "You going to tell me the truth about the pawn now?"

Her face shut down. "I told you, I didn't get any-thing—"

So she was going to play it that way. I ignored the disappointment and let the anger course through me.

Whipping a hand out across her chest, I pinned her to the seat. "I heard Victor's name."

The silver stake she'd been given was pressed against my throat in instant. She'd been quick enough that I could have been in trouble. Was it a lingering effect of the vampire blood?

Or were her instincts becoming so honed she'd known what was coming?

"Take your hand off me." Her blue eyes were locked on mine, hard as ice.

"Tell me the truth." I leaned into the stake, the silver burning my bare skin, the pain keeping me focused.

Ivan cleared his throat. "Ladies, perhaps we should save this discussion for when we're back in the air?"

From behind us, I caught a shimmer of movement as Antonio stood. "Tony. Stay the fuck in your seat. This has nothing to do with you."

"You're in an altercation with my lady friend. I believe this is my business," he said, sidling up the aisle.

I lifted an eyebrow at Rachel. "Lady friend?"

I let her go, knowing what would happen. She spun away from me, unbuckled from her seat, and stood in a single fluid movement. I grinned across the aisle at Ivan. He shook his head. "You two always fight like this?"

I shrugged. "Two strong personalities, both of us driven to do the right thing in her own way, haunted by our respective pasts. What do you think?"

Maybe that had been too much, because Ivan's eyes softened and filled with pity.

"Don't fucking pity us, dog," Rachel snapped. "Lea's right. What makes us a good team is that neither of us will back down. No matter what happens." She let out a slow breath. "Antonio worked for Victor, same as you."

Antonio let out a soft groan. "Do not trust her, *mi amour.*"

I stood, unbending myself slowly, knowing we walked a fine line. I was sure Antonio was a trained Cazador. Which meant that he was as fanatical about taking out vampires as I was. Yours truly included. But I knew when to compromise.

"Rachel, this is your call. You want him off the plane? If he can keep his weapons away from me, I think he could be useful."

She went still, and the engines started up again, the captain's voice coming over the speaker. "Please take your seats, we'll be taking off momentarily."

The four of us stood in a perfect standoff as the jet began to taxi. Rachel swayed and grabbed the edge of one seat. "Too late to kick him off."

"Actually," Ivan said, "it's the perfect time. Open the door, push him out, leave him behind before he can call the authorities."

Antonio glared at him. "Bad doggy."

The jet picked up speed, racing across the tarmac. Rachel was thrown to her knees by the explosion of speed. Antonio reached for her, and she jerked away. I grabbed her arm as it flicked back and yanked her onto the seat.

Her eyes popped wide as she landed. "Hey!"

"Better in the seat than in his lap," I pointed out.

"I'm sorry I didn't tell you." She paused. "I can't totally trust you. You understand?"

I shrugged, trying not to feel the sting. "I've saved your life more than once. And you've saved mine. I'd hoped we'd moved beyond the trust issue. If I wanted to kill you, Rachel, I could have done so many times over."

"Bragging?"

"Pointing out that you are safe with me." The distrust in her eyes told me it was time to do what I'd been avoiding. She needed to know about the bond. Fuck, this was not going to go down easy.

"What? You've got a look on your face like you've been sucking on rotten eggs."

I cleared my throat. "When you made the oath to hunt vampires with me. We clasped hands."

"Yeah..." Her eyes narrowed.

"The oath was more than hunting vampires."

Those blue eyes narrowed to mere slits. "What are you saying?"

I licked my lips.

"Spit it the fuck out, Lea."

"You replaced Calvin."

She frowned. "That's it? I know I replaced him, that's why he got his panties in a fucking twist."

"So you're okay with that?" I couldn't believe she was taking this so well. To be bonded to a vampire was no small thing. Her whole life would be tied to mine until the day she died.

She shrugged. "You obviously need the help, my friend."

Friend. Relief flowed through me. I realized how badly I had wanted to believe she was indeed my friend. That she wouldn't hate me for binding her to me. I really was going soft.

She reached below her feet and pulled out her laptop. Or, should I say, Derrick's laptop. "I'm going to see what else I can find. See if there are pieces that fit together now that we know more."

Just like that, the conversation was done. Ivan tipped his head at me, gesturing for me to come to him. I slipped past Rachel, who was already buried in the computer. Ivan scooted over to the window seat.

"She doesn't understand what you mean about her replacing this Calvin dude." He dropped his voice low enough that there was no way Rachel or Antonio could hear him.

"She's not stupid. She knows."

"From what little I know of her, she wouldn't be so nonchalant if she understood she was bound to you for eternity. It would be akin to me binding you to me. You two are peas in a pod, wild as they come and not eager to be tied to anything or anyone."

"You couldn't bind me to you." Of course that was the first thing I denied. Of course. He grinned.

"You sure about that?"

I scrambled backward and into the aisle.

Unable to keep still, I paced the jet from the cockpit to the service galley and back as the hours passed. More than once the captain told me to relax, throwing a grin over his shoulder. Finally it seemed he'd had enough. "We've almost reached Istanbul. Will you tell Victor? And sit down."

I leaned into the cockpit and put a hand on his shoulder. "Re-route to Arbil, Iraq." He stiffened under my hand and I increased the compulsion, drawing on my reserves. I hadn't fed in a full twenty-four hours, and was running out of juice.

The captain nodded, but the co-pilot looked at me and shook his head. "Take your hand off him."

Rather than comply, I dropped my other hand on his shoulder. "Be calm. Do as your captain says." The co-pilot slumped a little and then gave a quick nod.

"You're the boss."

I stood, watching over them as they overshot the Istanbul airport, ignoring the air controller's pleas to turn around and land.

Which is why I saw the telltale sparkle of a rocket headed our way as soon as we crossed the border into Iraq.

"Fuck." I grabbed two of four parachutes from behind the captain and co-pilot as they struggled to turn the plane around, a move I knew would not work in time to avoid the rockets. I ran into the cabin and threw a parachute to Ivan. "Take the limo driver."

I grabbed Rachel and hauled her to her feet. "Time to go."

"What the fuck is going on?"

I slipped the parachute on her back and buckled it up. "Don't say I never gave you anything."

Everything seemed to pause. I glanced at Ivan, who'd put the parachute on and grabbed Antonio by the arm. "You want me to let him drop?"

I shook my head as I turned back to compel the pilots to put on their parachutes.

And the world around us exploded.

Rachel reached for me and I grabbed her around the shoulders as we were flung from the plane. The scream of metal tearing apart was accompanied by bright flashes as the fuel lines erupted all around us. The dark night was lit up as we tumbled through the air. And I couldn't seem to do anything but stare and remember the previous plane crashes I'd survived. The people I'd lost.

The one I'd failed to save. He'd been my companion before Calvin.

"Lea, snap the fuck out of it! When do I pull the cord?" Rachel's voice cut through the mind-numbing memories.

I craned my neck back to see how high up we were. We

dropped through a cloud, the moisture slapping us in the face as the fluffy dark obscured my vision.

"Now?"

"Not yet."

I wrapped my legs tighter around her waist and leaned back so I could see better. A flicker of lights in the far distance. "Still too high. Another twenty seconds at least."

"Where are Ivan and Antonio?"

"They'll be fine." I didn't know that for sure. They could have been caught in one of the explosions and totally fried before they had the chance to free-fall. But if anyone would survive, a werewolf would.

"Fuck." She bit out the word.

The wind ripped around us, battering at our clothes. Above us, bits of plane fell in burning chunks. "Hang on."

I angled my body to change our trajectory. A piece of metal sliced the air right where we'd been. Rachel's body shook and her eyes were wide, but she held it together remarkably well. Better than I could have hoped for jumping out of an exploding plane.

"Pull the cord." I tightened my grip on her and she yanked the cord. The parachute popped up above us, billowing and snapping our headlong fall into what felt like a sudden stop.

My grip on her slipped and I grunted as I scrambled to re-adjust.

I ended up with my legs wrapped tightly around her hips, my arms around her shoulders and neck. We were pretty much nose to nose.

"I like you and all," she said, "but this is a bit much even for me."

I grinned, a giddy sense of relief flowing over me. "Imagine the position the boys are in."

She burst out laughing and I joined her.

For the moment we were alive, and that was worth celebrating.

Even if we both knew it was likely to be cut short.

CHAPTER 20

RACHEL

The parachute slowed us down, but the ground still hurtled toward us. Between the pitch black of the night and Lea's face in front of mine, I struggled to see how close we actually were.

Then Lea released her hold on me and landed on her feet, dipping into a squat. The parachute was still attached to me, so I was seconds behind her. I landed on my feet and then pitched forward when the parachute deflated behind me. The wind picked up, blowing sand in my face and grabbing hold of the chute, tugging me a little across the gritty earth.

I reached up and unbuckled the pack from my chest, frustrated as my fingers shook.

"Rachel? You okay?"

"Just peachy," I grumbled, dropping the pack to the earth. "You?" I glanced around to gauge where we were, but all I could see was scrub grass and pieces of plane raining down around us. Shit, this was not good. I dropped to my knees and started pulling the chute toward me.

"Fine." She walked closer. "What are you doing?"

"Trying to hide the evidence that we survived the explosion. Where are Ivan and Antonio?"

"I don't know."

"We need to find them and get the fuck out of here." I had most of the chute gathered around me and began stuffing it into the pack. The question was where could we hide it? The answer was nowhere. I would have to take it with us. "Where were we when we were shot down? Iraq or Turkey?"

"Iraq."

I pulled my phone out of my pocket and switched it on, glad I'd turned it off during the flight from London to conserve the power.

"You planning to make a call?" she asked in disbelief.

"No, I'm using the compass to see where the fuck we are." I pulled up the app, saying a silent prayer of thanks when the longitude and latitude numbers popped up. "Oh, God." I patted my hip, not surprised to find my bag wasn't there. "The computer. All the papers. They're gone."

"Fuck."

"The coordinates for the facility," I said. "Do you remember them? I can't remember the exact numbers."

"Yeah. I've got them." She rattled them off. "30.5 N 47.816 E."

I entered them into a message on my phone and then powered it off. "Based on our coordinates, we're fairly close to a town where I have some contacts. We can get supplies and a vehicle from them. We're too far from the facility to walk, but right now, we need to get your pet and the slime he carried with him and get out of here." With any luck at all, Antonio had plummeted to his death, but guilt washed in behind the thought. I didn't want him dead. I just wanted him gone.

"Maybe we can find some of our weapons in the rubble," Lea said, then pointed to the east. "It looks like a lot of debris landed that way. We might find Ivan and your friend too."

I slung the pack over my shoulder and started hiking in that direction. "He's no friend of mine," I spat out.

"You sure got friendly with him earlier."

"And you know why."

"Oh, yes. To get information."

I spun around to face her, stopping in my tracks. "I needed information and I used what I had at my disposal to get it. I will *never* let a man deceive me and use me again," I spat through gritted teeth. "Are we clear on that?"

She lifted her hands in surrender. "Sorry."

"The asshole needs to go. I say we find Ivan and leave Antonio behind."

"You know it won't be that easy," she said softly. "He will go where we go whether we want him to or not. It's better to keep him with us so we can watch him."

"And I say we can't trust him. I'd rather try to lose him."

Her chest puffed with irritation. "I am in charge."

Choose your battles, my father had always said. Just because Lea thought she had the last say didn't mean she actually did.

After we hiked several hundred yards, Lea called out Ivan's name.

"Over here," I heard the pain in his voice.

We found him sitting on the ground, his leg twisted at an unnatural angle. "Complex fracture to my femur." Spittle shot through Ivan's gritted teeth. "I couldn't set it myself."

Antonio was squatting next to him, looking up at me.

"Why didn't you set it for him?" I demanded as I dropped the parachute pack to the ground.

"Not my problem" was his harsh reply.

"You know werewolves heal fast, yet you left him like this?" I turned my attention to Lea, who gaped at me in surprise. Probably because I was showing concern for Ivan. "Can you reset it?"

"Yes, but it will take him several minutes to heal enough to walk." She lowered next to him, her hands already on his leg, feeling for the break.

Fury rose inside me and I delivered a roundhouse kick to Antonio's chest, sending him flying onto his back.

I caught him off guard, but he quickly recovered, bouncing off his back and into a squat before rising. So he knew how to fight, but I had already suspected that.

He held his hands out at his sides. "You don't want to do this, *mi amor*."

"I am not your fucking *amor*." I circled him, and he watched me, wary but alert.

"Not now, Rachel," Lea snapped.

"Let them fight," Ivan grunted, the pain cutting his words. "It's distracting me from the torture you're putting me through.

"Rachel." My name sounded sexy and exotic in Antonio's accent, which I was sure was his intent. "I am not your enemy."

"You are not my *friend*. My *friend* would have set Ivan's leg instead of stalling our escape for several minutes. My *friend* wouldn't be stalling, waiting for someone to come pick us up. Who's coming, Antonio? The U.S.? The Iraqis? Or perhaps some jihadi group?"

His eyes widened in surprise. "That was not my intent."

A snap filled the night air and Ivan released a sharp cry of pain.

"He speaks the truth," Lea said, sounding resigned. How would Lea know that? Because of their work for Victor?

"Bull-fucking-shit he does." I took advantage of the fact that he was looking at Lea and made my move, kicking him in the chest again. The hit landed, but he reacted quickly enough to grab my leg. I jerked free and followed with a strike to his head, which he blocked. He threw a strike of his own, but I ducked and swept my legs under his. He fell to his back, releasing an "oomph" as he hit the ground.

He was setting us up and I'd let him do it. I straddled his waist and held my blade to his throat. "Give me one good reason I shouldn't kill you now."

"Because you need me."

"Like hell we do."

"Not them. *You.* There is much you need to know. Things she refuses to tell you."

"That's between Lea and me." But when Lea didn't contradict him, I wondered if he spoke the truth. I didn't have time for doubts and indecisions.

A slow grin spread across his face. Was it because he saw the doubt in my eyes? Or because I was on top of him again? "Twice now you have held my own blade at my throat. Should you try a third time, there will be consequences."

"Let him go." Lea sounded weary as she climbed to her feet.

I swung my leg away from him and stood, but I still held my blade out in a defensive move. "You're coming with us."

He sat up and rubbed the back of his head. "That was the plan all along, *mi guerrera.*"

If Lea was surprised by my change in tactics, she didn't let on. But I didn't trust him not to run off and tattle on us.

"How soon until Ivan can move?"

"Another few minutes." Lea scanned the horizon. "Which way do we go?"

I pulled out my phone and waited for it to boot up. "The village is to the northeast. We can find a place to stay before sunrise." I paused. "The sun is brutal here, Lea. You'll barely make it, even with your full gear. If we want to travel by day, we'll need a transport truck of some kind. You can ride in the back."

"How far are we from the facility?"

I shot a glance at Antonio, then back to her. I wasn't sure we should talk about our plans in front of him. "Hard to say. I need a map. I'm sure I can get one in the village. Someone who lives in the area owes me. Once we get close to the village, I'll contact him. But it might take a day or so for him to get it together. It depends on where he is and what he's doing."

"Who is *he*?" Antonio asked.

I ignored him, keeping my gaze on Lea.

She nodded. "I'm going to see what I can salvage in the debris, then we'll go." She turned her steely gaze on Antonio. "She better be completely unharmed when I return."

He nodded, looking solemn. "You know I will not harm her."

I considered protesting—I'd just knocked his ass to the ground mere moments ago—but all four of us knew he'd let me take him.

The question was why.

CHAPTER 21

LEA

I found two silver stakes in the debris, the glimmer of metal beckoning to me through the smoke. I stepped over the pilot's mangled body. I didn't think he and his co-pilot made it out. A twinge of remorse cascaded over me, and quickly fled. For those who were looking for us, a couple of bodies would help solidify that the crash might have killed us.

I bent and scooped the two stakes up, tucking one into the top of my boot and tossing the other lightly in my hand, feeling the heat of the metal on my skin. "Rachel. Do you still have your stake?"

Through the smoke, I saw her nod and hold it up.

I flipped the second stake toward her so it buried into the ground at her feet.

"Here's a backup. Just in case." I turned back to the wreckage. A beat-up bag lay underneath a section of seats. With a tug, I pulled it out. Singed and battered, it had hooked onto the undercarriage of the seats. Inside the bag were Rachel's notes, her destroyed laptop and a few other odds and ends. I shook my head.

"Rachel, you aren't going to believe this." I held the bag up so she could see it.

"No fucking way!" She ran to me and I handed her the bag. "How is this even possible?"

"It hooked onto the seat."

A low groan brought my head around. Ivan was in a shit ton of pain—it all but rolled off him in waves. I sucked back the saliva pooling in my mouth at the thought of his wounds.

"Can't you give him...some blood?" Rachel slung her bag over her shoulder.

"No. I haven't fed in far too long now. If I give him any, I will be putting myself at risk."

"Can't have that, can we?" Antonio quipped. I turned to him, a slow anger building in my veins. Cazador he may be, but he wasn't really one of us.

My steps took me to him like a magnet drawn to steel. I stopped only when I could feel Antonio's breath on my face. "I would be able to help Ivan if I could feed."

He took a step back and pulled a silver stake up. "You could try. I do not think you would like how I taste."

I grinned. "Well, you can't be that bad. Rachel seems to like your flavor."

His jaw dropped and Rachel sucked in a sharp breath.

Ivan grunted, and when I glanced his way, laughter sparkled in his eyes. I went to him and helped him stand.

"Come on, wolf."

He slung an arm across my shoulders and gave me his weight.

It took me a few feet to realize we were the only ones moving. We slowly turned around. Rachel and Antonio seemed to be in some sort of stand-off. I blew out a sigh. We did not have time for this shit. "Rachel, you leading this circus?"

She shook herself and nodded. "Yeah."

No snappy comeback. Damn, I must have struck a nerve. She got in front of me and Ivan, setting a brutal pace considering I was all but packing two hundred pounds of werewolf. I said nothing about slowing down. We needed cover, and we needed it fast. I called over my shoulder to Antonio. "Think you can cover our tracks?"

"Already done, bloodsucker. Some of us are professionals."

Ivan let out a low growl that rumbled through me, but I tightened my hold on him until he stopped. "Not worth it. Right now, we can use all the help we can get." I paused and raised my voice. "Besides, Antonio is a killer, just like you and me, Ivan." Though Rachel's stride didn't falter, her head tipped ever so slightly to one side. Anyone else wouldn't have noticed, but I knew her well enough by now to pick up on it. I could almost feel her interest as if it were inside my own head.

"He doesn't even know you," Ivan grumbled. "Doesn't he get that we're out to save the world?"

"Feeling dramatic tonight?" I glanced up at him, saw the intense and serious way he was looking at me, and dropped my eyes.

"Cazadors don't get to know their prey. We kill them. End of story." Ivan's eyes were guarded, cluing me in that he'd already suspected. "It will mess with his head on more than one level if he realizes I'm not like the other vamps." I shifted where my arm tucked around Ivan's waist so I could grip his belt and use it as a handhold.

We walked for an hour before lights came into view. Not the kind of lights you would see in a city, but the flickering faint lights of a few candles lit in windows. "Rachel, your friend is here, in this village?"

"If it's Shwan, then yes. If not, then it seems unlikely."

She strode forward with impressive confidence. The village consisted of two streets set across one another, with homes and what looked like a few businesses scattered along the edges. Rachel dialed a number and lifted her cell phone to her ear.

After a minute, she nodded. "Baran, it's Rachel. Listen, you aren't going to believe this, but I'm in the area, somewhere south of Arbil, at these coordinates." She rattled off the longitude and latitude on her phone. "We're hoping for a place to crash. Somewhere people won't be looking for us." She shot a glance back at Antonio.

I glanced at the Cazador, who had us both in his sights.

"What's his number?" She paused. "Thanks, Baran. I owe you big for this. But I need some other things. Transport—something I can hide someone in—a map, and weapons if you can get them." She looked toward the village as she listened. "I am forever in your debt, my friend." Then she said something in Arabic and hung up.

"What did you say?" I asked.

She narrowed her eyes, obviously irritated by the question. "The literal translation is *peace be upon you*. We could use a little peace ourselves. Karma and all that." She entered a number into her phone, then held it to her ear. In the distance, I heard the telltale ringing of a phone. The timing was too coincidental for it not to be her contact.

I steered Ivan in the direction I'd heard the phone ring. Rachel made a grab to stop us, but I kept moving, forcing her to come along.

"Siyad," she said, then spoke to him in soft Arabic, looking furious that I had taken off without waiting for her to finish her conversation. She hung up and called out to me. "Slow your ass down, Lea. You can't just barge in on him."

"Watch me."

The house was at the far end of the village, of course. Which was good as far as I was concerned. I knocked on the door and stood back. Rachel stopped giving me a murderous stare for long enough to grab a scarf out of her bag and cover her head.

The door opened and a short, older man filled the threshold, looking like he'd just gotten out of bed. "Rachel?"

She stepped in front of us, adjusting the folds of fabric at her neck. "Siyad, I'm sorry for our late intrusion. We'll only stay one night before we continue on our way." Then she said something in Arabic.

His eyes widened as he took in Ivan and me. He swallowed hard enough that the gulp was audible. I narrowed my eyes as I let Ivan go. "You three stay here, I want to take a look around. Make sure things are safe."

Ivan gave me a nod. "Be careful." And he pushed his way into the tiny house while Siyad was still spluttering. Rachel pointed at Antonio and whispered out of earshot of our host.

"Get in or fuck off."

He shrugged and followed Ivan without a word. She fell in beside me. "Feeding?"

My jaw ticked. "I have to, or the threat to Antonio will become very real."

She drew a slow breath. "Don't be long."

It comforted me to know she was as safe as she could be with both Ivan and Antonio looking out for her. I backed up and headed toward the center of the village, following the scent of a flock of sheep out to the surrounding hills.

Movement ahead snapped my reflexes into action before I fully registered what I saw. I dropped to the ground, my belly flat against the hard-packed dirt and my side against the closest house.

A figure edged from the corner of the same house. I caught my breath; his scent was as familiar to me as my own.

Calvin.

With a burst of speed, I leapt to my feet and rushed him. We slammed onto the ground, rolling until we ended up against a large rock. I had my hands around his throat.

"You bastard, you set those demon dogs on me, didn't you?"

His hand clutched mine and he struggled to speak as I strangled him. "No choice. Please. No choice."

Damn him. I eased off and he sat up, but he didn't take his hands from mine. He squeezed them tightly instead. "You have no idea what I've been through. I have a master, I can't deny him. I can't even tell you who he is."

"I can take a fucking guess, Calvin. How long were you swapping blood with vamps? Months? Weeks?" I'd sensed this weeks—hell, even months ago. Why hadn't I called him on it?

Because I'd wanted to believe it wasn't happening.

His jaw tightened. "I didn't know, you self-righteous bitch." And he jerked me forward. I braced for a blow to the head, so I was completely caught off guard when he kissed me.

He slid his hands around my back, taking my arms with him, pulling me into his lap as his mouth locked on mine. I groaned and leaned into the kiss, remembering all too well the one night we'd shared years ago. The heat of his mouth, the feel of his hands and body. He cupped the back of my head and pulled his mouth from mine. "I hate you," he snarled, but it lacked the heat to make it truly dangerous. At least at *this* moment. Yet there was a glimmer in his eyes that suggested it was true. "This is your fault. You wanted me to be a vampire. But it won't work. I won't let you ever forget this is your doing."

I jerked back and slapped him hard enough for his head to slam into the rock behind him. "I never wanted this for you. Never. I loved you."

His head slowly turned back to me, blood trickling down his lip. "Past tense."

"What?" I scooted back, needing room. His proximity made me forget too much. Like his deception, his lies, and the shame that grew in me as he spoke.

"You said you loved me. Past tense. No more? Did you find some other human to latch onto? Or maybe you're fucking that pretty blonde, Rachel. I know I would have liked to." He stood, but I beat him to it.

I launched myself at him, but I was so weak from not feeding, from sharing my blood with both Rachel and Ivan. Calvin dodged me—barely—and was disappearing into the night before I could get to my feet.

"Only one of us will survive this, Lea," he called, his voice fading. I took a step, knowing I could catch him. Kill him. End whatever was left between us. I swayed where I stood from a wash of fatigue so strong it dropped me to one knee. If I didn't feed, I would be of no use to anyone.

The crunch of a footstep and the soft sound of whistling snapped my head around. I moved without thought, without really seeing. I tackled the man to the ground as I'd done to Calvin, only this time I bit into his neck and drew his blood into me as if I were dying of thirst and he was an oasis of water.

His memories flowed over me as I drained him. His life alone as a shepherd, his desire for the woman who'd married his best friend, his sense of honor for doing the right thing. Guilt and shame flooded me as his life slipped from him. I couldn't stop myself. My hunger and anger were too intense, and the shepherd's life slid away.

He lay limp in my arms as I swallowed the last of his life down. "Damn," I whispered. I pulled my stake out from my boot and slid it through the shepherd's chest, piercing his heart, just to be safe. There would be no coming back for him. I laid him on the ground, rolling him so he looked as though he were sleeping.

Anger, shame, guilt, love, pain. The emotions, most of which I'd pushed away for the last several hundred years, roared through me with the force of a hurricane. Like unstopping a dam. I stood, trembling as I struggled with myself, wondering how the hell I was going to deal with this new reality.

There was no going back to Rachel and Ivan in my current state. They knew me too well. Ivan would smell Calvin on me and ask questions I wasn't ready to answer. Rachel would see the pain in my eyes and probably guess. She knew the only one who could push me like this was Calvin.

I bolted into the darkness, not after Calvin, but in the

opposite direction. I would circle the village and keep watch from there. It was all I could do now.

Give myself some time and hope to hell I could get myself under control before dawn broke.

CHAPTER 22

RACHEL

L ea took off into the night and my stomach immediately churned with anxiety, which was ridiculous. She'd survived hundreds of years without me, and it was likely she'd survive a few hundred more. The thought of her life going on so far beyond my own left me strangely unsettled. That I would just be a whisper of her past one day and she'd likely forget me.

Siyad seemed deeply uncomfortable with the whole situation. "The big one is injured and needs sleep," I said to him in soothing Arabic. "We will be gone at first light." I hoped. Baran had promised he'd have a truck at the edge of the village before dawn, along with weapons. The sooner, the better, as far as I was concerned.

Siyad set up two pallets on the floor of the main living area, apologizing profusely that he only had bedding for two. He continued to shoot worried glances toward Antonio, the person he obviously saw as the most immediate threat. Antonio paced the small room, sending off anxious vibes that it didn't take a vampire to pick up on.

"You're freaking him out, Antonio," I growled. "Tone it down a couple hundred notches."

He gave me a look that let me know he didn't like the reprimand, then shot out the front door without a word.

I would have said good riddance, but he knew too much about us and posed a direct threat to Lea, who was God knew where. I would get Ivan situated and then track him down.

Siyad cast a nervous glance at the door.

"He has gone after our other friend," I said in Arabic. "Thank you for the hospitality you have shown us. We've put you to enough trouble. Please go to bed."

He nodded, then left the room, slipping into what was probably his bedroom and shutting the door behind him.

I turned back to Ivan, who had sat in a kitchen chair the entire time, watching everything without speaking. After everything we'd been through, I'd come to realize he put off a laid-back, clueless vibe, but he was anything but. He saw everything and filed it away for future reference.

He stood and I helped lower him to the floor. He released a long groan as he stretched out.

"I want to look at your leg," I said, leaning closer.

"It's fine. It's set. I'm only hobbling because I need rest."

"Do you make it a habit to get hurt this often?" I asked

with a teasing grin. "I'm guessing you know from experience."

The flickering of the kerosene lantern lit his dark eyes as he chuckled and folded his arms behind his head to make a pillow. "I usually lead a boring, mundane life." He grinned, but something dark lurked in his eyes. "You girls are bad luck."

"So why stay with us?" I asked carefully, wondering what his answer would be today.

He winked. "The thrill, of course."

A bullshit response. "What do you think about Antonio?"

His eyes darkened further. "Be careful with him, Rachel. He's dangerous. Especially with you."

I nodded, but Lea seemed like the more obvious target given his attitude about the supernatural. "I suspected, and I can take care of myself."

He gave me a sly grin. "I saw the cut on his neck when he emerged from the back of the plane. I know you can take him. I was talking about your heart."

I snorted. "You have no worries there, my friend. He's no threat to my heart. I'm more worried about him cutting out Lea's. He has an agenda, and while he claims he wants to stop Stravinsky, I have this feeling there's more to it."

He gave me a curious glance. "Like what?"

I pushed out a sigh. "All I know is that we have a huge dilemma on our hands. He could be useful, but how do we know he won't turn on us once we get to the complex? I'm not sure it's worth the risk."

He studied me for a moment. "I'm certain he wants the same thing we do—the destruction of the facility, Stravinsky, and everything that mad vampire created. But beyond that, I suspect we have very different agendas." A protective fire burned in his eyes.

"Lea."

He gave a sharp nod. "I will defend her to the death."

I shook my head. "But why? Why does she mean so much to you?"

"She's the only one who can defeat Stravinsky." He paused. "The two of you are."

"Why are you on this quest? You have to know we might not be coming back from this." When he didn't answer, I pushed on. "Lea called you a lone wolf. An enforcer. I don't know much about werewolves, but I do know they need a pack. Where's yours?"

"Gone." He shifted, clearly uncomfortable. "She's right on both counts. I was an enforcer. I had been sent to take care of someone who was out of line. My pack was from Canada, and this guy had traveled pretty far north. I was gone for nearly two weeks. When I got back, the pack was gone."

"Do you live in communes?"

"No; unlike vampires, we try to fit into society. That's the most disturbing part. They disappeared one by one. The disappearances had started before I left, but we didn't recognize what was happening at first. Tobi, the runaway, was the one who told me. He was terrified when I found him. He said a monster had come for him one night, but he'd escaped. Tobi was no lightweight. I thought he'd lost his mind, especially when he told me he couldn't shift."

"You mean into his wolf form?"

He gave a sharp nod. "But I knew something was off. He smelled differently and there was a rash on his neck." When I didn't react, he said, "Werewolves don't get rashes. We don't get sick.

"When I tried to bring him back, he flipped out. He was acting so oddly, I called the pack to send someone to help me. But I couldn't reach anyone. Tobi got hysterical and said *he* was coming for all of us. That he'd never let *him* take him again. When I asked who he meant, Tobi said a single word. Stravinsky. Then he pulled out a gun and blew out his own brains."

I cringed.

"I looked around the cabin and found some notes, but none of them made sense. Stravinsky's name and a list of several countries. Canada, the U.S., Iraq. A few random references. I grabbed what I found, torched the place and headed back…to nothing. Everyone was gone."

"In less than two weeks?"

"Yeah." Worry filled his eyes. "It's not easy to take a werewolf, Rachel. Let alone a whole pack."

"How did they do it?"

"A toxin." He paused. "It was in Tobi's notes. He had an address too. By the time I got there, everything was gone, but a pile of bodies was stacked in the back. The thirty-two members of my pack, minus Tobi and me. They hadn't bothered to get rid of the evidence.

"They'd experimented on them. It was the dead of winter, so the bodies were frozen. Some were stuck in mid-transformation. Others had tumors on their bodies. But there were animals too. It looked as if they'd been in the process of shifting—a dog to a pig. A horse to a sheep. A monkey to a…"

He shook his head, and his eyes were haunted when he continued. "I swore I'd track down the bastard and kill him myself with my bare hands. But I've fumbled around for ten months, tracking leads in New York City. And then I heard about what you and Lea did to the facility there, and I knew you were the ones who could find the bastard. The vamp murders around the city made me realize she was a Cazador, which meant she could really find and kill the bastard. I only planned to tail you until Lea hopped into my taxi. Then I knew it was my destiny to help you two, that you would finally help me avenge their deaths. Her death."

"Whose death?" I asked quietly.

"Patricia." His voice was rough. "My wife."

His eyes were glassy with unshed tears. Stravinsky—and the people behind the Asclepius Project—had stolen someone from both of us. I fully understood why he was here now. I put my hand on his arm. "You need some rest, my friend." My voice broke, so I cleared my throat. "You need to sleep if you're going to have the energy to rip Stravinsky's head off with your bare hands. I'll do my best to make sure that honor is yours."

His eyes sank closed and I made a quick check of my bag. While it still contained my laptop, it was broken into pieces. At least I could probably rescue the hard drive. I had a thirst to get moving, to track down Stravinsky, the bastard who'd destroyed life after life. But I knew I needed to deal with Lea and Antonio first.

I slipped out the front door and lifted my face into the wind.

Sayid lived on a dirt path, and while Antonio had hid our tracks as we fled the crash scene, he hadn't bothered to cover them here. His footprints led around the back of the buildings, then inside the outer wall of the town. I found him lying with his stomach on the hood of a Jeep, looking out at a rare field of grass dotted with sheep.

"If you're trying to sneak up on me, you have failed miserably," he said, not changing his position.

"If I had intended to sneak up on you, we wouldn't be having this conversation."

"You should get some rest, *mi guerrera.* You'll need all your strength for the fight."

"What are you? Really? And don't give me some vague answer."

His eyes filled with appreciation as he turned to glance at me. "What do you think I am?"

"A Cazador. Lea thought there might be another. So she's not alone?"

"No, *mi amor*. She is not."

"So you're along for the ride because you want to kill Stravinsky and every vampire we find in the facility? Like we're handing you a Disney Fast Pass?"

He chuckled and straightened, moving slowly toward me with the grace of a panther. "I like you more than I expected."

"I have no idea what that means, but you better keep your fucking hands to yourself, Antonio."

He stopped in front of me, resting his hand on the driver's door. "You are this delicious combination of bark and bite."

"You haven't fully been introduced to my bite," I said with a sneer. "But I can pull it out for you if you'd like."

He chuckled again, then snaked an arm around my waist and pulled me to his chest. But I was ready for him. I spun away from him and assumed a defensive stance.

"Why can you not give me a chance, *mi amor*? We are good together."

I rolled my eyes in disgust. "Save the happily ever after shit for someone who buys it. Besides, we have more important things to worry about. Like surviving."

"I fully intend to survive, Rachel. And I fully intend for you to survive as well. I need a partner who is my equal."

I snorted. "In case you hadn't noticed, I already have a partner, thank you very much."

"A partner or a yoke?"

"What the hell does that mean?" I shook my head. "I would love to leave you behind, but we need all the help we can get. So—against my better judgment—you can stay."

A slow grin spread across his face. "I thought that was a given."

"Nothing is a given. *Nothing*."

His smile faded.

"When this thing is done, you fucking walk away, do you understand? You walk away. You touch a hair on Lea's head before you go, and I will hunt you to the ends of the earth and kill you myself. Go it?"

His eyes darkened. "You don't know what you ask, *mi amor*. I must free you of your bond."

"That's my decision, *Cazador*," I snarled. "Not yours."

"It was never your decision, *mi guerrera*. It was made for you."

"What does that mean?"

But his body had stilled, his muscles tensed. He balanced on the balls of his feet, his fingertips twitching.

"What's out there?" I whispered, letting my hands relax at my sides as I slowly dipped down. The tips of my fingers brushed the top of the blade in my boot. I didn't sense anything, but he obviously did, and while I didn't like this cocky bastard, he had far more experience with the supernatural realm.

He looked me square in the eye, his eyes full of…was that pride? "Werewolves."

"How many?"

"Six."

"Can you take them?"

His mouth curved into a sexy grin. "No, *mi amor*. But we will together." Then he charged.

CHAPTER 23

LEA

Werewolves were not to be trifled with. Werewolves on leashes held by men I wasn't entirely sure were human posed a whole other problem. From a low rolling hill, I watched them sweep the area. It didn't take a genius to figure out who they were after.

Six pairs fanned out across a swathe at least the length of a football field. No matter how clever Antonio thought he was in covering our tracks, there was no way the wolves would miss our scent.

The werewolves were in wolf form, their noses to the

ground, muzzles latched over their elongated snouts. The low whimpering in the back of their throats, the way they pulled on the chains; they already had our scent. I had hoped for a little more time.

"Shit." I rose to a crouch. If Rachel had a transport coming at dawn, we had to wait. Which meant I had no choice. I had to kill the werewolves and their handlers. And I had to do it before—

"The dogs have the scent. Release B3, B7, C9."

The click of chains being unlatched sounded as loud to my ears a bullet report. Three of the werewolves leapt forward. They tore each other's muzzles off and then the center one tipped its head back and howled. The sound wasn't the cry of a normal wolf—it was more of a guttural roar that twisted into a high-pitched scream.

I bolted parallel to the wolves; slow enough so they would see me, fast enough to stay ahead. If I could draw them away, Ivan might be able to handle the remaining three. At least he'd have a chance.

The wind shifted, bringing me the smell of their fur— musky and rank with urine. That was not natural to were-wolves—by nature they were clean, almost fastidious in their...I shook my head. Not the time for tangents. The wind shifted again and brought me a scent that snapped my feet to a standstill. "Rachel, what the hell are you doing out here?"

Now that I knew she was outside, it only took me a moment to pinpoint her and Antonio down at the edge of the village. But in that moment of stillness, the first were-wolf launched at me. Full of the shepherd's blood, I was too fast for it. By a fraction of a second. I threw myself to the ground as I spun, driving my boot into the wolf's rib-cage as hard as I could.

Ribs exploded under my boot, shattering like glass,

and the beast's side split open. The scent of decay rolled over me. The werewolf didn't even whimper. It landed and immediately spun and faced me, its side hanging open, teeth bared, eyes glassy with a death it didn't know it held.

"Fuck me, zombie werewolves?" I whipped my stake out as a second wolf shot forward, its belly skimming the sand as it lunged toward me. I stabbed the stake down hard and fast right before the wolf reached me, driving it through the creature's brain until I felt the crunch of sand on the tip. A burst of blood, bits of flesh and a bright green liquid I couldn't identify spewed out of its mouth, and I gagged on the rancid scent that coated my tongue.

The moment of distraction cost me.

The first werewolf grabbed my leg and jerked me off my feet. I hit the ground on my left side, and it dragged me, shaking me hard enough that the stars above blurred into white streaks. The third wolf bit down on my left shoulder, teeth driving through flesh and cracking the bone. Pain arched my back and a grunt escaped me as I swallowed the scream. No, if I screamed, it would draw them to me.

Away from Rachel and Ivan. I screamed, the sounded echoing into the night. The chorus of wolves that answered was loud enough that I knew it would work.

Now I had to move my ass.

I reached up with my free hand and grabbed hold of the wolf whose teeth were still locked into my shoulder. I dug my fingers into the thick, rotting ruff of fur around its neck, searching for the windpipe. The corded muscle quivered under my fingers and I grabbed hold, ripping it free.

The wolf didn't let go.

"Fucking mutt!"

The wolf on my leg jerked hard enough that my knee popped out of joint. The scream this time was not intentional. One more pull like that and I'd lose my leg.

Wrapping my free hand around the neck of the wolf on my shoulder, I sat up and yanked it with me. Its body flipped over and landed on my legs, knocking its buddy off my foot. Then I booted its head with my good leg and scooted back on my ass.

With as much speed as I could, I grabbed my dangling leg and jammed the knee back into the socket with a grind of bone on bone. A hiss of pain escaped me, but at least my leg was mine again. For the moment.

The sound of paws thumping across the sand behind me sent a shiver down my spine. The two wolves in front advanced, their red eyes glowing, their teeth clacking together over and over. I pushed myself to a crouch, my stake gripped in my right hand. What I wouldn't give for another weapon or two.

"Come on, boys," I beckoned to them, and they obliged.

A dark furred shape shot between us, tackling the two wolves at the same time. His scent was as clean and pure as theirs was rancid and foul.

"Ivan! Take their heads. It's the only way."

I had to trust he could handle them. Because the other wolves hadn't shown up, and the sound of fighting from the edge of the village was all I needed to know that Rachel was in trouble. Limping, I ran toward the snarling and snapping of teeth, the sound of Rachel cursing out the zombie wolves.

"You fucking bastards!"

Shouldn't have been funny, but it made me smile for a split second.

I ran over a low hill, and there they were in front of me. Antonio and Rachel were standing back to back, each facing a wolf. There was no sign of the sixth and final wolf. Not good, but I would deal with it after—

Rachel spun away from Antonio, drawing the wolf she

faced with her. The werewolf followed like a good doggy, and she caught it under the jaw with her boot, snapping its head back. Before it could even recover, she leapt forward and drove the silver stake through its brain.

"Good girl," I whispered and made my way down the slope. Antonio...I didn't really care if he survived or not, but if he fell, the wolf would be at Rachel's back. I crept up behind the oversized canine and grabbed its tail. It let out a yelp as I reeled it in to me. Climbing onto its back, I clamped my legs around its torso and drove my stake sideways, in through the right ear and out through the left. The wolf slumped under me, blood and that strange green liquid pouring out in a rush of sewage that made me gag.

"Shitty time to have highly tuned senses, isn't it?" Ivan said from behind me—back in human form. I nodded and stumbled off the wolf's body.

"There's one more. I counted six," I said.

Rachel nodded, her whole body vibrating. "We caught the first one off guard. It's dead."

"And those who held the leashes, did anyone see them?" I asked.

Ivan shook his head. "There was no one else, Lea. Just the wolves."

I blinked and touched the side of my head. I was not seeing things. I couldn't be. Because if that started…

I swallowed hard, but Antonio spilled my secret.

"If she's seeing things, she's more dangerous to us than ever before. Vampires, as they age, grow stronger. But the years they live weigh on them and they slowly lose their minds. Isn't that right, bloodsucker?"

Fuck, I did not want to have this conversation, certainly not in front of Ivan and Rachel, both of whom were staring me down.

"Partly true, Cazador," I said, letting myself slump to

the sand. "Partly true. With great age, a vampire can lose their mind. But not if they know what they are doing, and I assure you, I know what I am fucking doing." I lifted an eyebrow at him. "Rachel, walk with me a minute."

"Do not do it, Rachel. She's not safe." Antonio stepped between us, but Ivan dropped a hand on the Cazador's shoulder and yanked him back.

"Don't get between them. Ever."

Madre de Dios, I did not want another reason to like Ivan. But he made it damn hard. Rachel held a hand out to me and helped me up. It worried me that I needed her help. Already I could feel the bites from the wolves coursing through me, like a sickness tightening its hold second by second. Vampires didn't get sick...I could only imagine what was happening to me.

How long would I be able to remain standing?

"How much of what Antonio said is true?" Rachel asked. "And don't blow me off. I'd like a real answer."

I kept a hand on her shoulder, steadying myself as we walked up the slow sloping sand dune and out to where I'd seen the handlers with the wolves. I'd seen them; I *knew* I had.

"Vampires can lose their minds. But it happens to those who do not bond with a human from the era they live in. I was bonded to Calvin, and he helped me adjust to how much the world had changed from when I was turned. Without him to steady me, I would have lost my mind."

"Fuck, but you don't have anyone now? How long can you go without a human bonded to you?"

I closed my eyes as disappointment flowed through me. Apparently I hadn't communicated the truth to her after all. I'd wanted to believe Ivan was wrong, that Rachel had understood what I'd told her on the plane.

For now, I would let her believe she would be free of

me one day. "I have time. Calvin has not been gone long. Barely a few weeks."

"So when?"

"In the next year. What I saw on the dunes, though...I think I might know what they were, but I need you to look. I...I want you to see what I saw."

Because if I wasn't going crazy, then what I saw was a big fucking problem. The kind of supernatural problem that was legendary even to a vampire of my age.

I found the spot where I'd first seen the handlers and their wolves, and I pressed my fingers lightly into Rachel's arm. "There, do you see the wolf tracks?"

"Yes. Big-ass motherfuckers that they were, they're hard to miss, aren't they?"

I guided her toward a chunk of chain and leather half buried in the sand. "Get that."

She moved away from me and I swayed where I stood. Whatever good the shepherd had done for me, I'd lost it and then some in that fight.

Rachel scooped the leash and bits of muzzle up. "Fuck me. Who could hold a werewolf on a leash and survive?"

I went to my knees, my throat convulsing as the sickness from the werewolves spread. I knew what I needed, but there was only Rachel. "Shadow men. They..." I couldn't get the words out. "I need to feed, Rachel. Now." I put some weight on the words, but I couldn't look at her. Shame filled me that I had to ask my friend for her blood. Shame and fear. If she turned from me, I wasn't sure I wouldn't tackle her and take what I needed regardless of her wishes.

She dropped to my side, going to one knee, though her movements were heavy with hesitation and unease. "Will it hurt?"

I shook my head and grabbed her arm, the pulse in her wrist beckoning me. "I'm sorry."

"Don't fucking apologize. Just don't turn me into a vamp."

I swallowed and lifted her wrist to my mouth. "Deal."

CHAPTER 24

RACHEL

I prepared myself for the puncture, telling myself it would be over in a short time. But the bite dredged up memories of the first time I'd come face to face with a vampire. How he'd almost bled me dry. And how Lea had saved me.

So while I hated every fucking minute of feeling my blood being sucked out of my veins, I was willing to do it for her. And while I wasn't about to volunteer the information, I'd do it again if the need arose.

"What the fuck are you doing?" Antonio snarled, grabbing Lea's shoulder, and throwing her off me.

Lea hissed, but I had rolled to my feet, and the blade from my boot was already in my hand and pointed at him.

"Stay out of this, Cazador."

Lea looked stronger than before and ready to attack, but I shot her a glare. "Lea. No. Let me handle this."

She showed me her fangs, and I suspect anyone else would have had their head ripped off.

I turned my full attention to Antonio, who seemed more than ready for a fight.

"You let that parasite feed from you."

"I helped my friend, something you don't seem to understand."

He burst out laughing. "That abomination doesn't know the first thing about being your *friend*." He spat the word out like he'd choked on spoiled milk. His glance darted to my blade and he growled. "How many times do you plan to threaten me with the blade I gave you? Can you not see that I am only trying to protect you?"

My eyes narrowed as I continued to hold out the blade. "You neglected to tell me the blade came with strings, but if you want it back, too damn bad. It's mine now."

"*Strings?*" he demanded. "I gave you a way to protect yourself when your friend—who knows the world you dally in—did not. I was the one to watch over you when Stravinsky's men followed you after you met Hades in the Financial District."

"I can take care of myself!" The insinuation that I couldn't pissed me off. I didn't need to prove *anything* to him.

His expression softened, but only slightly. "My blade helps you do that, *mi amor*. What has the bloodsucker given you?"

"Why do we keep having this conversation?" I snarled, my grip tightening on the blade. "I'm sick to death of talking about it. I've made my choice, and if you can't deal with it, go the fuck away! It has nothing to do with *you*!"

"Choice," he snorted. "You think you have been given *a choice*?"

"Enough." Lea stormed past me and grabbed his arm. Dragging him backward, she said, "We need to chat about boundaries."

"Nice knowing you, Antonio," I called after him, surprised he wasn't giving Lea more resistance.

"Why do you hate him so much?" Ivan asked from the darkness, moving slowly toward me. He was still limping, but it didn't look so bad considering he'd had a broken femur an hour before.

I squatted and stuffed my blade into my boot. "Jesus, Ivan. I don't have superhuman sight or hearing like you and Lea. A little warning would be nice."

"Sorry, but you evaded the question."

I shook my head and groaned. "I refuse to discuss my feelings for that asshole."

"Your feelings could get us all killed."

That pissed me off, and my exhaustion sure didn't help. I grabbed his shirt and pulled him closer. "Don't you ever suggest I would do something to intentionally hurt any of us."

"I didn't mean you'd do it intentionally. All I meant was that you need to face why you hate him so much. And this—" his eyes shifted to my hand, "—looks pretty damn intentional."

I shoved him away, cursing under my breath. He was right. Antonio threw me off balance. "I hate him because he represents everything I ran away from growing up. The kind of men who always told me I wasn't smart enough, wasn't strong enough. Wasn't good enough. That I was weak because my chromosomes were different than theirs.

"I've busted my ass to prove them wrong—in everything I've done. When I was a reporter here, I had to be tougher and stronger and braver than all the men just to prove myself their equal. I've proven myself over and over, and I'm done. So if that asshole finds me lacking, he can go fuck himself."

What I didn't add was that I'd let men use me and trick me, and I was officially done. Men were good for two things: opening jars and a good fuck. As far as I was concerned, Lea could open all the jars I needed and my vibrator would take care of the second.

He gave me a short nod. "I understand. I'm sorry."

That caught me by surprise, and a smile curved my lips as I put my hands on my hips. "Imagine that. A man who apologizes. Lea should snatch you up." Still, he was a reminder that all men might not fit into my very narrow lens. But now was not the time to get philosophical.

He grinned and started to say something, then paused abruptly. I knew he'd just been alerted to something.

"What is it?" I asked.

"Vehicles. Coming this way."

"How far?"

"Outside of town but approaching fast."

"It could be Baran's transport. He was trying to put a rush on it. The more road we put between us and the village before daylight, the better." I could hear the low rumble, but without binoculars or night vision goggles, I couldn't do anything. "Where's Lea?"

He nodded to my right. "She's on the hill with the thorn in your side."

"We need to get her. Now. If it's Baran, we won't have much time." Without giving him a chance to answer, I jogged over to a Humvee that had stopped at the corner of a nearby building. A man got out and looked around before his gaze settled on me. It only took a few seconds for me to recognize my friend.

"Baran," I said softly as I started toward him.

He pulled me into a hug, thumping me on the back. "I never expected to see you again." His gaze shifted and I realized Lea was standing behind me.

"Have you heard of a facility that is conducting experiments? Human experiments?"

"We are always hearing rumors."

"Anything I can count on?"

"What kind of story are you pursuing?" he asked.

"It's better you don't know. And hopefully I can get it shut down before you ever do. Did you get everything I needed?"

"Yes." He led me to the truck and showed me a bag on the passenger seat. "Laptop, tools, weapons, explosives, GPS locator, maps, and satellite phone. Food and water in the back, a few extra goodies just in case."

"You are amazing to get this together in such a short time," I murmured. "Now you and I are even."

But he scowled. "After everything you did to help my family, we will never be even as long as you draw breath."

I put my hand on his arm. "Thank you, Baran."

He nodded and walked toward an idling truck as I grabbed the bag and pulled out the GPS. "Now, we have a real chance of finding this place." I grinned at Lea. "We can plug in the coordinates Hades gave me." My gaze landed on Antonio. "Do you still want him to come with us?"

Her eyes darkened. "Yes."

"Then he can drive so I can back up my busted computer onto my new one. I estimate we'll be there in about seven hours. Lea, you wait in the back and stay hidden." I grinned at her. "And maybe take a nap. With Ivan."

She opened her mouth to say something, but I cut her

off. "I'd keep Ivan up front with me, but I don't want to leave you alone, and I sure as hell don't trust Antonio with you. Which means Ivan goes in the back."

I expected an argument, but she got into the back and dragged Ivan with her. Then she stopped and studied me with a strange look on her face.

"Rachel?" she asked, her voice heavy.

"Yeah."

"Don't let Antonio get to you."

I scowled. It was too damn late for that.

CHAPTER 25

LEA

The back of the truck was littered with wooden boxes, a few blankets and what looked like a large rug rolled up against the cab. Using a foot, I pried the rug open and spread it across the surface.

"You look like shit, Lea." Ivan put a hand under my elbow as the truck lurched forward. I would have shaken him off if I could have spared the energy. I had nothing left in the gas tank, and I'd be lucky to get into the truck without help.

I let my weight drop and he helped lower me to the

thick rug on the bed of the truck. My wounds ached, the bite marks from the werewolves burning with a fire I couldn't put out. An ordinary werewolf bite would have been healed by now. Whatever Stravinsky was doing, his new weapons were dangerous even to me.

Ivan sat behind me and scooted so my shoulders were against his lower back. "The fact you aren't arguing with me is rather concerning."

"Ivan."

"What?"

"The Cazador is going to come at me soon. When he does, don't interfere. Even if he kills me."

"That's not going to happen."

"Promise me you won't interfere between him and me."

"Fine, I won't save his scrawny ass from you." I could almost hear the smile in his voice.

My discussion with Antonio had gone poorly at best, but my point had been made and that was all that mattered.

As soon as we were out of sight of the others, his fist slammed into the side of my head. The lack of blood and the injuries my body fought to heal on the little bit of blood I'd managed to take from Rachel made me human-slow.

Still, he'd take a cheap shot and I couldn't have the conversation I wanted from a position of weakness. I went to one knee, grabbed both of Antonio's ankles and jerked him to the ground. I climbed up his body with the drive to feed so strong it gave me the energy I needed to move faster than he could react.

I pulled back at the last second. My mouth hovered over the throbbing vein in his neck while I kept both his hands trapped deep in the sand. "You see, Cazador. You aren't strong enough to keep her safe. And if she turns from me now because you tell her she is bound to me, you will strip her of my protection. Imagine an army of vampires, Cazador, coming for you and her. And no one to stand between."

"I don't need you to protect me, puta de sangre!" he snarled.

Blood whore. I hadn't been called that in a long while. I leaned in and nipped the skin on his neck, breaking it open. Sweat beaded on his face. I smiled, though the pain of not feeding on him all but seared my throat.

"You see? Not so tough. Fragile is actually a good word for you and your oh-so-tearable skin." I tightened my grip on him even as my strength faded. I had to end this conversation fast. "I still hold the deal I offered you."

"I'll make no deals with a monster." He tried to head butt me, but I avoided the blow.

"Until this is done, we work together. When the other vamps are dead and gone, I will lay my heart bare for you to take. A clean blow. Just as I promised."

He went still below me. "Lies."

Time to lay it all on the table.

"I was a Cazador, Antonio. I hunted the monsters before I became one. And now I use their strength against them. When the time comes, I will not fight you. But until then—" Using the last of my reserves, I jerked up to my feet, yanking him with me. "Know your place in the food chain and keep your fucking mouth shut."

He took a few steps back, but I had to give credit where it was due. He didn't run. "And if I tell her that you bonded her soul to yours? That she is damned as long as you live?"

"She'll believe me over you. You are on her shit list, my friend. I saw into her mind and she does not want you in her life," I said, hoping to hell the first part was true. The second was a lie. Rachel's thoughts regarding Antonio were at best, complicated and at worst, intrigued. The fact that I could read them at all without bringing her to the edge of death was confirmation of our bond.

But we just had to get through this mess before I told her. Besides, if we played it right, maybe I was soon to be the last vampire if I had my way. Which would leave only one final bloodsucker for Antonio to kill and no need for Rachel to know anything.

Ivan brushed a hand over my head and I cringed from his touch. "Do not get fond of me, mutt."

"Too late. You need to feed still?"

I curled tighter around myself. "It can wait."

"I can smell the hunger on you, Lea. You can't hide from me." He put his arms around me and spun me around so I was straddling his lap. I found myself staring right into his eyes. This was not the plan.

"Damn you," I whispered as he tipped his head back, offering me his throat. I closed my eyes, fighting the urge. With Rachel, there was friendship and a growing trust.

With Ivan, I wanted more than I had the right to ask for. The more I leaned on him...the more I would need him.

"There is a chance I will see your memories," I said, struggling to find a reason not to feed on him, but instantly regretting that one. I had no plans to drain him—although I was hungry enough I might lose the ability to stop. My attraction to him was stronger than I cared to admit, which left me open to another type of bonding.

"I doubt that. We're trained to lock them away from vamps for fear of releasing information about our packs. Safe houses. Number of members. Weaknesses." His chartreuse eyes locked on mine. "You won't see a thing."

The smell of his skin and the blood pumping just under it were too much for my hunger. Even though he was healing too, I knew I could take a little from him without weakening him. It would get me through the day, and I could feed again when we stopped after sundown.

I sunk my teeth into his neck without touching him anywhere else, doing my best to keep it clinical and distant.

Ivan was having none of it. He wrapped his arms around me, his hands soft and gentle, urging me closer.

No, this couldn't happen. I dug my fangs in hard

enough to make it hurt, tearing and grinding instead of only puncturing.

"I didn't know you liked it rough. You'd make a good wolf," he mumbled as his hands grabbed hold of my ass and jerked me toward him, pressing me against the rather obvious attraction in the front of his pants.

His blood hit my tongue, the first werewolf blood I'd ever taken, and all thoughts of holding back fled.

Now I knew why vamps would seek out the werewolf packs. An ounce of human blood powered me for a few hours, but an ounce of werewolf blood would last days. I took four gulps and pulled back, wiping the back of my hand across my mouth.

"Thanks."

He grinned at me. "Anytime, but that's not a proper thank you." His lips were on mine in a flash, demanding and sweet at the same time, the taste of his blood in my mouth making the kiss that much more pleasurable. I clung to him, wanting it all, knowing it was a bad idea. Knowing also he was strong enough to stand with me.

Knowing he didn't hate me, didn't loathe what I was. Unlike Calvin.

Calvin.

His name snapped through me as surely as if I'd been doused with a bucket of ice-cold water. I pulled back, all but scrambling away from Ivan. "I need to rest."

He tried to kiss me again, but I slid the rest of the way from his lap. I did not want more attachments than I already had. It was bad enough I'd bonded myself to Rachel. I knew that bond would at least be sundered with my death. But to start having feelings for the wolf? I glanced at him, and he grinned at me.

Part of Rachel's memories surfaced in my mind—a discussion she'd had with Ivan. About his past, about what drove him.

I steeled myself not to feel what I was about to do. "Your wife was beautiful. But I think you need to work on keeping your memories to yourself."

Ivan paled and his whole body shook. "No."

I turned away from him. "I warned you. I'm not one of the pansy-ass vamps who stalk your people. They were weak enough to be blocked. I will not be blocked from your mind."

He slammed me into the floor without warning. I let him, knowing him well enough to know that after the rage faded he would hold his distance from me. He pinned me the same way I'd pinned Antonio, arms to the sides, his mouth next to my neck, teeth bared.

"One bite and I could tear your head off," he snarled, his body quivering with barely suppressed anger.

I snorted. "I let you tackle me, Ivan. You're good at what you do, but with your blood coursing through me, there are very few who could match me." I turned my head, pressing it against him until he got off me. He slumped in the corner, acting as if I'd whipped him soundly.

"Why, why would you say that?"

The truck hit a particularly bad bump, sending us both sprawling and opening one of the boxes.

The glittering silver stakes that spilled across the rolled-out rug cut short any answer I might have given them.

"Fuck. Maybe Rachel isn't your friend after all," he said, picking up a stake and rolling it across his knuckles. He looked over his shoulder at me, just the corner of one eye visible.

Damn him for being so fucking sexy when I needed to distance myself from him.

I made myself sit. Act like nothing bothered me—neither what I'd done to him nor Rachel's failure to mention she'd acquired more vamp-killing equipment. It made sense, we were going after vampires and the surest way to kill them was a silver stake. Yet I felt...betrayed. She should have told me.

The night faded around us, and the canvas covering of the truck slowly lightened up. Neither of us moved or spoke.

God, what a mess. A Cazador who wanted me dead in the worst way, and was threatening to tell Rachel about the bond I'd forced on her before she was ready. A lovesick werewolf who had played on my sympathies and long-buried desires while he sought to revenge his dead wife. Then there was Rachel and our tenuous friendship. Add to that the fact we were driving into enemy territory filled with rotting werewolves, shadow men, and vampires old enough to make me look like a child.

The day didn't feel like it could get any worse.

I put a hand to my forehead. "What day is it, Ivan?"

"What?"

"The day of the week. Which one?"

He was quiet a moment. "Monday."

I laughed, unable to contain it. Why was I not surprised? I lay down on the floor and closed my eyes. Might as well sleep it away and hope that Tuesday would be a little bit better.

One could hope.

CHAPTER 26

RACHEL

After Lea and Ivan climbed into the back, Antonio gave me a strange look, and I suddenly felt like a specimen under a microscope. But I could tell Lea had whipped him good. That thought filled me with more smug satisfaction than I cared to admit as I walked past him and around the front of the truck.

"You're driving, so why are you still standing there?" I climbed into the cab and pulled my bag strap over my head.

Without a word, he got in and turned the engine over and waited.

I put my bag in the middle between us to set up some boundaries. When I realized he hadn't started driving yet, I started to get snippy. Then I realized I hadn't told him where to go.

What if Ivan was right? What if my anger over Antonio was distracting me enough to put us in danger? I reminded myself I'd fought off werewolves with him at my back. I might not like him, but I knew I could count on him in a fight. Like it or not.

I dug Hades's coordinates out of my bag and plugged them into the GPS. "We need to head out of the village, then northwest."

He nodded and started to drive, keeping his attention on the road.

I narrowed my eyes. Why was he being so uncharacteristically quiet? I set the GPS next to him so I could focus on the problem of transferring files over from my salvaged hard drive.

After I hooked up my phone to the charger Baran had included, I pulled out the new laptop first, "new" being a relative term. It was refurbished but functional.

Next came what was left of my laptop. I used one of Baran's screwdrivers to open the pieces. Unbelievably, the hard drive looked intact. That boded well.

I opened the new laptop, replaced its hard drive with my old one, and held my breath as I rebooted the computer and opened the drive.

"Thank God," I muttered under my breath when I saw everything was intact. I grabbed one of the thumb drives from Baran's bag, inserted it into the USB port and transferred the files.

"You seem to know what you're doing."

It was a statement, not a question, and my gaze jerked

up in surprise. "My first two months in war-torn desert country taught me if I had computer issues, there was no Geek Squad around the corner to take care of things for me. So I learned to do it myself."

He didn't respond to that, but snuck glances at me as I finished the transfer and swapped the old hard drive for the clean one. Once I had it all together, I went through my messenger bag to make sure everything else was in there.

"Your friend just happened to have supplies?"

"He just happened to have *my* supplies." I shot him a sardonic grin. "I was on the move a lot. I found it helpful to have emergency backups scattered around."

"Why would that man bring you a Humvee as well as all the other things you requested and deliver them within hours?"

"Have you ever been in a war zone, Antonio?"

His shoulders rolled back. "I am at war every day."

I rolled my eyes. "Not a war of your own making, *real* war. Ugly and deadly, where people hate each other for no reason other than the color of their skin, a line on a map, the possession of a fossil fuel, or a belief in different gods—a violence that sweeps across a land and destroys everything and everyone in its path. That is war. Not your grudge match with Lea."

I turned more to face him. "I've stared into the faces of the victims. The children who watched their parents die. The man who lost his arm and can no longer work on electronics to feed his children. They are the ones who pay the price for the decisions of a bunch of assholes in suits. I'm sick of it."

"And how does Baran play into this story about a man who lost his arm and can no longer work on electronics?" A pleased grin lit his face. "I can put things together."

"How Baran plays into it is no business of yours."

"Fair enough…unless we can't trust him and we're walking into a trap."

"If we were walking into a trap, you would have been killed when Baran drove into the village." I leveled my gaze. "You are a participant in this thing, but you're not one of us. If you don't trust Baran, you're free to go. I'm done with my computer, so I can take over." I pointed out the window at the endless barren landscape. "That looks like a good place for me to drop you off."

"I'm staying with you and you know it."

"Then keep out of my past."

Exhaustion overcame me. I was tired of sparring with Antonio. I needed to save my energy for the facility, especially since we had no idea what nightmare we would find there.

I leaned my head back and closed my eyes, dozing for what seemed like a few minutes. The ringing of my cell phone woke me up, and when I opened my eyes, I was shocked. Based on the sun's position in the sky, it had risen several hours ago. I reached for my phone, but Antonio already held it in his hand.

I snatched it from him, and my mouth dropped open when I checked caller ID. It was Hades.

"Hello." I still sounded groggy from sleep.

"Did I wake you?" he asked, chuckling softly. "I'm trying to picture you in bed."

"I'm in a truck cab with drool on the side of my face—" I swiped my cheek with the back of my free hand, "—so try again."

"Are you in Iraq?"

I put a foot on the dashboard. "No." I still didn't trust Hades. Yes, he wanted me to go to the facility, but I didn't trust his motives. Especially after the werewolves on the train warned us against them too. He was asking me to destroy what was essentially his life's work, yet he hadn't offered a reason that satisfied me. So let him think we were a day or more away, not that we were about to come knocking within hours.

He was silent for several seconds, and I wasn't sure if he was about to call me out for lying or hang up. Finally, he said, "I thought you took this threat seriously."

"I assure you that I do," I said, sounding irritated. "But Iraq isn't exactly an easy country to get into."

"A resourceful girl like you should be able to find a way."

"What do you want, Hades? Because I'm pretty damn sure you didn't call to belittle me for my travel troubles."

Antonio shot me a glance.

"I called to assist you in your quest, but if you won't be there in time…"

I tensed. "In time for what?"

"The beginning of the end."

"And what does that mean?"

"You will find out soon enough."

"So if you called to assist me, start assisting."

He paused. "I will send you a file that will help you take out the entire facility. Hit it where it is most vulnerable."

"You mean blow it up?"

"What better way to destroy it all?" His voice lowered. "But it will be too late if you aren't there by tonight."

"I'll do the best I can." Which was basically the same as telling him I'd do better. Hello, possible trap.

"There will be a reward for you when you are done."

"Oh…" I said in a dry tone. "A job well done is its own reward."

But he'd already hung up.

Sure enough, less than a minute later, an email showed up on my phone with an attached file. I hooked up my hotspot to the laptop and downloaded the file, sucking in a breath when I realized it was a close-up view of a schematic.

"What is that?"

I consider hiding it from him, but I was a reporter, not a demolitions expert. He'd probably know how to approach this better than I did. "A way to blow up the facility."

"No shit."

"No shit," I confirmed. It was a ventilation room, but its location was a complete mystery.

Then something hit it me. Hades's file was titled APX… I'd seen that title on Derrick's computer. Buried deep in a utilities folder.

I pulled up Derrick's buried files, and found the schematics for the medical facility. After scrolling and zooming in, I placed the image Hades had sent me over the top.

"Bingo."

A shiver ran down my spine. Derrick had known about this place for over a year.

"Where did you get the complete plans?"

"My friend." It pissed me off that my voice cracked. "He gave his life to try to stop these people, and now I'll probably have to give my life too." My back stiffened. "He may have failed, but I won't."

"What makes you think your quest will have a different outcome from his, *mi amor*?" Antonio asked, giving me a quick glance. His dark brown eyes bore into mine, but instead of the accusation and belittlement I expected, I saw understanding and approval.

"Because I can hold a grudge. And I'm not dying until I get my revenge."

He gave a slight nod. "Then we will get it together."

CHAPTER 27

LEA

The day passed in absolute silence in the back of the truck. Ivan didn't try to talk to me and I didn't even look at him. Tension did not begin to describe all the unsaid words hovering in the air between us. I told myself I'd been right to push him away, even if it didn't feel like it.

Besides, he'd been using me, making me think there was something between us when he really wanted revenge for his wife and his pack. A stab of jealousy I did not like arced through me.

Ivan turned and lifted an eyebrow, but I closed my eyes.

I didn't care what he smelled on me. For all he knew, I could be feeling jealous of the budding relationship between Rachel and Antonio.

Their voices reached me, the conversation lighter and starting to flow more easily. Of course, I wasn't up there with them. And if I were being honest, I was a huge part of the reason those two didn't get along. Okay, the whole reason.

"*Madre de Dios*," I whispered. What a fucking mess.

It would hurt when I had to walk away from both of them. Ivan was already treating me like the monster I was, and while my friendship with Rachel wasn't over yet, the end was coming. This was better though, and with all my years of experience, I knew it. But a part of me mourned the loss of my friends. That was the problem with allowing myself to recapture a piece of my humanity. The pain was too hard to bear.

As the sun faded, the truck slowed to a stop and the engine cut out. Ivan was gone in a flash, not even pausing to look at me before he leapt from the back.

I followed, slower, thinking about the challenges that lay before us. Rachel and Antonio slid out of opposite sides of the truck. While I'd put distance between Ivan and me, it looked as though Rachel had eased up on the Cazador.

Good and bad. I approached her while I scanned the area around us. "Nice to see you two getting along."

"How can you possibly know that?" She frowned at me and I shrugged.

"Tension has a feel to it. It's eased." I winked at her. "And I could hear you talking from the back."

She snorted. "Some friend you are. Me and Antonio have come to...an understanding at best."

Ivan stared out over the sand dunes. "Rachel, which direction are we headed?"

Rachel grabbed a map from the front seat and unfurled it with a flap. She pointed to a spot on the map. "We're going here." Then she opened the laptop, and an image of the facility popped up on the screen. A giant square block with spokes reaching out into the desert. The thing looked like an angular octopus.

"These are the entrance tunnels." She jabbed a finger at the long spokes. "But they are heavily guarded and it looks like there's a lot of cameras and additional security Derrick couldn't quite pin down."

Ivan nodded. "I'm going to check it out."

"That's not a good idea," I said. "They're going to be watching for us. Stravinsky is a lot of things, but stupid isn't one of them."

"And you think I can't get close without being caught? That I'm too much of a dumb mutt to manage even this small task?" he snapped at me, a low growl following his words.

From the corner of my eye, I saw Rachel suck in a sharp breath. "So I make nice with dickhead here, and you go and piss off the werewolf?"

Ivan spun and was gone in a spray of sand and snarls.

"You can't just let him go like that." Rachel grabbed my arm, but I shrugged her off.

"I can't stop him, Rachel. As you pointed out, he's a werewolf. The fact that he's played nice for this long is a fucking miracle."

Her blue eyes narrowed. "Because he's got it bad for you. What the hell did you say to him?"

Antonio laughed softly and we turned to him in unison. "We're thinking about breaking into a facility filled with monsters that could tear us apart in a matter of seconds and you're worried about the love life of a werewolf and a vampire?"

Rachel snarled as if she were a wolf herself. "Ivan is more a part of this team than you are, and if he gets killed, we are down a man."

"He's doing it on purpose, Rachel. Some boys only know how to seek attention by hurting the one they desire." I pulled her back until she stood beside me. "He'll figure out how stupid that is one day, but by then, we'll be gone from his life and he'll have lost his chance."

I lifted an eyebrow at him, wondering if he got the double meaning. Not only his chance at Rachel, but his shot at taking my heart.

His dark eyes glittered in the dusky light and his chest rose and fell as he struggled to collect himself. "How long do we wait for the dog—*wolf*—to come back?"

Trainable. That was a good thing if he could keep it up, but I doubted this was anything more than a bid to keep Rachel and me happy.

"We give him an hour," I said, my eyes drifting in the direction Ivan had gone as I sniffed his scent on the breeze. "Then I will go after him."

"Now, wait a minute—" Rachel spluttered.

I held up a hand. "I will not go into the facility without you. If Ivan is retrievable, I will bring him back. If he's been taken, I won't go after him. Either way, I will come back for you."

And so the waiting began.

Antonio went through the boxes in the back of the truck systematically, laying the weapons out, side by side. I knew the exact moment he found the box of silver stakes.

A long, low chuckle rumbled from him. "Rachel, I like

your style more and more." He held up two stakes, tucked one into the back of his pants and swirled the other around in a circle on his palm.

Rachel looked up from where she sat, surprise in her eyes. "I didn't ask Baran for those."

Well, damn.

"Then who put them in there?" Antonio asked the question before I could.

My eyes shot to Rachel's. "There is only one person it could be, and he's been leading you on from the beginning."

"Hades." She breathed his name. "But that means he knows we're already in Iraq...oh fuck. Ivan."

I pointed at her. "I won't be long." I glanced at Antonio. "If I don't come back—"

"In this we are in agreement, vampire. Rachel comes first." When our eyes met, he nodded, and Rachel let out a pissed-off squawk not unlike that of a cat I'd seen dunked into a pond once.

"You two fuckers can't just order me around. I'm coming with you, Lea. I'll follow you if you make me."

I paused, thinking about how much more dangerous that would be for her. Because I didn't doubt her—she'd find a way around the Cazador to come after me. "You're right, you have a stake in this. So let's make our lives count for something."

I strode to the back of the truck and opened one of the last boxes of weaponry. I stuffed several of the explosives into a bag I slung over my shoulder, then took a good length of rope and looped it around my waist. Back in the bunker in New York, there had been more than one moment when a bit of rope would have come in handy.

"If it goes badly, you'll know. I'll make a big bang to draw them to the far side of the facility. That will allow you time to get in, set the rest of the explosives and get out. Do you understand? We can't do this together, not if we all want a chance to survive. If it's quiet, that means I'm coming back to you and we can try another route in."

I already knew it wouldn't go easy. Hades knew we were here, and it didn't look like he was on our side. At least not in the way he'd led us to believe.

Rachel touched my arm. "Be careful, Lea."

Antonio grunted but said nothing. For just a moment, I considered giving Rachel some of my blood to boost her strength. She must have seen it in my eyes because she shook her head.

I nodded. "You be careful, too."

Explosives tucked away, I headed after Ivan, following his scent and watching for any booby traps along the way. The first arm of the facility rose out of the sand like the lurching monster it had resembled on paper. Ivan's scent pulled me around to the far side, away from Rachel and the entrance she would likely end up using, so at the very least, that was good.

When I got within a few hundred yards, I lay in the sand and watched for movement. Ivan's scent curled around me and beckoned me forward. The idiot had gone right down to the edge of the building. I could see cameras every ten feet or so, and there were guards circling the facility at three-minute intervals. But I had to give Ivan credit where it was due: it looked like he'd made it all the way down the sand dune without getting caught.

"Stupid mutt."

The sound of a footfall on the sand was the only warning I got. I rolled to my back and had a silver stake out even as Calvin dropped down beside me. He raised an eyebrow.

"Still pissed? Usually you hold it together better than this."

He could help me, I knew it. *He* knew it. Time to put aside any anger and our past issues.

"One last time, Calvin. Will you help me end this?" I weighted my words with the power and strength I'd taken from Ivan.

Calvin's eyelids drooped and his voice slurred. "I only ever wanted to help you, Lea."

Ooops. Maybe a little too heavy on the suggestion there.

"Calvin—"

"I loved you once." He leaned toward me and I froze. Caught between the old desire and my new reality. I didn't love him. Not like that. Maybe I never had. Maybe my feelings for him had just been my first attempt to regain my humanity.

I turned my face away and pulled back. "No. What's done is done. We aren't going back to that. Help me, Calvin. One last time and then I will end it for you. If that's still what you want."

His eyes cleared and he shook his head. "Your wolf got taken, but I can get you in there. I have access." He flicked a badge on his chest. A damn badge.

Because he was one of them. Even if it wasn't his choice.

"Wait here for me. I'm going back for Rachel."

"No time. If they took him as a wild wolf, they'll drop him into the tanks right off the bat. He'll be fighting for his life already against werewolves that have been twisted, made stronger and less vulnerable to injury. For all I know it could be too late for him already." Calvin stood and brushed sand off his shirt. "You coming?"

This might be my only chance to get in. My only chance to save Ivan. Fuck. I glanced back the way I'd come.

Rachel was going to kill me.

"Yes, I'm coming."

CHAPTER 28

RACHEL

I let out a long groan. Vampires and werewolves were about as reliable as a drunk surgeon as far as I was concerned.

"She's been gone for thirty minutes. What do you want to do?" Antonio asked.

I let out a string of curses that would have made a sailor blush.

He shifted his weight. "I hesitate to suggest this, but it needs to be said."

I glanced at him, giving him a look that told him to proceed carefully. If he recognized I wouldn't like what he was about to say, it couldn't be good.

"She might have abandoned the mission."

I snorted and shook my head. "She wouldn't do that."

"Why? Why *wouldn't* she leave? We're about to enter a facility that's holding vampires as prisoners and our goal is to kill them all."

"No." I enunciated the word slowly and distinctly. "My goal is to get as much evidence as possible of what they are doing in there and then destroy their work by blowing up the facility."

"And blowing up the vampires inside."

I held up my hands. "Can vampires die in an explosion?"

"They will be weak and defenseless after their bodies burn. If they don't feed, they will be slow to recover. And the young ones *will* die. The monsters will burn."

I put my hands on my hips. "So what's your plan? We burn them up and then you stake them in the back?"

"You bet your very sweet ass."

So we were back to the whole egotistical pig thing. That truce hadn't lasted long. And then the truth plowed into me so hard, I took a half-step backward.

I was so, so stupid.

Antonio had been in a lot of coincidental places. He worked for Victor—who had helped finance the facility on Rikers Island. He'd tailed me after my meeting with Hades. Then he'd picked us up after our train adventure.

I looked him in the eye. "Why is there a case full of silver stakes in the back of this truck?"

His eyes hooded with suspicion; he didn't like where I was going with this. "How the hell would I know?"

"How did Baran manage to get the truck and supplies that weren't my own belongings to us so quickly?"

"He was your man, Rachel. You tell me."

I gritted my teeth. "Try again."

He stared at me in disbelief. "The bloodsucker claims it was the work of your mysterious Hades."

"How did Hades know we were already here?"

Irritation washed over his face. "How the hell would I know?"

I held out my hand. "Give me your phone."

"*What?* Why?" His mouth dropped open. "You think *I* called him?"

"It's not outside the realm of possibility."

"You're climbing up the wrong tree. The werewolf is the likely suspect. If his job was to get you here, he's completed his task. It makes sense he would find some petty excuse to take off and get out of the line of fire."

What he said made sense, but I dismissed it within half a second. Yet the delay was enough to tip up the corners of his mouth. Damn him! I jerked my hand toward him. "Your phone."

He held his hands out at his sides. "My right front pocket. Come get it."

I cursed again, which brought a burst of laughter from him.

He dropped his hands and gave me a satisfied smirk. "That's what I thought."

Perhaps he was amused, but I was not. Holding his gaze, I strode toward him. I kept my gaze neutral as I stopped in front of him and reached into his pocket. His eyes danced as my fingertips brushed his inner thigh. I pulled the phone out, keeping my face a blank slate.

"Enjoy feeling me up, Rachel?"

"I'm sorry," I quipped, swiping his phone screen. "Was there something in there to feel?"

He laughed again and tried to take the phone from me, but I held it out of his reach.

"I just want to enter my password."

"Just tell me."

"Four-one-six-two."

I opened the phone app as soon as the screen unlocked. Most of the entries in the call list belonged to one name. "Who's Skylar?"

"Have we moved to the next phase of our relationship? We're now ready to share our friends with each other?"

"Cut the shit, Antonio. Who's Skylar?"

"I told you. My friend."

"I had no idea guys were so chatty with each other on the phone." I looked up to stare into his face. "You talked to him six times the day I met Hades."

"I've made no secret I was watching you. And I've told you I work for an organization that oversees supernatural creatures. I'm not sure what you think I'm hiding."

"Your duplicity mocks everything I shared with you today." God, I was *so* stupid.

He moved closer and lowered his voice. "Rachel, there is no greater honor than avenging your friend's death. I swear on my life I was sincere when I said I would help you. I have not betrayed you, but there's a good chance someone has. Entering this facility was dangerous in the first place. Now there's a good chance we're walking into a trap. We can hole up and wait a few days. It's probably advisable."

I studied him, certain he was bullshitting me, but the earnestness in his eyes told me otherwise.

There might be hope for him yet.

"No, it has to be tonight. Something big is going down and we have to stop it. End of the beginning and all that shit Hades said."

He nodded. "Then we do it tonight. Which tunnel do you want to enter?"

I took a breath and grabbed the map. My finger tracked the facility grounds and then pointed to a tunnel entrance on the northeast side. "Derrick seemed to think this entrance was the most easily accessible, but his intel was nearly a year old. Everything could have changed by now."

"Your call," he said, his gaze on the map. "I trust you in this."

I took a deep breath and pushed it out. "Let's get ready."

We'd already prepared a battery of weapons and explosives, so we grabbed our packs. As I slid my straps over my shoulders, Antonio held out several stakes.

When he saw my irritation, he shoved them toward me. "Don't let your stubbornness get you killed. You need to be prepared to defend yourself against every type of enemy."

I agreed with everything he said, but I was worried about two supernatural creatures in particular. "Fine, but if we see Lea or Ivan, you have to swear not to kill them."

"They betrayed you."

"You don't know any such thing. Swear it. On your life."

He handed me a blade, then covered my hand with his, staring into my eyes. "I swear on my life I will not kill Lea or Ivan tonight."

I jerked loose. "I caught the 'not tonight.' Just so we're perfectly clear, any time after midnight still counts as tonight."

A slight grin lit up his mouth. "Agreed."

We crossed the dunes in no time and made a wide sweep around the perimeter of the building. When we got to the tunnel entrance, we studied it for signs of movement.

"Derrick's intel still holds," Antonio said, lowering the binoculars and handing them to me. "Only one guard."

I grabbed the binoculars and peered through them. "I don't want to kill him."

"That's ridiculous. He'll die in the blast anyway."

"Probably not. He'd be far enough from the blast."

"Maybe. Maybe not. This is your mission, so I'll do it your way." He gave me a knowing look. "But next time we'll do it mine."

"There will be no *next* time."

"We'll see." He stuffed the binoculars into his backpack. "So what's your plan?"

"Shoot him with a tranq dart. I found a gun in the back of the truck."

He shook his head, his dislike for my plan evident. "Your circus. You take the lead. I'll follow."

"What about the cameras?"

"They make a sweep, so once it moves past us, we'll take him out and run for the entrance. I'll tell you when."

We waited for nearly a minute before he said, "Take him out."

I was surprised he didn't question whether I could make the shot—he just accepted I could. I got the guard in my sight and squeezed, thankful when he staggered and then crumpled to the ground.

"Go!" Antonio took off running for the entrance, and I followed. He tugged the key card from the guard's shirt and handed it to me to hold over the card reader.

When door slid open, Antonio dragged the guard into the empty hallway. "We need to find a place to stash him."

"How about there?" I asked, pointing to a door. It had been listed as a janitor's closet on the schematic. To my relief, that was correct.

"Where to?" Antonio asked after he dropped the guard's legs on the floor in the closet.

"This way."

The plans indicated the laboratory was close to the ventilation room. It couldn't hurt to see what I could discover. The reporter in me couldn't help it.

We'd gone down a flight of stairs and made it around a corner when I heard voices. I grabbed Antonio's arm and tugged him toward a nearby door. To my relief, it was unlocked. I dragged him in with me, though I almost regretted it when I discovered we were in another cleaning supply cabinet.

Antonio gave me a ghost of a smile as his chest pressed against mine and his arm snaked around my back, pulling me closer. But his body was tense as he strained to hear the conversation from the hallway. I wasn't surprised to hear them conversing in English.

"—difficult to be done in time," a woman said, her voice growing louder.

"I don't care," a man responded in a short tone. "The time table has been accelerated and it happens tonight."

"Sir, the suits haven't been fully tested," the woman protested. "Our people might not be protected."

"Ms. Danvers, we are about to annihilate an entire village of two hundred and thirty men, women, and children. There are always casualties in war. We shall deal with losses, even if some are on our side. Is the antidote ready?"

"We think so." She sounded flustered.

"Then put the antidote in the canisters like we discussed and hose them down. That should be sufficient."

"But it hasn't been fully tested. Can I offer a suggestion?"

He sighed. "Yes."

"Your original plan was to drop a bomb with the toxin in it. But what if you send in a tank and spray the village? I think it will help with the problem of the toxin getting caught in the wind and carried to a nearby village."

The man was quiet for several seconds. "Fine, it's a good idea. Make sure everything is in motion within the hour." Their voices faded and Antonio looked down at me, his mouth pressed into a tight line.

Suddenly, this thing had gotten a whole lot bigger.

CHAPTER 29

LEA

The T intersection in front of us beckoned along with Ivan's scent. And the scent of several other werewolves. But there were no signs of struggle, no claw marks dug into the walls; worse, there was no *smell* of a struggle. Ivan's adrenaline should have been through the roof, throwing off a scent trail so strong, a blind man could have followed it.

But there was barely a whiff of him.

"He went willingly," Calvin confirmed. "This place is good at bringing people in without a struggle. They've perfected it."

"How?"

"Was his pack taken at some point? I assume so, since he's here with you." Calvin looked down the left hand branch of the intersection, then ducked back. "Camera."

I nodded. "Yes, his entire pack was killed, but..." The conversation I'd seen in Rachel's memory was so strong. The way Ivan had spoken of his wife, the pain on his face.

"He'd have followed her anywhere," I whispered. And the truth slammed into me like a ten-inch silver stake.

I was a fucking moron.

I swung a hand at Calvin, grabbing him around the throat and lifting him off the floor. "And you were *my* bait, I suppose?"

He scrabbled at my hands, but Ivan's blood still sang in my veins, making me stronger than Calvin by ten-fold. As if he were a mere human again.

"Not like that," he bit out. "Helping."

I tightened my hold and then threw him into the T-intersection, slamming his body into the far wall hard enough to send him through it. A high-pitched alarm went off, and a chorus of howling sounded from the depths of the facility, carried to us through the filtration vents.

"You're going to get us both killed!" Calvin slowly pulled himself out of the hole. "I swear I can get you to them!"

"And then walk me right into a trap? I think not, my friend." *Madre de Dios*, I was a fool's fool. I had more than one problem. I couldn't leave Calvin loose. He'd already confessed he was doing his master's bidding.

But I wasn't sure I could kill him, in spite of our agreement. Even I wasn't that cold. He took a slow side step away from me as his eyes widened. "You can't kill me, Lea. Not yet. I'm not done yet."

"You know the rules, Cal. No witnesses."

His eyes widened as I leapt at him and tackled him to the floor. We rolled down the hall, fists flying hard and fast. I pulled a stake from the top of my boot and drove it into his shoulder, twisting it until it ground against bone.

Calvin screamed, his body arching under the silver. "Fuck!"

I left the stake where it was and steeled myself. "I'm sorry, Calvin." And drove my fangs into his exposed neck. I drew down his blood, gulping it until I felt as full as a bloated tick, my body barely able to contain everything I took. Sweet blood, the blood of my friend and the one person I'd trusted for so long. Tears trickled down my cheeks. I was the monster he'd accused me of being so many times.

I unlatched my mouth from his neck and his eyes flickered. I'd taken enough to make him too weak to follow me, but not enough to kill him. Even now, I couldn't make myself end his life.

"Damn you," he whispered.

"I *am* damned, no need to remind me." I rose and lifted him easily into my arms. I slid into the first open door I found and settled him inside the room. Until someone came along, he'd be going nowhere. "If I can, I'll come back for you."

He glared at me and I shrugged.

"No, you won't." He said.

I didn't argue with him, just bent and took his pass card from around his neck. I couldn't say goodbye, not again. So I backed out the door and closed it softly. A distant howl caught my ears.

A howl I knew all too well.

"Fuck it all, Ivan," I snarled. "You're going to get us all killed."

I sprinted down the hall, following his scent to a wide open room—a small ballroom by the looks of it. But why would there be a ballroom in a facility like this one? I took one step inside before the room's lights dimmed. I froze and watched as an image flickered to life in front of me, about halfway across the open space. A tall auburn-haired woman with pale gray eyes smiled at me.

"Ivan." She breathed his name and held a hand out to me. "My love, come to me." She glanced over her shoulder, a full body shudder rippling over her. The scent of roses and fear wafted into the room.

Fuck, whoever had put this hologram together was good. I could see the glimmer of sweat on her brow, the flicker of uncertainty in her eye, even the twitch of her muscles as she seemed to fight something.

I held my ground and she went to her knees, pleading. "Ivan, don't leave me here. Please!" The words sang between us. She tried to move toward me on her hands and knees and then flipped onto her back, her whole body convulsing as if electricity were being run through it. "IVAN!"

From below us came a howl full of pain and grief.

"Fuck, this is going to get ugly."

Unraveling the rope from my waist, I tied it around both sides of the doorknob behind me and then made a slip knot on the other end. I grabbed the knot and tightened it around my wrist, grabbing the rope as well.

I gritted my teeth and walked toward the image of Ivan's wife. Each step I took shuddered beneath me—a portent of what I knew was coming. Ivan would have run to her, never noticing the shift in the floor.

As I reached her, the image flickered and went out, and the floor dropped out below me. I swung down into the darkness. The jerk at the end of the line snapped my body sideways and I slammed into a slick metal wall.

"Ivan."

Something shifted below me, and I looked down. There

were four werewolves, three with glowing red eyes. Their bodies were hulking, huge and covered in dark fur. Except for the one whose coat was several shades lighter. *He* looked up at me with a pair of chartreuse eyes I had grown rather fond of.

"Ivan, move it, wolf. Despite my propensity for a long life, I'm not going to wait forever."

He leapt up to me, his claws digging into my hips. I gritted my teeth, biting the words out. "Get your ass up here."

He climbed up my body, pausing only to lick my cheek before continuing up. A lick from a werewolf should not have made me smile.

Damn the grin on my face.

As soon as he was above me, I started up after him. And was grabbed from below by a set of teeth that clamped into my left foot. "Let go, you fucker!"

I lifted that one foot high enough that I could slash at the werewolf with my free hand. The silver stake cut across his face diagonally, popping one of his eyeballs. Screaming, he fell back to the ground with a thud.

Then the rope jerked upward and I was out of the hole in a matter of seconds.

Ivan's body had returned to his human form. And he was buck fucking naked. I snapped my eyes upward, doing my best to un-see what I'd seen.

"Come on, we have to get back to Rachel," I said. "Knowing her, she's already on her way. I've been gone for almost forty-five minutes."

"Why did you come for me?"

I untied the rope and pushed past him. "We've got to move."

"Lea, why did you come for me?"

I could have lied, could have told him he was just a part of the team. That Rachel had made me come after him.

I spun around, grabbed his face and kissed him. His arms wrapped around me, crushing me to him. I pulled back after a few seconds. "Because."

"Because?" He grinned, and there he was. The wolf I'd first met in the taxi.

"Yeah. Because. No gloating. Let's get Rachel, kill Stravinsky and blow this place the fuck up."

"I notice there was no mention of finding clothes for me," he said.

"I assumed that was automatically on the list."

He snorted. "I think you like the show."

"Well, you certainly like giving it."

He burst out laughing. "Oh, Lea. Every time I think I have you pegged, you surprise me."

We were already out of the ballroom, headed back the way I'd come. He grabbed my shoulder and tugged me back toward the last intersection, his nose in the air. "Wait."

Oh, fuck no. "Don't tell me she's in here already."

He grimaced and shrugged. "Both of them. She's got Antonio with her. And there are wolves on her ass if I'm smelling right."

I pushed him. "Go, go!" Another time I would have enjoyed the view, but fear coursed through me. Rachel was already in here, and with only Antonio to help her...*Madre de Dios,* we were all going to die.

CHAPTER 30

RACHEL

"We have to set those explosives and get the fuck out of here," Antonio hissed in my ear.

"Not until we stop them from killing those people."

He grabbed my shoulders and leaned back to look into my face. "How do you propose we do that?"

"I don't know, but I have to at least try." I tried to jerk loose, but he held me in place.

"Stop and think this through. There are only two of us against all of them. It's one thing to sneak in here and set explosives, but it's another thing entirely to take them head on."

"Then you go set the explosives, and I'll take on the other mission."

He cursed in Spanish, then pulled me closer. "And if I drag you out of here?"

I snorted. "You can try, but I highly doubt you'll be capable of fathering children if you do." His hesitation irritated the shit out of me. "You would seriously let them kill those people?"

"It's not like I'm pulling the trigger," he said defensively. "And if the odds were even slightly bent in our favor, I would consider it. But it's a suicide mission. If we do this, then we run the risk that we won't get to set the explosives. If we don't destroy this place, a lot more villages will be destroyed."

He had a point, as much as I loathed admitting it. "Fine. We set the explosives first, then stop them from gassing those babies."

"We still have to figure out *how* to stop them."

"The man in charge agreed to the plan of spraying down the village. Which means they'll use some kind of vehicle, which is probably in the underground garage. I saw the location on the schematics. I know how to get there. We set the bombs, then find the garage and figure out how to proceed from there."

"And if we make it to the garage and still don't see what we're looking for? Or if we get detained while the bombs are ticking down?"

"I never asked you to help, Antonio. This was never your mission. It's mine. So why don't you help me set the explosives and then get out of here. Wait for me by the truck, and if I'm not back when the place blows, you'll know I didn't make it."

"Are you insane?" he asked. "You think I would leave you here?"

"Why would you stay?" I asked, just as incredulous as he'd sounded. "You only met me days ago. You feel no obligation to save that village. Why would you feel differently about me?"

He opened his mouth to say something, then closed it and leaned his head closer to mine.

I pulled back. "If you try to kiss me, I will seriously hurt you. Fucking priorities, dude." Then I shoved him back and opened the door, bursting into the hall, which was a stupid thing to do. I should have at least checked to make sure the coast was clear.

But Antonio drove me crazy, because part of me wanted to kiss him, and another part kept reminding me of how Sean had tried to seduce and use me. I couldn't fall for it again.

I took off toward the ventilation room, Antonio on my heels. I'd essentially memorized the plans, so I knew the laboratories were close. It made sense that this area would be more heavily guarded, so it didn't surprise me when I heard the faint sound of voices at the next intersection we reached.

Antonio must have heard it too, because he pulled a handgun out of the holster at his side.

I moved with my back against the wall, drawing my own gun. "The lab is sure to have the antidote."

"Remember our deal? Explosives first," he whispered into my ear. "Then we can do it your way."

This plan was a huge risk. We were damn lucky we hadn't been caught yet. And we'd be even luckier to set the bombs and get out alive. Now we'd added another two major tasks—finding the antidote and tracking down the truck delivering the toxin. It really *was* a suicide mission. Not that I was changing my mind.

But first we had to make it past the hallway without being noticed.

I peered around the right-hand side and saw two guards clustered further down the hall. They stood outside of what I was fairly sure was the lab. We'd deal with how to get in there later. I decided to take a chance. People had been wandering the hall earlier. We were far enough away that if they saw us, we could pass as employees. Besides, they were so engrossed with their conversation, they probably wouldn't even notice us.

My plan almost worked. I crossed the hallway opening without being seen and Antonio was almost across when I heard one of the guards shout, "What are you doing in this section?"

"They sent me to maintenance to get a tool kit," he said. "They're having issues with the coupler again."

"Yeah," the guard said. "Whatever. Hurry it up. This section is off limits for the next half hour. We're about to move a toxic chemical."

"Yes, sir," Antonio said, then joined me on the other side. He looked amazingly calm for having nearly been caught.

The ventilation room was locked, but Antonio pulled out the employee badge from the guard we'd tranquilized and held it up to the card reader. The door popped open and we slipped inside.

Setting up the explosives was easy—so much so, it made me nervous. I had to grudgingly admit Antonio was better at this than I was. He set up five bombs to my three, then set the timer. Looking up at me as he finished, he said, "You get forty-five minutes, *mi amor*. No more."

More generous than I'd expected.

We hurried to the door. "If we can intercept the toxin in the hall, we can stop it from even getting to the transport," he said. "Then we can get the hell out of here."

"Maybe so, but it will be heavily guarded," I said. "Not to mention that we're dead if it spills. It would be safer to sabotage the transport vehicle or maybe even steal the vehicle it's stored in." Not to mention getting Ivan and Lea out before the place blew. If they were even inside.

"This is a crap plan," he said.

"I know. Think of a better one and I'll entertain it."

But he didn't. He remained remarkably stoic instead as he followed me down another hallway my map said led to the garage.

It was quiet when we got there. Quieter than I had expected it would be if they were loading a truck for a mission. I had learned enough from hanging around U.S. military missions to tell something was terribly wrong here.

"Hands in the air," a deep voice said behind us.

Antonio's face was expressionless as he prepared to turn. He gave me a look that suggested we fight like hell, but the minute we turned, I knew it wouldn't be easy to slip out of this one. Eight men had machine guns pointed on us.

"Bind them," someone said, and before I could react, my arms were jerked down and bound behind my back with a zip tie. Shit. A quick glance to Antonio confirmed he was in the same situation.

"Come with us," the leader said and turned, his long legs moving quickly down the hall.

My stomach was in knots and I re-examined my decision to try to stop the extermination of the village. But I couldn't be sorry, even if we didn't survive. Doing something honorable—even if I failed—was far better than doing nothing at all.

The man led us down several halls before finally opening a door into what looked like a large control room. It was dimly lit, with multiple TV screens spread along the back wall.

"Ah, Ms. Sambrook. Welcome," a dark-haired man called out from the front of the room. His tall, lanky body was dressed in khaki pants and a polo shirt under a long white lab coat, and his eyes were a steely blue. "I had hoped you would bring your new friend Lea with you."

"Sorry. I didn't realize the plus-one required a specific guest. Maybe next time."

He gave me a patient smile. "Please, introduce us to your friend."

"You know Lea, but you don't know Antonio?" I asked. "That tells me you're not someone of importance."

He released a short laugh, but I could tell I'd offended him. Good.

"You have no idea who I am, do you?" he asked.

"No, and I really don't care."

He advanced toward us with a grace that revealed him as a vampire. So it surprised me he didn't know Antonio. All the vampires seemed to know Lea, or know *of* her.

"You really *should* care." He leaned close and sniffed my neck, his fangs extended. "I'm sure you're quite delicious."

My face held contempt and indifference, but there was nothing I could do to hide my now-rapid pulse from a vampire. He lifted his eyes to mine, a menacing smile on his lips. "I can smell your excitement. Do you want me, Rachel? Maybe you've enjoyed a bite or two already from Lea?"

"You still don't know who I am," Antonio said, nonchalantly.

The man straightened and turned his attention to Antonio. His eyes narrowed. "No, but you aren't like most weasels I meet. I'll admit, I'm intrigued."

I wasn't sure it was a good idea for Antonio to tell this sick bastard he was a Cazador. After all, we were both bound with our hands zip-tied behind our backs. I suspected it would be a death sentence for at least one of us.

"Are you the man in charge?" I blurted out before Antonio could speak. We were short on time. We needed to figure out a plan and fast.

"And if I were?" he asked.

"I'd ask you why you're wiping out an entire village. How can you live with yourself?"

He released a short laugh. "I'm not killing anyone."

My eyes narrowed. "How can you deny you're murdering two hundred and thirty people? We overheard your plan about spraying them with toxins."

"I'm not killing them. I'm re-creating them."

"What does that mean?" Antonio asked.

But I already knew. I'd come face to face with his creations several times in New York—both loose in the city and tucked away in his secret lab. I sucked in a breath. "You're Stravinsky."

His eyes lit up. "I'm sure Lea has told you about me."

This guy had quite the ego trip going on. "Nope. I think I read your name on a few files in the Rikers lab. In the failure pile."

He snarled, but a door opened just then and several men in military uniforms walked in. One in particular caught my attention.

"What do you mean re-creating them?" Antonio repeated.

But Stravinsky, apparently bored of taunting us, turned his attention to his visitors. "General, I trust you've accommodated the change of plans?"

The man I recognized nodded. "As long as it works this way, I prefer it. This type of weaponry won't be sanctioned, and it would be too easy for the airplanes dropping the packages to be tracked. It'll much better to use ground transport—easy in and easy out and no one's the wiser." He grinned. "Because the monsters aren't going to talk."

Stravinsky grinned.

I'd heard and seen enough. "General Hamm?" I asked in disbelief. "How can you condone something so evil?"

"Rachel Sambrook?" His eyes widened. "What are you doing here?"

"She and her friend were trespassing. We are detaining them."

"General, please," I pleaded. "You have to stop this. Have you seen what this man has created? They are monstrosities!"

He gave me a sympathetic look. "I know. That's what we're trying to create. Their appearance is intimidating. This test is to see if they can be trained in the field."

"But the children!" I protested. "What about the babies?"

"The children can be of use, though I confess the babies are a burden more easily disposed of."

I gasped in shock, although perhaps this was to be expected. If he could condemn an entire family, what were a few babies?

At that moment, the ceiling caved in and Lea jumped down, landing on her feet. Ivan was right behind her, wearing nothing but a pair of pants. And then there was one more person—a man whose presence filled me with dread.

"Calvin," I whispered.

Lea cast a quick glance my way and I nodded sharply, letting her know I was happy to see her.

"Lea," Stravinsky said. "I wondered when you'd show up."

She gave him a wicked grin. "You know how I like to make an entrance." She pulled out a silver stake. "Let's get started."

CHAPTER 31

LEA

"Lea," Stravinsky purred my name, "you are so predictable." He strolled between Rachel and me, but he didn't touch her. "You always bind the most interesting humans. How do you find them?"

I couldn't look at Rachel, but I still saw her jerk at her bonds. "What?"

Stravinsky grinned at me and turned to her. "You didn't know? Lea bound you to her. You are her human servant until one of you dies. Have you not noticed an increase in your speed and stamina? An almost preternatural sense of knowing where she is?"

Rachel glared at him. "Mind games are not nice, you dirty fucker. Don't make me call—"

"He's not lying," I said softly, drawing her eyes and every other eye in the room to me. This wasn't the way I'd hoped to tell her, but I could use it to our advantage. "I bound you to me the night Louis died, the first night I saved you from dying." I walked slowly toward her, holding a hand out as if I were pleading. I dipped my eyes ever so swiftly to her hands. If she spun at the right moment, I could cut her bonds and we'd have a chance.

Her jaw ticked and fury rolled off her in waves, but the slightest flicker of her eyelids was enough for me to know she would follow my lead. She took a step toward me, a snarl on her lips, blue eyes flashing like summer lightning. "You bloodsucking whore!"

I bowed my head. "I'm sorry."

"You'd apologize to her, but not me?" Incredulous, Calvin pushed between us. Fucking idiot.

I shoved him back. "You were a piece of ass at best, Cal. Nothing more. As a servant you were so much less than her, it's laughable." My feelings for him were complicated, but it took everything in me to hurt him this way.

He choked but didn't stumble away as I'd hoped. No, he leapt at me, hands outstretched. I spun on my heel and swung my other leg up, driving it into his solar plexus and throwing him over my head. While he hovered in the air, I shot forward, Rachel spun around, and I slashed through the zip tie.

Chaos exploded around us along with machine gun fire. The engine of a truck roared to life in the other room and Rachel screamed at Antonio. "Stop them!"

"Busy, *mi amor*!" He backed away from two men, keeping them at bay with well-timed kicks. I flicked a finger at them and Ivan shot forward, tackling them both at the same time. Bullets spilled through the air, but the gunmen were obviously not used to their weapons, and the guns' recoil sent the muzzles into the air.

I ran toward them, a stake in one hand, and a knife in the other. I ran down the line of men as they struggled with the oversized and overpowered guns, slicing their throats. Bullets zipped through the air; two nicked my left side but the soldiers' fear made them sloppy. Blood sprayed in my wake as I turned at the end of the line to wipe my weapons on the suit of the final soldier.

"What were you saying about predictability, Stravinsky?" I lifted an eyebrow at him. Rachel was next to Antonio, cutting his bonds. Ivan was with them. We were down one.

Calvin hit me from behind, taking me out at the knees. I snapped forward, catching my weight on my palms and rolling to my back.

Calvin clung to my legs, but his eyes flicked to something above me. Something that blurred through the air and slammed into the side of my head hard enough that the crack I heard was not external. Black lines and dots flooded my vision and I lolled to the side, blood trickling from my nose and mouth.

Voices. Screaming. Someone scooped up my limp body. My head hung backward over his arm as he took me from the room. Ivan and Rachel made a move toward me, but Antonio stopped her.

Stay. I mouthed the word. Stay. Ivan froze, his face a mask of torture. But there was no point in both of us being taken. Stay.

My eyelids fluttered and the motion of the walk made my stomach roll dangerously. I managed to get my head tipped to the side, gagging on nothing, feeling as though my head would split and my body would follow close behind.

"Did you have to hit her with the silver spiked club?" Calvin asked, his voice wavering on the edge of my periphery.

"Did you notice it didn't kill her? The fact that she's alive tells me Stravinsky is right. We need her blood for the final tests. We'll hook her up to the machine and sedate her."

Well, this sounded lovely. I let my eyes roll. The longer I could play dead, the better.

"She's playing dead," Calvin said.

"Really?" A hand touched my face and turned it side to side. "No reflex response. I doubt she's even aware yet."

"You don't know her, Mac."

Mac was about to get a shock. I snapped my right hand up...or that was the plan. The only thing that actually happened was a twitch of my thumb. Horror flickered through me. In all my years as a vampire, I'd never been this defenseless.

I was hoisted onto a table and strapped down: wrists, waist, ankles, and forehead restrained with thick leather straps. I drew in a deep breath, trying to pinpoint things around me. Antiseptics, blood, vampire, and werewolf rolled through my nose and coated the back of my throat. Ah, so Mac was a werewolf.

Mac chuckled softly. "I never thought I'd see Ivan again. Damned if he didn't look as stunned as she was."

"You know him?" Calvin asked, shuffling to one side. I forced my eyes open. The room was sterile, full of sheet metal, surgical tools, bright light and not much else.

Calvin startled, his eyes meeting mine. I glared at him, baring my teeth even as blood dripped down the side of my head. A studded club—it was brilliant really, even if it hurt like a motherfucking son of a bitch. You didn't have to hit the heart to drop a vamp, and they were incapacitated well enough that a heart shot was like a walk in the park.

Mac turned around, and when he saw my open eyes, he put a hand on my arm as if he hoped to hold me down on his own. "How old is she?"

"Old enough," I whispered, "to outlive you, *Mac*." I weighted his name as heavily as I could, putting the last of my strength into controlling him. He let out a whimper and his eyes glazed over. He'd been compelled before, which worked in my favor. "Kill Calvin."

Calvin jumped the moment before Mac leapt at him. They tangled on the floor, biting and snarling. I wasn't sure Mac could take him, but it would buy me the time I needed. With a sharp jerk that took everything I had left in me, I brought my head forward, splitting the leather strap.

The wristbands came next. I bent and undid the waist and ankle straps while Calvin and Mac continued to smash around the room, like a tornado unleashed indoors. There was a yelp and then Calvin stood. Mac whimpered on the floor, his back at an impossible angle. At least, impossible to survive without a reset.

"What the hell is wrong with you, Lea? Do you not trust me?" Calvin yelled.

"No. Get away from him." Shockingly enough, he did as I asked and moved to the doorway, peering out.

"If we hurry, we can catch up to Rachel and your other friends. We have a few hours left of dark."

I ignored him, dropping to my knees beside Mac as the

world spun and sparkled, the injury to my head anything but healed. I was about to change that right now. "Thanks."

"Don't hurt me," he whispered.

"You betrayed Ivan and his pack—" I brushed his hair back, "—didn't you?"

"Yes."

I dropped on him and buried my fangs into his neck hard, grinding them through muscle and tendons, deliberately keeping the pleasure from him. He screamed, but I slapped a hand over his mouth, holding him down while I drank him down, letting his werewolf blood heal my injuries at light speed.

His memories cascaded over me, most of them of his life in the barracks here, of the borderline sadistic things he'd happily done. But then came the memories of his pack life before...of how much he'd resented Ivan and wanted his wife. How he'd been the one to betray them all and how he'd started kidnapping the pack for Stravinsky, then deliberately took the rest while Ivan was gone.

To hurt the enforcer as much as he could.

In short, Mac was the asshole of assholes. I was glad I'd killed him—and even happier I'd made it hurt. As soon as he was dead, I checked his body for weapons. I took his gun and the spiked club. It was smaller than I'd thought it would be, just a black club the size of a police baton studded all over with half-inch silver stakes. I held it up, looking past it to Calvin. He blanched.

"I'm on your side, Lea. I'm fighting with you."

"You tackled me."

"If I hadn't, his blow would have embedded you with more of the stakes in that club." He pointed. A part of me knew he was right, I'd seen Mac's memories of that incident too.

"Three strikes and you're out. You've had two, so in other words—" I tipped my head to the door, "—don't fuck up again."

CHAPTER 32

RACHEL

All hell had broken loose, keeping me busy enough not to think about what Stravinsky had said about me being Lea's servant. I knew she'd played the situation to grab an edge—and I had played my part—but deep inside, I also knew he was right.

But I had to focus on getting out of this melee. I wouldn't be anyone's servant, least of all my own, if I didn't survive.

While General Hamm was here, it was obvious the

men he'd brought with him weren't real soldiers. They were poorly trained, poorly coordinated, and out of their element against a vampire, a werewolf, a Cazador whose hands were still bound, and me.

We were making good progress, but I noticed a group of men moving toward an open garage door I hadn't noticed in the back corner—and an armored vehicle, specially equipped with nozzles and hoses attached to big tanks. The engines revved.

I was fighting off two guys, but Antonio was closer to the tank. "Stop them!"

"Busy, *mi amor*!" he shouted as he fought off two men with several good kicks since his hands were still bound.

Lea cut a path of blood and destruction as she made her way across the room, getting closer and closer to Stravinsky. After disposing of my two attackers, I got close enough to Antonio to cut his zip tie.

Lea finally made it across the room to Stravinsky, but I didn't hear what she said—I was too busy watching Calvin tackle her just as a tall guy with arm muscles the size of my thighs swung a thick silver club covered in spikes square against Lea's head.

I'd seen her take many hits before, but this was different from all the others. Her body went limp and I released a scream as Ivan roared in anguish. I started to rush toward her, but Antonio grabbed my arm and held me back as a new wave of guards rushed through the open garage door.

The muscled man scooped up Lea like she was a rag doll, her bloody head drooping over his arm. Ivan hesitated, torn between wanting to go to her and staying to fight, and released another roar.

I lost sight of her as we fought off the fresh guards, not an easy task since we were out numbered five to one. I fought off my rising panic. Lea had looked *dead*. I reminded myself vampires were hard to kill, but she was defenseless. Calvin had followed them and he wasn't to be trusted. If she wasn't dead, she would be soon. I had to get to her.

Especially before the bombs went off.

Oh shit. How much time did we have left?

We also needed to stop that tank, but I couldn't do it with this gaggle of asshats in my path.

A new burst of rage channeled into energy, and I took out three men as Antonio and Ivan cut down the men surrounding them.

I had a clear shot to both the garage and the hall Lea had disappeared down, but who to follow? My head told me to try to save the village, but I felt a strong tug toward Lea.

Was it because of our friendship, or did I really have a supernatural bond to Lea that superseded everything else? It pissed me off to think she'd tricked me into something so permanent without my approval, but I'd deal with it later.

I had to get to her.

I heard the first explosion as I bolted across the room.

I gasped and shot a glance toward Antonio and Ivan.

"Time to go," Antonio said after his fist connected with his last attacker's temple, sending the man crumpling to the floor.

"I have to go after her," Ivan said, but I grabbed his arm.

"This whole place is going to blow, Ivan. We have to get out now." But even as I said the words, I felt the same urge.

"Lea…"

"Is a vampire. She'll survive this too." If she was still

alive, but I had this weird sense that she was. "We'll come back and find her."

He started to protest, but another explosion shook the building and sent a chunk of the ceiling crashing to the floor.

Ivan's mouth pursed, but he nodded and we ran toward the garage. Shots rang out, ricocheting off the concrete walls. I ducked behind a tool bench and tried to assess the situation. A group of men were on the other side of the garage—a concrete tomb that could fit half a football field—hidden behind several pieces of machinery, but as soon as they realized we weren't shooting back, they began to advance, sending a wave of bullets toward us.

Antonio cursed next to me. "They took our weapons." He shot a glance toward Ivan, who was hiding behind a transport truck.

Ivan held up his empty hands.

Shit.

Blade still in my hand, I was prepared to take out the first man who rounded the tool bench. I press my back to the cool metal, waiting to make my move.

Only the first threat came from the opening behind us. Two men stood in the doorway, smiles curling their lips as they lifted their weapons to fire.

Instinct took over and I threw my knife at the one on the right. The blade lodged in his throat and surprise filled his eyes as he reached for it, dropping to his knees.

His friend turned to him in shock, giving Antonio the opportunity to follow my lead. He leapt at the guard, slitting his throat and sliding his gun across the smooth concrete floor. I caught it and peered around the side of the bench to take stock. I had no idea how many bullets were in the clip, but knew I had to make each one count. I saw three men across from me. I ducked back around the bench as bullets sprayed toward me. I took a deep breath, then peeked around the side again, aiming for the man on the end.

He fell as I ducked back to safety.

Several shots went off beside me, and I swiveled to see Antonio shooting a semi-automatic rifle while Ivan wielded a handgun.

I swung around to shoot again, taking out a man less than six feet away.

The gunfire cut off abruptly, and I glanced at Antonio. His jaw was set and his eyes glittered with anger, but they softened when he glanced down at me. "Let's go."

The temperature in the garage had risen and smoke now filled the room behind us, burning my lungs.

I nodded and got up to make a break for the exit, but an anchor bolted my feet to the floor, my body insisting I run back into the fire.

"Rachel!" Antonio shouted. "Come on!"

I tried to take a step forward and fell to my knees, fighting the urge to turn around and run toward Lea. "I can't," I said in a panic. "I have to go back for Lea."

"*Mierde*," Antonio spat out in dismay. "The bind is calling her."

"Shit," Ivan said, looking torn himself. "It means she's still alive."

"She's not alive!" Antonio shouted. "She's already dead, and for you to go after her would mean certain death for you too!" He looked furious. "I know you want to save her, but the bind works both ways and you know it. If Lea's actually alive, what will she do when she finds out you let Rachel die trying to get to her?"

Flames flicked at the space behind us and the lights flickered.

"We have to go!" Antonio shouted. "The door is electrical, and we won't be able to get the garage door open once the power is out." The large garage door was at the end of a twenty-foot-wide and thirty-foot-long tunnel, and appeared to be our only way out.

"Fuck," Ivan growled, then grabbed me and tossed me over his shoulder.

But the urge to fight him was overwhelming. I kneed him in the stomach as I beat on his back, trying to evade his hold.

His arm pinned my legs tight against him as a new terror rose inside me, eclipsing the fear of being crushed underneath the walls and ceilings of the collapsing building.

The large garage door groaned in protest as it opened in a jerky movement.

My pulse pounded in my head, exacerbated from hanging upside down. "We're not going to make it!" And part of me—a part that freaked the shit out of me—didn't want to make it. Not without Lea.

"We'll make it." Ivan's voice was a low rumble.

I fought him with every step he took, even as he ducked to make it under the partially opened door.

Then it crashed to the ground with a thunderous noise that sent panic through me.

Ivan continued to run, not stopping until we were several hundred feet from the building. As soon as he let me slide to the ground, I bolted toward the building. He grabbed me around the waist and hauled me back.

"This is for your own good, *mi amor*," Antonio said as something smashed against the back of my head.

Bright streaks flashed in my eyes, followed by darkness. As my consciousness faded, I heard Ivan's voice, drenched with relief. "If she's fighting this strong, we know Lea's still alive."

Chapter 33

LEA

A sharp pain sliced through my head that had nothing to do with my own injuries and everything to do with Rachel's. I stumbled and pressed a hand against the wall closest to me as the building rumbled like a beast in the throes of death. I had no doubt the explosions were Rachel's work.

"If we don't hurry up, we're going to fry like Sunday chicken." Calvin grabbed my arm and jerked me forward.

"Did you ever feel me when we were bound?" I didn't look at him as we ran down the corridor.

"No."

That's what I'd thought. In all the years I'd worked with Calvin, I'd never been able to sense where he was, or if he was hurt. To be fair, I'd never had this strong of a bond with any of my servants. I'd heard of bonds this powerful between vampires and their servants, but hadn't really believed it until now.

I didn't need Rachel's scent to find her anymore. The pull toward Rachel was too strong. A secondary explosion rocked the building and the lights flickered, dimmed, and went out.

Calvin grabbed my hand and led the way. "The main garage is full of idiots with guns. If we go out the side exit, we'll avoid the worst of them."

"Last chance, Cal." I whispered the words, knowing full well he heard me. Some gut instinct compelled me to say it.

We took a left at the next T-intersection, kicked open a locked door and there he stood in front of us.

Stravinsky.

"What a good pet you are, Calvin," he murmured, the weight of his words crushing the air out of me.

Calvin dropped his head, shook it once. "No, I didn't... Lea, I didn't know he was here. This was an exit. I know it."

Stravinsky laughed, the sound echoing in the rounded-out room. "That's what I let you believe. I made you, Calvin. I can get inside your head whenever I want."

Calvin's head jerked up. "No, that's not true. Peter never controlled Lea."

Stravinsky smiled. "May I point out, you have neither Lea's fortitude nor her mental strength. From what Peter said, she fought him from the beginning, her faith in her quest giving her all she needed to deny him. While your anger, confusion, and quest for revenge make you weak and easily manipulated."

"Calvin." I said his name with as much emotion as I could. "Calvin, he doesn't own you."

Stravinsky tipped his head to the side. "You want to use him as a prize? See who he comes to? Who can break his mind first?"

Calvin's eyes shot to mine and I shook my head. "No. He is my friend, no matter how much hate he carries for me."

The words seemed to soften something in Calvin, but Stravinsky snapped his fingers. "To me, Calvin."

Cal took a step toward his master, stumbled a bit and then took another as an explosion rocked the foundation under our feet. This was not the time for our contest of wills.

"Calvin—" I didn't lift a hand or try to manipulate him with words, knowing him well enough that it would send him the wrong direction. "You fight him on your own, then come with me and we'll take them down together. I will not force you, not even in this." I took a step back. Rachel's heartbeat tugged at me, the steady thrum that hummed along the bond the only thing that gave me hope that Ivan and Antonio were keeping her safe.

I took another step back and waited. We didn't have a lot of time, but this was one of those moments that couldn't be rushed.

"Kill her," Stravinsky snarled.

Calvin tensed and so did I. I held my ground. "We can take him, Cal."

Just the truth, nothing more.

"You...know me better than I thought." Calvin grinned over his shoulder at me, and for the first time in years I saw the life in him. Ironic, now that he was dead.

I held out a hand and he slapped his palm into it, jerked me forward and threw me at Stravinsky. I shot through the air, yanking a stake from the top of my boot as I came down on the vamp.

Except that one second he was there, and the next he wasn't.

"You think you're the only one full of werewolf blood, Lea?" Stravinsky was on the other side of the room, and I hadn't even seen him move. It was normal for humans not to see vampire movement. But vamp to vamp, both of us loaded with werewolf blood? Shit, how old was he?

A cold chill ran down my spine. Stravinsky waved to me, but I spun around and ran the way we had come, away from whatever trick Stravinsky had planned for me.

Call it a hunch, but—

The explosion behind us sent Calvin and me flying out the door and down the stretch of hall, our bodies tumbling and then smacking onto the cement. I rolled onto my back, away from the fire, putting out the flames burning the back of my shirt. Calvin reached over as if to pat one out and then pulled his hand back. "That would be stupid."

"Yeah, flammable, remember?" I rolled to my knees and led the way.

Technically Calvin had struck out by taking me to Stravinsky as he'd done.

But I'd let it slide...because this was Cal and I wasn't sure I could kill him even though I'd promised. There was too much history, too much shit between us. And not enough time to make any sort of rational decision.

Rachel was moving away from me, though not quickly. That meant they were on foot, which was good and bad.

Calvin kept close, but said nothing about me taking the lead. In less than a minute, I had us back in the main garage where we'd started.

Bodies lay where I'd left them, the big-ass truck was gone and there was no sign of anything moving. Of course, that wasn't to say we were in the clear. "Can that main gate be opened?" I pointed at the oversized steel-plated door that cut us off from the outside world.

"Yes, but even now, I couldn't do it on my own. The hydraulics are out with the power."

I followed him to the mechanism. He pointed at two sets of chains with links thicker around than my forearms. "Those are the backups. They pull them with forklifts if something goes sideways."

I grabbed a chain in each hand and tipped my head back. "Get to the door."

His eyes widened. "You aren't Superwoman, Lea."

"Do it," I snapped. There was no time to fucking argue.

Calvin headed to the door and I took a deep breath. This was going to be a test even for me. I thought about Ivan and Rachel; they were waiting on me, so it was now or never.

Teeth gritted, I leaned back, putting my body, muscle, and heart into this. If I didn't get out, Rachel would die. I knew in my gut that more trouble was coming our way; she was going to need me.

I couldn't let her down. Especially not now that she knew the truth about the bond. With a scream, I hauled the chains a foot, then another, then another. There was nothing but the pull of metal on my skin, the pain of muscles being pushed beyond limits, followed by the snapping of something in my left shoulder. A joint maybe, I wasn't sure.

"Lea, I'm through. You'll have ten feet," Calvin yelled.

It would have to be enough. I gave the chains one last jerk, let go and bolted for the door with all I had.

The steel door raced to the ground as I dove toward it.

It was so close the back of my shirt got caught behind me.

"Lea, you've been holding back on me all these years."

"Shut up, Cal." I was on my feet and running toward Rachel before I'd even finished speaking. She was close.

And as pissed as she'd ever been.

I ran across the sand, about three hundred yards before the building behind us exploded into the night air with an eruption that sent shock waves across my skin.

"That's going to bring the rain," Calvin said.

I was pretty sure he didn't mean clouds and a gentle patter of raindrops.

"Fuck."

"Yeah."

I bolted toward Rachel. As I drew close, all I saw was Antonio standing over her. He was yelling; she was holding a hand to her head.

Like he'd hit her.

Something in me snapped loose. I was on Antonio and strangling him before he could draw another breath.

"Lea, no!" Rachel touched my shoulder and the spell snapped. I backed off Antonio and shifted my attention to Rachel. There was a bruise growing on the side of her head. "Did he hit you?"

She grimaced. "Not like you're thinking." Damn, she was protecting him. I shot a glance at Ivan, who shrugged.

I scooped her up, slinging her onto my back. "Time to go. Rain is coming."

Calvin nodded. "They'll set the hounds on us."

"How is that possible?" Antonio slowly got to his feet, rubbing his neck. "Are they not all dead in the explosion?"

Calvin and I shared a glance. I nodded. "Shadow men will not die in a fire, and they can still make things happen. Antonio, will you be riding the wolf or the vamp?"

"Riding?"

"We have to move fast," Ivan said. "And you're a slow-ass human."

Rachel tightened her hold around my neck. "It's not so bad, kind of a souped-up pony ride."

Ivan laughed. "Souped-up, nice play on words."

I *felt* her smile, and was more than a little freaked out by the way I was picking up on her movements and gestures. Was it the same for her? Or maybe it had something to do with the situation?

Ivan grabbed Antonio and slung him onto his back. "Tally ho!"

Rachel snorted and I took off as fast as I could. "I hate to say it... But I'm glad you brought the wolf. He's been...a good addition."

Why was she saying that now?

"Because I'm still not sure Antonio was a good idea. And Calvin gives me the fucking willies."

I swallowed hard and did my best not to think any more questions. As long as she didn't realize I hadn't spoken out loud, maybe—

"Oh my God. You didn't say anything, did you?"

I shook my head.

"Not now, Rachel. We'll deal with this, but not now."

"Why the fuck not?" she yelled.

"We're being followed!" Ivan called out.

CHAPTER 34

RACHEL

I couldn't stop to think about the implications of the fact that I'd heard Lea's thoughts as clear as if she'd spoken them aloud. We had bigger issues—literally. The werewolves from hell were headed straight toward us, and I had a feeling we couldn't fight these bad boys.

"How did they survive the explosion?" I asked.

"I suspect they were kept somewhere else."

I still had the gun tucked in the back of my pants, so I pulled it out, then lifted it up to turn off the safety.

"A gun won't kill them," Lea shouted.

"It might if the bullets are silver." It made sense. The guards worked in a facility that housed supernatural creatures, many of whom were not there on their own volition.

I leaned back, trying to take aim, but Lea's steps weren't exactly smooth and I was sure the shot had to be through the brain. It didn't help that the back of my head throbbed where Antonio had hit me. But I had to do something fast. "Lea, they're gaining on us."

"Impossible."

"Yet true."

"How many?" She glanced at Ivan, who struggled to keep up, Antonio looking none too happy on his back. Calvin ran like he was out for a Sunday stroll, his face devoid of emotion.

"I can't tell exactly. At least fifteen."

"Not great odds."

I snorted. "Since when do we do great odds?" I sucked in a breath, shocked at what I was about to suggest. "We need to stop and fight them. We'll never outrun them. Antonio and I are slowing you two down. We stand a better chance taking them on face to face. It's better than them grabbing us from behind."

I could sense her emotions, her struggle to do what she thought would be safest for me. It was equally reassuring and alarming.

"We're stopping," she shouted to Ivan and Calvin. "Be prepared to fight. On the count of three."

The glare Ivan shot her suggested he wasn't a fan of this plan, but he gave a sharp nod.

"One," Lea counted.

Antonio noticed my gun and prepared his. I briefly considered grabbing my knife out of my boot, but I couldn't hold onto both weapons and Lea. The gun would work out of range of the werewolves' claws and teeth, but I had to calm my nerves and steady my hands. It all depended on my aim, how many bullets I had, and if they were silver. There were a lot of ifs there.

God, I hoped I'd made the right choice.

"Two."

Antonio shot me a cocky grin that said, *You can do this.*

Damn right I could.

"Three."

Lea turned sideways so my right hand aimed forward as she skidded to a halt, sending a plume of dirt into the air around us. The dust filled my nose and stung my eyes, but I didn't dare blink in case I missed my opportunity.

I lifted my gun and aimed for the eye of a werewolf approaching us at full speed.

Doing my best to keep the gun steady, I squeezed.

The recoil jolted my arm. The werewolf continued his forward momentum—spittle hanging from his open mouth, sharp claws out, ready to grab me—and for one horrifying moment, I wondered if I'd made the wrong call. But his body was just several seconds behind the misfiring dying synapses in his brain. His feet twisted beneath him and he fell forward, his body skidding on the ground to a stop.

Confused, two werewolves behind him looked at him, then stared at us, their eyes glowing red. They were pissed.

"One down," Lea said as I jumped to the ground and lifted my gun. "Fourteen to go. You take the one on the left."

"Got it."

She pulled out a short blade, her face looking like a statue of an Amazon warrior.

I took careful aim at my mark and squeezed the trigger

just as Lea leapt onto the back of her attacker and jabbed it in the eye with her stake, digging deep.

Antonio had shot several rounds from his semi-automatic rifle, but the werewolf he'd targeted just looked pissed. Not a good thing.

"You're the only one with silver," Antonio shouted as he evaded the reach of another werewolf. "Make them count, Rachel."

The problem was I had no idea how many bullets I had left.

Ivan was in a tangled mess with two werewolves. Even Calvin was in a fight with a werewolf, although I still didn't trust him.

Another werewolf bounded for me, and I stood my ground as I aimed and shot. The werewolf fell, its body skidding to a halt at my feet.

Lea was in her own messy situation. I tried to see if I could take a shot at one of her attackers, but they were too close to her, not to mention their movements were too jerky to allow me a clean shot.

"Rachel!" Antonio shouted. "Behind you!"

I crouched and spun on the balls of my feet, staring up into the face of a snarling werewolf. I grabbed the knife from my boot with my left hand and swung it up, slashing the creature's throat. While I knew that wouldn't kill it, the wound might slow it down. I gagged as the smell of rotting flesh filled my nose. Its claw was in a downward arc toward my face.

Then there was a blur of movement behind me, and someone tackled the beast to the ground. I gaped in shock when I realized it was Calvin.

Had he really just saved me?

I didn't have time to dwell on it. Another werewolf was

already charging toward me. I picked up my gun, forcing my nerves into submission after my close call, and squeezed.

Nothing.

My heart rate increasing, I squeezed again. Still nothing.

"I'm out of bullets!" In a desperate move that was probably foolish as hell, I threw my silver blade for the werewolf's head, using every ounce of strength I had.

Unbelievably, the blade jammed in its eye socket and the creature fell into a heap, my blade buried somewhere underneath it.

Calvin ripped off the jaw of the werewolf he'd knocked off me, then reached deep into its head through its mouth and pulled out something I was fairly certain was the werewolf's brain.

He turned his cold eyes on me.

I stood, tossing my now-useless gun aside as I edged toward the werewolf I'd just killed. It was then I realized we were a good twenty feet away from the others, all of whom were busy in battles of their own. We were next to a transport truck I hadn't noticed before. "Get away from me, Calvin."

"I just saved your life."

And while that was undeniably true, the glint in his eyes told me he had an ulterior motive. "Is this the part where I'm supposed to say thank you?"

He grinned, but it didn't reach his eyes. "Probably not. Death by werewolf would have been better."

"What the hell do you want?"

"You stole her from me."

"Who? Lea?" His non-answer was enough. "Are you shitting me? We're doing this now? *Here*?"

He continued to advance and I edged closer to the werewolf I'd killed. I had to retrieve my blade. "Here and now is perfect." He was ten feet away, stalking toward me like the perfect predator.

"It didn't take you long to adapt to becoming a vampire." I rolled the creature over with the toe of my boot, keeping my eyes on Calvin as I squatted and pulled my blade free.

His grin was more genuine. "I've watched the best for decades."

He slid to the side when I stood, blocking me from the others, driving me toward the truck. "What do you want from me, Calvin? I'm sorry you became a vampire. I'm even sorrier if you blame me for it after you begged me to kill you to keep it from happening."

"No," he said earnestly. "I was wrong. Today has been a revelation to me. Turns out becoming a vampire was the best thing that ever happened to me. I wasted so many years blaming Lea for being what she was, when in truth, she's beautiful in every way."

"You love her."

"Yes, more than you could possibly understand. We would be the perfect match, the perfect mates."

I wanted to ask him why he'd treated her like shit for years if he really loved her so much. "Ivan might have a thing or two to say about that."

He scoffed. "She could never love him. He's a dalliance. A distraction after losing me. But now I'm here and I'm hers."

"So go get her. Help her fight off the werewolves instead of acting like an angsty middle-schooler with a crush. Do you want me to ask her if she wants to go steady with you?"

"No. I want you dead."

I felt so, so stupid. How had I not seen this? The trap.

His real plan. We were behind the truck now, hidden from the others' view.

"You feel threatened by me."

"Not feel, Rachel. I am. You have a bond with her that will prevent me from being her true partner."

I lifted my hands in surrender. "Hey, whatever you're thinking is off-base. I don't swing that way."

He moved closer and I held the blade in a defensive stance.

"It's deeper than sex, Rachel. You have a true blood bond she never shared with me."

"Because you fucking wouldn't let her, you uptight prick. You broke her heart for decades and now you think she's just going to start something with you? *Because you changed your mind?*" I was pissed as hell on her behalf.

"I've seen the error of my ways. I love her. Love her with a depth you could never understand, but Lea and I will never share a true bond if you stand in the way. So I need to eliminate you. Stravinsky made me special. I'm stronger and more durable than any other vampire created. With Lea by my side, no one will be able to defeat us. We can rule the world for eternity."

"Then you never really knew her at all," I spat. "Because that's the last thing she would want."

He was only two feet away now, and he bared his teeth, his fangs glistening in the moonlight. "I would tell you this wouldn't hurt, but that would be a lie," he sneered. "I want it to hurt. I want you to pay for stealing her from me."

I swung my blade upward at his chest, but his hand darted out too fast to see, knocking the knife from my hand hard enough to break the bones. It clattered against the side of the truck.

He slammed me against the truck, his hand around my

throat. Bright lights shot through my vision as the already sore spot on the back of my head screamed with pain. I gasped for breath, clawing at his arm, but he just grinned, showing me his other hand. Claws sprang from his fingertips.

"I can make this look like an unfortunate werewolf attack." He slashed at my right arm. "And Lea will never know the truth."

Hot burning pain filled my bicep, but my scream was stifled from my constricted airflow.

He tilted his head. "I could go for the humane kill—a deep slash to the gut—but where's the fun in that? I've learned I like to play with my victims."

He slashed at my left leg, tearing through fabric and flesh. Blackness had replaced the bright lights, and my lungs were burning from the lack of air. I tried to kick him, but my un-oxygenated muscles lacked the coordination to make it effective.

He grinned as he lifted me to eye level, my feet dangling beneath me. "Naughty girl. I would love to play longer, but I think it's time for the kill."

"You're fucking out of time, all right," Lea growled as she crashed into him, throwing him sideways to the ground.

I could feel the fury radiating from her as she smashed his head with her fist, over and over until his grasp on my neck loosened.

Strong hands pulled me away from the now blurry pile, and I breathed deeply, trying to refill my lungs as tears stung my eyes.

Antonio swung me up into his arms, strode to the side and handed me to Ivan.

"What the fuck do you think you're doing?" Ivan asked, gently taking me.

"I'm going to fucking kill him."

Ivan's smile was grim. "I think you'll have to fight Lea for it."

CHAPTER 35

LEA

Calvin jerked in my hands, but I tightened my grip on his forearm until the bones ground together. He stared up at me. "Kill her, Lea. She's the only thing between us."

I saw it in him, something that happened to many young vampires. He was not the Calvin I'd known; his mind had cracked under the strain of the change, and I'd been too stupid and blind to see it. There was no way I could let him go now, not like this. And there was only one way to truly help him—to honor the person he'd been.

I pulled him with me, dragging him toward the carnage of the werewolves. Back the way we'd come, a second chorus of howls lit up the night air. "How many more are coming, Cal?" As I purred the words, I could hear Rachel barking something at me. She wanted to know what I was doing, and I couldn't blame her. He would have taken her life if I'd gotten there a moment later.

Killing him kindly. His mind is broken.

I knew she didn't fully understand what I meant, but she relaxed—which allowed me to focus. Whatever information Calvin had, I wanted. It might just save us. But that would mean drinking him down. I pushed him to his knees. "I'm going to bind you to me."

His eyes lit up, like a child in candy store.

I ran a hand over his head and tightened my grip on his hair, tipping his head sideways. I didn't give him warning, but I softened the bite and pushed a sense of pleasure into it. A final goodbye. He sighed and dug his fingers into my waist, gripping me hard.

His memories flowed through me. I saw myself through his eyes, the mix of love and hate, of pride and disgust he'd felt for me throughout the long years we'd spent together. And then the night Stravinsky had turned him and broken his mind, how he'd put him back together just enough to function.

An image of the old man he'd been wavered in my mind, the old man I'd loved with all I'd been able to give him.

"You've done good, Lea. You have. Don't forget it, no matter what happens. You were right to bind her to you. It's the only way you'll both survive this. I never really was a good bond, I know that." He let out a sigh and snorted. *"Go on, save your friends."*

"You are my friend, too."

"I know. Now get the fuck out of here, bloodsucker. Go save the world; that's your job now."

I jerked my mouth off his neck. His heart was still beating, but it faded fast. Judging by the sound, the second pack was at best a mile away. I drew my silver stake and drove it through Calvin's heart, twisting it once for good measure. "Goodbye."

I ran from him, tucking the blade back into my boot as I moved. I scooped up Rachel as I went by, ignoring Antonio's protest that he could carry her. "More wolves."

"Yeah, we heard. Calvin?" Rachel asked.

"Dead."

"For sure this time?"

"I drank him down."

Ivan grunted. "His memories, was there anything in there to help us?"

Fuck, I'd barely paid attention to that. I fast-forwarded through the last weeks of his life as we bolted across the desert. "There's an oasis up ahead. Weapons and the antidote to the toxin are stashed there."

"Now, that's what I like to hear," Antonio said.

A trickle of concern rolled between Rachel and me. I nodded. "Yeah, some of Stravinsky's boys could be lying in wait. But that could work in our favor. The pack behind us is big."

"How big are we talking, and how the fuck can you tell?" Rachel spat out, the words jarred by the bumping of my stride—which also made her wince with pain I could feel as if it were my own. I looked at Ivan and gave him a nod.

"The howls are the Alphas calling their packs to them," he said. "There was at least four sets of howls."

"Four packs. Are you serious?" Her heart rate escalated against my back. "And you said packs can be—"

"Roughly twenty members. On average," Ivan said.

Antonio grunted. "So close to a hundred zombie were-wolves on our asses?"

"But they will kill anything that gets in their way," I said, "and the oasis holds weapons and cannon fodder."

At least, I hoped it did. Rachel's injuries from Calvin had to be handled too. She wasn't going to like the solution, but it was the only way.

"Fuck me," she muttered. "I don't want to drink blood again."

"What the hell are you talking about?" Antonio spat out.

Rachel shook her head and I said nothing. There was no choice. She had a broken hand, plus a slashed-up leg and bicep. Without my help, there was no way she'd be able to stand on her own, never mind fight.

"The village is the other way," Rachel said. "I won't leave without trying to help them."

"Neither will I," I said.

A large sand dune rose ahead of us and we charged up it. Ivan put out a hand, slowing us. "Voices." He breathed the word, and I dropped to my knees to let Rachel slide off. Once she was beside me, I handed her a knife and held up my wrist. "No time to be squeamish."

With hunched shoulders, she took the knife and slashed my wrist with more force than necessary. I didn't flinch. I lifted my wrist and looked away as she drank from the wound.

Antonio choked and Ivan put a hand on his shoulder. "Rachel will slow us down and probably die if she isn't functioning at full speed."

"That doesn't mean I have to fucking like it," Antonio snapped.

Rachel drew back from me and I took her hand, making sure the bones were all in place. I counted the heartbeats, sensing her body heal.

"Twenty seconds," I said.

"We've only got a minute before the wolves are on us, so I hope you're right," Ivan said.

I counted down the seconds, and Rachel's eyes popped open by the time I hit twenty. "I'm ready."

The four of us belly-crawled up the last ten feet of the hill to peer over.

Calvin's memories had been on point. The oasis was bigger than I had realized, though, easily covering a twenty-acre area—the palm trees and bushes thickening deeper into the center. There was movement within the trees..Stravinsky's men, I had no doubt, and I could see several Humvees.

I looked behind us, and could see the four packs coming in fast and hard. "We've got to move. We've got cannon fodder, the antidote, and weapons ahead of us. Rachel, stay with me. Antonio, stick close to Ivan."

"Meet at the water?" Ivan asked.

"Weapons first," Rachel said. I nodded.

"Weapons first. Water second. Trees if we have to. We'll take the antidote when we leave." At least, that was the plan. The four of us stood and ran down the side of the sand dune. Rachel kept pace with me easily, though I had to put out a hand to help her keep her balance a couple times when she lost her footing.

And for a fucking miracle, she didn't snap at me.

"I'm not that big of an asshole," she said, reading my thought.

"Sometimes you are," I said.

She grimaced, but there was humor under it. Maybe this mind-reading thing wasn't so bad.

All of those thoughts fled, though, as we raced toward the oasis and the soldiers saw us. The rapid staccato of gunfire filled the air at the exact moment the wolf packs hit the top of the sand dune.

I ran straight for the first Humvee. I yanked the driver out of the seat, snapping his neck with a sharp twist. "Rach, check the back."

"Already on it."

Three more soldiers came at us, and I dispatched them—breaking backs, arms and legs—and kicked away their weapons.

"Kill them!" Antonio yelled at me.

"No. They are a better distraction this way. Wolves like live things to play with," I said.

Antonio cursed me, but didn't argue. Rachel came up triumphant. "Guns and silver bullets. And a shit ton of antidote!"

The triumph didn't last long; the wolves swept into the oasis, flooding us with the scent of death and wet dog.

I grabbed Rachel, shoved her into the front of the Humvee and climbed in after her. I cranked the engine on and backed the truck up as a werewolf leapt onto the hood. Rachel took aim and shot it through the eye, and the beast rolled off without a sound. The windshield cracked, but didn't shatter.

A thump came up from above us. "Go, go!" Ivan yelled.

"I hope he remembered Antonio," I said as I hit the gas. Dawn was only a few hours off, and if Calvin had remembered it right, we were still a two-hour drive from the village. I glanced at Rachel. She nodded.

"Why, you like him now?"

I grinned at her from across the cab. "No, but you do."

"Get out of my head, Lea," she snapped, but there wasn't a lot of heat to it.

I waited until the sounds of gunfire and werewolves faded behind us. I tapped the roof of the truck and Ivan leaned in through the passenger side window. "You remember the Cazador?"

"Was I supposed to?"

Rachel went absolutely still beside me. I raised an eyebrow at Ivan. "Don't tease her, it's not nice."

He reached in and patted Rachel on the head. "I got him. Even if he's grumpy about not being able to do it on his own."

She eased back in her seat, reclining her head and closing her eyes. "Do you think we can save the village?"

I flicked through Calvin's memories. "From what I can see, it's not looking good. The strain they are using is virulent, violent, and based on what Calvin knew, they aren't even sure the antidote will work."

"Fuck."

I agreed with her. But with two hours on our hands and the boys in the back of the truck, I had to say something.

"I'm sorry."

She didn't need to ask for what. "I'm going to be real mature about this, Lea. Real fucking mature. Don't get excited by what I'm going to say because I'm only saying it once."

I braced myself, tightening my hands on the steering wheel. "Okay."

"I'm not."

I blinked several times, fighting the urge to shake my head. "You aren't?"

"Fuck, I'm not sorry. It's not that I like the idea of being bonded to you, but we are a kick-ass team. Admit it, Calvin didn't have a thing on me." She grinned at me.

I burst out laughing. "No, he certainly didn't."

"What happens, though, after this?"

I shrugged. "Depends on if we're both still alive. Chances are good I'll be dead, and you'll be free of me forever."

"And if we both survive?"

I glanced at her. "I'm not sure. I've heard of bonds like this, true bonds between vampires and their servants—"

"I'm not bringing you fucking oatmeal in the morning."

"I'd never ask. The point I'm trying to make is I've heard of this sort of thing, but never experienced it. Not with any of my helpers. Which tells me something about you is truly special."

She went quiet for a moment, thoughtful. "You thought you were telling me about the bond on the plane, didn't you? You tried to fess up, but I didn't catch the drift."

"Yes. I thought you understood."

"Well, even I have my moments." She gave me a wink as she ran a hand through her blonde hair. I laughed under my breath.

"You did not just make a blonde joke, did you?"

"Of course not, that's fucking ridiculous."

I shifted the truck into a higher gear and pressed the gas. "Try to sleep. I'll wake you when we get close."

She nodded. "Lea?"

"Yeah?"

"No more secrets. One more fucking secret and my head might explode."

You think we can keep secrets from each other right now? I thought.

She groaned and I grinned.

Maybe we would die before dawn, but at least we'd die as friends. That had to count for something.

CHAPTER 36

RACHEL

I jarred awake, sitting up in a panic. I rubbed my arm, surprised there was no more pain. Sure enough, the claw marks were now pink streaks on my skin. My leg too. "They're healed." I looked over at Lea, but she didn't look surprised.

"Beauty of the blood," she said. "Though it was faster even than I thought. Probably the bond is helping too."

I looked around, realizing why I had woken up. "Why are we stopped?"

"I think we're here," Lea said, staring out the windshield of the now-stopped Humvee.

A village lay ahead. It was an hour or so before dawn, but there should have been some kind of light—even a candle. The village was completely dark.

"How can you be sure?"

"I smell death," she whispered.

My heart jumpstarted. "They killed them all."

"We don't know that." But she didn't contradict it. "We need a plan. If Stravinsky's boys have already been here, you know it won't be pretty. In fact, it will probably be dangerous."

"Which is why we have the antidote."

Lea grunted softly. "We don't know it will even work. Or how long it will take to work."

"Lea, we have to try."

"It's probably too late for them, Rachel. We should focus on making sure we've stopped Stravinsky for good before he moves on to his next location."

"No. That's not good enough."

"Why are you so dead set on this? Why do I think this is personal?"

"What's wrong with wanting to save an entire village?" I asked a little too defensively.

"Nothing." She paused. "But—"

"I *knew* there would be a but."

"I think you're too close to this. Your personal feelings make you dangerous. They could get you killed."

"You don't know anything about why I feel so strongly against this, Lea. Let it go." Then I started singing the alphabet song in my head in case she tried to sift through my thoughts.

"That's mature," she grumbled.

"I'm not the one digging into someone else's head." Although I had to wonder what I would find if I tried.

"Don't even think about it."

Ivan's face appeared in the driver's window, standing next to the door. "So what's the plan?"

"For Lea to stay out of my head!" I snapped.

Ivan gave her a strange look, but she simply shook her head. "Don't ask."

"I wasn't planning to."

"The plan," I said, "is to go into that village and save as many people as we can."

Lea and Ivan shared a look and I shook my head. "Stay here if you want. I'm going."

"I'll go with you, *mi amor*," Antonio said from behind Ivan.

"Shut up, Cazador," Ivan growled. "We all stick together in this."

"We need to investigate," Lea said. "And to do that we need to get closer."

The guys climbed back onto the truck and Lea drove us closer to the village, turning the truck around to point away, as though ready for an escape.

As we met at the back of the truck, eerie moans and cries echoed in the darkness, which I had to admit was creepy as shit.

Lea's hand tightened on the steering wheel. "We need to presume Stravinsky's men have done their job."

Ivan nodded. "I smell the concoction." Lea's eyes widened, but Ivan gave her a reassuring smile. "The toxin works immediately, then the residual chemicals break down quickly." When she started to protest, he put a hand on her arm. "I know from what happened to my own pack, Lea. I found some papers about how it works."

"So the toxin is only a threat immediately after it's sprayed," Antonio said, his gaze sweeping between Ivan and me. "After an hour or so, it's no longer toxic?"

"Minutes," Ivan said. "Seven, from what I've read."

"There's no sign of Stravinsky's men," Lea murmured. "So it's been longer than seven minutes. The toxin isn't a problem. It's the residents. Or what they've become."

"The canisters appear to be ready," Antonio said, keeping his eyes on me. "The antidote is slightly different from the toxin. The toxin only has to be in the air you breath, but the antidote needs to be sprayed on the infected person's skin." He paused, making sure he still had my attention. "But from the looks of the canisters, you have to be close for the nozzle to reach. I'm guessing within ten to fifteen feet."

"Close enough they can attack you," Lea said in a dry tone. "We need to come up with an alternate plan to deal with the creatures if we can't cure them. And we need to be prepared to execute it immediately. We give the antidote a few seconds, and if it doesn't work, we eliminate the problem."

"*No*," I said, shaking my head. "The antidote might need more than a few seconds. It might need minutes. Or hours. Or even days," I pleaded. "You can't make a snap decision like that."

"Even though Stravinsky and his people have bigger problems, he's so invested he's probably going to send his people back to check on the results of his experiment," Lea countered. Her matter-of-fact tone was a sharp contrast to my impassioned one. "Not to mention we don't have hours or days. We have a half hour max to get in and get out before the sun rises. This needs to be quick and decisive. Either the antidote works or it doesn't. One thing is certain: no monster will be left alive when we leave."

Her words hung heavy in the air as her gaze held mine.

"You will do as I say, Rachel."

Tendrils from her words slipped into my brain, curling around my will, and I found myself wanting to nod and agree with her. I shook violently as rage mushroomed inside me. "You're pulling your servant bullshit mumbo jumbo on me?" I demanded through gritted teeth. "How fucking dare you!"

"I'm protecting you."

"By taking away my free will?" I shouted, taking several steps back. "I am not a child!"

"Then stop acting like one." Lea's tone was cold. "I am handling this in a professional manner. You are not."

I pointed to the village. "There are children in there, Lea. Defenseless children. Babies." I stood straighter, throwing back my shoulders. "I refuse to be cold and calculated about killing innocent children. I refuse to kill them at all." I swung my finger to point at her. "So you better stay the fuck out of my head, got it?"

She studied me for a moment before nodding. "Then let's get going."

"Not cool, Lea," I heard Ivan say as he leaned over her.

Antonio moved directly in front of her. "When this is done, you will release her."

Lea gave him a look that would have made lesser men run for their lives, but he stood his ground, his eyes full of danger and defiance. "This does not concern you," she insisted.

"If you are a Cazador, you know the tales. She is the one. She must be free of you."

"The tales are nonsense. Fairy tales."

"What if they're not? What if they are true?"

They both turned to study me, a new interest filling their eyes.

A slow grin spread across Lea's face as she turned back to him. "What makes you so sure *you* are the one?" She chuckled. "If your theory is true, then it must mean *I* am the one. I am the one who is bound to her."

Antonio looked like he wanted to strangle her.

This conversation irritated the hell out of me. They were talking cryptic nonsense about me as though I wasn't even there. "What the fuck are you talking about?"

Antonio cocked his head, giving his full attention to Lea. "Because I am a true Cazador. You are like a ghost that doesn't realize it is no longer alive. You are the very creature you seek and destroy. She needs a *real* Cazador to help her complete her mission."

"I agree with Rachel," Ivan said, his voice hard. "What the fuck are you talking about?"

Lea remained still for two agonizing seconds before turning and grabbing a canister of antidote from the truck. "It is nothing we will discuss now." She shot a glance at Antonio. "We need to keep our focus on this village." She handed the canister to me. "You and Antonio spray any villagers you see. Ivan and I are the protectors."

I shuddered, knowing what she would do as my protector. "Let's go."

The four of us were quiet as we entered the village, the tension between us thick and taut. Part of me wanted to kill Antonio for adding just one more layer of anxiety to an already anxiety-packed night. But another part of me wanted to know what he and Lea had been discussing.

It was obvious Lea hadn't kept it from me purposefully. Whatever he'd proposed had clearly never occurred to her. Right now, the mystery was just one more thing added to my monstrous pile of things to worry about. But if it didn't affect the outcome of what we were about to do, Lea was right—it could wait.

The moans were louder now that we were closer, and my muscles were as tight as coiled springs. I wasn't sure I was prepared for what I was about to see. I wasn't sure I could handle the slaughter of children. Again.

Lea shot me a quick glance.

Get the fuck out of my head, I mentally shouted at her.

I heard a scraping sound, followed by the click of shattering glass. Twenty feet away, a door swung open and a man staggered out. Or what was left of him. His face looked like it had been partially melted, leaving a beak-like nose with a long hook. His hands looked like bird talons with sharp claws. When he saw us, his still-human eyes rounded and he lurched toward us as best he could with his bent and twisted legs.

When he got close enough, I aimed the nozzle of the can on my back and drenched him from head to toe, which only seemed to infuriate him more. He let out a long squawk that drew squawks from deeper in the village.

"Shit," Ivan mumbled. "I don't like the sound of that."

The drenched man continued toward us, lifting his talons as if preparing to strike.

"It's not working," Lea said, lifting her gun to shoot.

"You don't know that!" I argued. "Give it a minute."

"Rachel." Her voice was tight as he moved closer.

"No." This man didn't deserve to be turned into a monster. Didn't deserve to be killed for the grisly fate someone else had forced on him. Maybe that was why I didn't fully understand Lea's self-hatred—her vendetta against her own kind.

How could she wipe out an entire race simply because they existed? She was proof enough that just because a person's warm blood turned cold, they were not destined to prey on the lives of innocent people. If anything, she strove to protect them—even if she saw the deaths of some innocent humans as collateral damage. How did we know none of these villagers could be saved? They were victims, and I couldn't bring myself to destroy them.

"We don't want to hurt you," I told the man as he continued to approach us, blind rage in his eyes. "We only want to help."

"Rachel." Lea sounded more panicked.

"*No*," I spat.

"I'll do it." Antonio's hand dropped to his side and he lifted his handgun before I even realized what he was doing. The blast echoed off the stone buildings and the man dropped face forward to the ground.

"Why?" I demanded.

"Because in this instance, she's right."

But the gunshot had set loose a cacophony of moans and shrieks, and doors began to burst open all across the village. Within seconds we were facing close to fifty men and women moving toward us at a slow gait. I could have handled the sight of all of them and more, but a figure in the front made me freeze in horror.

The pack was led by a child. A toddler who lifted the talon that had once been a hand and let out a cry of anguish and anger.

I took a step back, bumping into Lea's chest.

"Oh, fuck," Ivan groaned.

I couldn't agree with him more. My worst nightmare had come true.

CHAPTER 37

LEA

I grabbed Rachel's shoulder with one hand and held my gun tightly with the other. "Ivan, circle around with Antonio. We'll give them as much time as we can."

Rachel's eyes flicked to mine. *Why now?*

"Get spraying." I pointed her in the direction of the shuffling villagers even as I pulled her backward. The twisted creatures lurched after us, slow and uncoordinated. They weren't exactly what I'd call a success if Stravinsky was trying to create a super army. Terrifying? Yes.

"You didn't answer my question." Rachel stumbled, but I managed to keep her upright.

"Contrary to what you think, I have no desire to see them all dead."

But that wasn't the reason, and we both knew it. The child lurching toward us was all it had taken for her emotions to crack and spill over into me. I could no more deny Rachel this opportunity for personal redemption than I could have denied Calvin his one last chance.

Hopefully the outcome here would be better.

"How many?" Rachel bit out as she sprayed another man in the face even as I kicked out, connecting with a woman who'd drawn too close. The woman grunted, but didn't go down. She barely flinched, actually, and I suddenly understood why Stravinsky was making them this way. They were like the zombie werewolves—pain didn't register.

"Two hundred. Maybe a little more." The numbers weren't huge at first, but they could be. And that was the key.

The sheer number of them could overwhelm even the staunchest fighters. If Stravinsky had hundreds of thousands of these creatures at his disposal, say if he released the toxin in New York City, the panic and chaos would be beyond anything the world had ever seen. But the U.S. military wouldn't want this on American soil. They probably saw it as a way to win the war against the Middle East extremists.

I kept Rachel moving as she sprayed the antidote from side to side. "I'm almost out."

"Us, too!" Ivan hollered over the unwieldy mob.

"Rachel—"

"I know. I know." She bit the words out, coating them in bitterness. "This can't happen again, goddammit."

I deliberately kept my thoughts to myself. I cut through the straps of the tank on her back as the last drop sprayed into the face of a teenage boy.

"How many did we get?"

I lied. "All of them, I think."

Hope filtered from her for a brief flash before fading. "You're a shitty liar."

We circled around the mob, Antonio and Ivan moving in tandem across from us. A trickle of light slid across the top of the village roofs. *Madre de Dios*, were we ever going to catch a break?

A cry that lifted the hair from the back of my neck drew my eyes to the center of the mob. The little girl who'd led the group was standing there, human once more, her tiny hand pressed to her eyes. "*Al'umm!*"

Mommy. She was saying mommy in Arabic.

"It worked." I breathed the words, unable to believe what I was seeing. The villagers paused as if her cry had drawn them to her. "Oh, fuck."

I wasn't sure I could get us both through, but there was no way Rachel would be willing to stay behind. "Stick close, Rachel!"

I slammed my shoulder into the man nearest to me, his hooked beak whipping toward my eyes. I jammed the heel of my hand up into his chin, snapping his neck, holding off just enough not to kill him and leave him as prey and hoping it worked.

"What are you doing?" Rachel screamed at me. She hadn't heard the child. I purposely covered my thoughts as I struggled with what to do. I could turn around, tell her I had been wrong. Save us both by pretending the people here were all dead even as they walked about us moaning.

But the desire to do the right thing, to save someone so new to the world had bled too strongly from Rachel into me. I couldn't turn back any more than she could. Damn her and damn us both to hell.

I plowed through the villagers as if they were stick people. A few got jabs in on me, but nothing major. We reached the center of the mob and I scooped the kid up, tucking her under one arm right as two villagers dropped to their knees and swept clawed hands where she'd been.

"Oh my God," Rachel said. "It worked."

"Ivan, lead them away!"

"Trying," he hollered. "You smell good; they like you two."

Even now he was flirting. Wolves had no shame.

Rachel snorted. "You love it."

We still had a monster problem on our hands, no pun intended. I held the howling child tightly to my chest and hunched my back. "Up, Rachel."

She leapt onto my back and I took one deep breath before I rushed into the mob. Bodies bounced off me, and hands ripped at both Rachel and me. Several of the beaks jabbed into my arms, and one landed in the side of my neck, but the pain was minimal compared to most of the injuries I'd sustained over the last few days. We were free of the worst of them in ten seconds and Rachel jumped off. Wobbling, I dropped to one knee. My vision sparkled with dancing lights and I slapped a hand to the wound in my neck, which had closed to a tiny pinprick.

I tried to speak, but the words were at best slurred and they faded into my native tongue.

Venomous, was the only thing I could think.

"Fucking serious? Kid, come here." Rachel took the girl from me and murmured something to her in Arabic as the cries of anguish and horror around us shifted to shrieks of terror.

"Lea, you have to get up."

When had I lain down?

"Get up," Rachel continued, "the antidote is working, but not fast enough. Some people are coming back—"

I'd seen them—human once more but in the midst of the monsters.

"And those who do," Antonio came into view, "are being attacked by those who haven't fully returned to themselves. Silly monsters, they're harmless. Ugly as—"

"They're venomous," Rachel said, and someone, I assumed Ivan, scooped me up.

"Lea, do you need to feed?" Ivan tipped me so I could look at him. I tried to shake my head, but nothing happened. Damn it. I didn't think feeding would help, but I wasn't sure what would.

"She's full up," Rachel snapped. "Is there any antidote left?"

"Drops." Antonio shook his pack, and the smallest sloshing noise was audible. Ivan put me down and ripped the tank in half. This was intolerable, being the weakest one of the group, dependent on someone else to save me.

"Welcome to the club," Rachel muttered. I shot a look at her. I'd never thought of her as weak. She gave me a tight smile.

Slow as molasses in February, but not weak.

"Keep it up, we can always leave you behind," she snapped, but there was no real heat behind the words. Ivan grunted. "If you two are done." He held up the bottom half of the broken tank of antidote. Antonio grabbed my head and forced my jaws open. "If it works on the skin, this might make it work faster."

His gaze stayed fixed on my fangs as Ivan poured the remainder of the antidote into my mouth, making sure to get some on my skin. My throat convulsed, the liquid sticky sweet and tasting faintly like melons, of all things.

"That's all of it. Now we wait." Antonio let go of me, dropping me the short distance to the ground so my head bounced a little.

Ivan snarled and the two men were suddenly nose to nose. I glanced at Rachel as best I could. Apparently we weren't the only ones who sometimes had difficulty getting along.

"Boys," Rachel snapped. "Perhaps you can have your pissing contest another day? The sun is almost up, and we've got to get under cover."

Lying on the ground, I felt the wolves pounding toward us before I heard them. Werewolves. I all but screamed the word in my head.

Rachel's head snapped around and her hand came up with a gun. Two shots fired off. Ivan hit the ground beside me, three of the twisted half-dead werewolves on him.

And I could do nothing to help them.

CHAPTER 38

RACHEL

The werewolves had us surrounded, but there were only six this time and they seemed most interested in Ivan. Several were attacking him at once.

I pushed the crying girl behind me as I shot off several rounds, stopping a werewolf that was headed straight for Lea and me while Antonio shot the two who had knocked him to the ground. "I hate these fuckers," I mumbled as I turned my weapon on one of Ivan's attackers and fired. But they were moving so quickly it took several shots for me to kill one. Ivan killed another with his bare hands.

That left one zombified werewolf for the men to handle, allowing me to give my attention to another pressing matter.

The little girl clung to my leg, her crying subdued as she watched the werewolves in horror. I pried her arms from my legs, saying in Arabic, "We will keep you safe."

She nodded, staring at me with terror-filled eyes.

I only hoped I hadn't lied to her.

I squatted beside Lea, checking for signs the antidote was working. But she remained unmoving, her eyes dull and blank as they stared up into the last stars before dawn. Her reaction to a few simple scratches scared the crap out of me. I thought of her as invincible. I sure as hell didn't think one of those awkward creatures in the village could kill her.

The moans still filled the night behind us, but screams now joined them. I felt sick to my stomach. *I hope Stravinsky's heart got pierced by a stainless steel beam.*

I'm sure he got out. He's on the loose.

I shot her a glare, letting anger overcome my fear. It was an easier emotion to stomach. "Then you better get your ass off the ground and help me find the son of a bitch. Stravinsky isn't going to get away with this."

"So happy to hear you agree," a woman with a thick accent said in the darkness.

I jumped to my feet and lifted my gun, unsure of what I was aiming at, keeping the child behind me.

Vampire was Lea's thought.

"Shit," I muttered.

Antonio pulled out his blade, but I kept my gun aimed in the darkness.

A yelp came from the last werewolf as Ivan ripped the top of its head off and tossed it down in front of him. "Friends of yours?" he asked in disgust.

"My welcome committee," the woman said.

That surprised me. From what little I knew, vampires and werewolves usually hated each other.

They do. They are pets.

Since these weren't genuine werewolves, it made sense that a vampire would use them to do her dirty work.

"You're with Stravinsky?" I asked. "You've come to retrieve us?"

"We've come for you, but we are no friends of Stravinsky." She stepped out of the darkness as if appearing out of thin air, and a group of six people trailed behind her. She was gorgeous with long, flowing dark hair and pale skin that reflected the light of the full moon. She wore tight black pants and a long-sleeved black shirt that dipped low enough in the front to leave little to the imagination about the size of her breasts.

The group behind her was similarly dressed—three women and three men—although there was absolutely no doubt of who was in charge.

The leader turned her head toward Antonio. "Cazador, I've been looking forward to this day."

A low snarl released from his throat as his grip tightened on his blade, his gun now in his other hand.

She gave him the sort of smile a mother gives a demanding toddler—a look of forced patience and false humor. "Is that any way to greet your queen?"

"You are not my queen, Elena." He spat, sending a glob of spittle down in front of her feet.

She bared her teeth and hissed, the sound sending shivers down my spine.

The little girl clung to my leg again, releasing tiny whimpers.

Get your ass up, Lea.

Her lack of a response sent a new wave of panic through me.

Elena swung her gaze to me so sharply, I expected her to have whiplash. "It is true."

I froze, then forced myself to say, "That Stravinsky is creating monsters? Yes. The evidence is behind us."

"Yes. They are being dealt with." She flicked her wrist and gunshots filled the night, accompanied by screams and the cry of the bird creatures.

"You're killing them?" I asked in dismay.

She looked bored with my question, but she took several steps toward me. "Do you not destroy canines with rabies?" She flicked a glance toward Ivan and grinned. "Do you have rabies, *dog*?"

"Rot in hell," he snarled.

Her smile widened as she turned her attention back to me. "You are a curious creature. You show no fear toward me."

"Should I be afraid of you?"

Her brow lifted into a smirk. "Oh, Lea. You have chosen well with this one."

I snuck a glance at Lea, more worried than before. She wasn't speaking in my head.

"She's dying," Elena said.

"We gave her the antidote."

"It's not working." Elena gave me a pretend pout, then moved behind me, circling to stand behind Lea. "It's for humans. Not vampires."

I sucked in a breath, overwhelmed with panic. I snuck a glance to Ivan, who looked like he wanted to rip someone else's head off.

"Who are you?" I asked. Both Antonio and Ivan seemed to recognize her, and she had called herself queen.

"Yes, my dear. I am Queen Elena. I have ruled the vampires for two hundred years, and you and I have a common enemy."

"Stravinsky?" I asked. "Why would I believe that? The werewolves you sicced on us were his creation, weren't they?"

Her gaze held mine. "We held similar goals once," she said, her voice soft and alluring. I could feel myself wanting to please her.

"Don't look her in the eye, Rachel," Antonio shouted.

I cast my eyes down, feeling like an idiot. That was Vampire 101. "Can you save her?"

She laughed. "There is protocol to follow here. I am royalty."

"Fuck your protocol. Can you save her?"

"Yes," she said in a satisfied tone. "I can save her."

I shook my head. "What is the price?" I cast a glance at her, then quickly looked away. "Because I know how the world works, and there's always a price."

She moved next to me, trailing the backs of her fingertips down my cheek and my neck, sending a shiver all the way to the base of my spine.

The little girl started to cry.

"You will not feed from her!" Antonio shouted. A scuffle broke out, and it sounded like Ivan was holding him back.

Elena looked amused. "I will do as I please," she said. "But she will give me her permission."

"Will you kill me?" I asked, trying not to show my fear. "Or turn me?" I'd drank from Lea recently, which made me wonder if it was a possibility.

She leaned in to sniff my skin, running her nose up my neck until it reached my ear. "No," she whispered. "I will let Lea have that honor."

"And if she's dead?" I whispered back.

"We shall see if she dies."

"So you'll save her if I let you take my blood? How do I know you even can?"

She glided over to Ivan and looked up into his face, trailing her hand down his chest. He looked to the side, evading her gaze. "You know I can save her, don't you, dog?"

"Yes."

I gasped in surprise. I figured she had been playing mind games.

She gave Ivan's chest one last stroke, then turned her attention back to me. "I know you distrust me, so as a sign of good faith, I will give her my blood first. I will drink from you when she begins to revive. You will let me." She flicked her finger toward Antonio. "And he will watch."

"The hell I will," he growled.

I steeled my back. "Then do it. Save her."

"What else do you want?" Ivan asked. "There has to be more. You could force yourself on her and let Lea die."

"Aren't you a cunning wolf?" She moved in front of me. "There is one little thing, an errand of sorts."

"What kind of errand?"

"I need you to retrieve the Book of Life."

"Excuse me?"

Antonio swore in Spanish and Elena smiled. "Yes, you are correct. She is the one."

"What are you talking about?" I asked, certain this had to do with Antonio and Lea's earlier conversation about me.

"You, my dear, are the one who's fated to find the Book of Life. Once you promise to retrieve it and deliver it to me, I will heal Lea, then you and I will drink from one another to seal the covenant."

"I'm not drinking from you."

"Then Lea dies."

"Don't do it, Rachel!" Antonio shouted. "You're selling your soul!"

"Lies," Elena sneered. "Ask the dog."

I looked at Ivan. He cast a glance at Lea, then back up at me, pleading.

"Ivan. Will she own my soul?"

He shook his head. "No. But she will own you until you complete her task."

"How hard will it be to find this book?"

"People have searched for centuries and never found it."

"A piece of cake," I said, looking down at Lea. *Shit.*

"She wouldn't want you to do it, Rachel," Antonio pleaded. "She would never ask this of you."

I lifted my gaze to meet Ivan's. His shoulders were tense and his voice shook as he said, "He's right. She would never ask this of you."

No, she would never ask, because that wasn't her style. She didn't ask for help. She was so freaking sure she could do everything on her own. That she didn't need anyone or anything. Calvin had broken her, but she had begun to revive, like a Phoenix in the ashes.

And I couldn't wait to see the look on her face when she found out she needed someone after all.

"Do you have any clues at all about where to find this book?"

"Yes," Elena said, "contrary to the wolf's dire prediction, we have excellent clues."

"So why not retrieve it yourself?"

"It needs to be a human. A special human like you."

"Why?"

"Legend says it can only be retrieved during the brightest part of the day."

"Can't a minion do it?"

She gave a slow shrug. "I have my reasons for asking you." She cocked her head to the side, looking lost in thought. "Your window to save her is quickly closing. I need your answer now."

"Yes," I said without hesitation.

Her smile spread wide. "Excellent."

"Rachel! No!" Antonio shouted.

But Elena had already dropped down next to Lea, quicker than I could see with my naked eye, and was holding her wrist over my friend's parted mouth. A thin ribbon of blood flowed down, rolling over Lea's lower lip and filling her mouth. Lea's body jerked, then twitched as Elena stood and gave me a smile that made my heart stutter.

"Sangre de la bruja, you are mine."

CHAPTER 39

LEA

Elena's words echoed in my head, and her blood sang in my veins as I came around, vaguely aware that Elena and Rachel were exchanging blood.

Sangre de la Bruja.

Blood of the Witch.

I jerked to my feet, my limbs as sloppy and uncoordinated as if they'd been dislocated repeatedly. Elena laughed softly as she delicately wiped the corners of her mouth.

"Oh, how I wish I'd met you years ago, when Peter first

turned you from the light. You could be queen one day, Lea. You have the strength for it."

"Fuck you." I spat the words at her, along with what was left of her blood in my mouth. Her eyes tightened at the edges as the vampires behind her shifted back a few steps. She raised a hand.

"I would no sooner break a prized broodmare than destroy her now. There is too much left for her to accomplish before she bows before me. But to be sure—" She bent and scooped up the girl hiding behind Rachel's legs.

"No!" Rachel lifted her gun and pulled the trigger in a single motion. One of the other vamps shot forward and took the bullet for his queen, right in the head.

Rachel's thoughts mirrored mine. *No fucking way.*

The little girl wrapped her arms around Elena's neck as the vampire queen cooed softly to her. "She will not be harmed. But if you don't come to me soon enough, she will make a lovely meal for Timothy." She paused in stroking the girl's hair, her eyes locking with mine. "Timothy created Caine. They have...similar tastes."

I took a wobbling step forward. Caine. The monster I'd killed in New York who liked his victims young and terrified. *Madre de Dios*, I could not let this happen.

"We'll do it. We'll get her back," Rachel said, iron in her voice. Iron enough for the both of us.

I glanced at my friend, and the knowledge of what she'd done washed over.

Her life for mine. Rachel gave me a nod. "We have a trip to make. You up for it?" But I could feel the questions swirling in her head.

I turned back to where Elena and the others had stood only a moment before, but they were gone. Of course they were. They had only lingered long enough to stir shit up.

The village was silent as the sun peeked over the horizon. Gingerly, I made my way to where Elena had stood. In her place was a small leather-bound book, a thin piece of leather wrapped around it several times and knotted on the front.

"Why did she leave a book if she wants a book?" Rachel asked in frustration.

"I suspect it's a rumored mythical guidebook. There were whispers the vampires once had a book with clues to find the Book of Life."

"It's true," Antonio agreed, not sounding happy about it. "I'd heard that Elena's people found it in the ruins of an ancient Greek temple."

I nodded. I'd heard them as well but dismissed them as nonsense.

The knot...I slid my hand over it, feeling the perfectly round tangle of leather against my palm. "It's called a death knot."

"Not real subtle, is she?" Rachel asked as I held out the book to her. "Why don't you open it?"

"The guidebook can only be opened by one family line." I frowned. "A family of witches so powerful, they were hunted to extinction during the Salem witch trials. At least, that is how the story goes. The book will only open for one of its own."

"What do you mean, one of its own?" Rachel didn't touch the book.

"The leather is made of human skin. The last witch who was taken allowed them to do so only after she'd had her daughter skin her back."

Rachel recoiled from it. "If they were so powerful, how did they get captured?"

I looked at Antonio and Rachel followed my gaze. "You Cazadors are real assholes sometimes, aren't you?"

I couldn't help but smile. "Antonio and I, we are the

nice ones. We only hunt the bloodsuckers. There were other Cazadors, though they did not call themselves that."

From the way he grunted, I could tell he was fighting a laugh. I knew what it would do to him to laugh with me and realize we weren't all that different. I'd been like him once.

"So what's this Book of Life? Why does Elena want it so badly?"

Antonio glanced to me, then to Rachel. "It's believed to contain the history of the origins of the species...but not only that." He paused. "It supposedly breaks it down enough that the owner of the book could create his or her own supernatural species."

"Like Stravinsky."

"Exactly," I said. "Only no mutants. Pure supernaturals. Elena probably wants it to fight for control."

Ivan moved to my side and slipped an arm around my lower back. I leaned on him, letting him take much of my weight. "It's a long story, Rachel. And we have a long trip ahead of us. And you may not like the story once it comes to light. Sangre de la Bruja is not for the faint of heart. Even more so when you realize that it is your bloodline, my friend."

"You don't know that." Her eyes flashed. I tossed her the book, and when she caught it out of reflex the knot untangled in front of us, slithering apart like a serpent.

"I do know," I said. It made all too much sense, and the coincidences that had brought Rachel and me together no longer seemed so coincidental. Fate had a funny way of making things happen.

Ivan and I moved away from the silent village toward where the Humvee sat waiting. I slid into the front seat, Ivan into the driver's seat. Rachel squished in next to me,

Antonio flanking her. The sun wasn't bothering me for the moment, and I knew why.

Elena's blood coursed through my veins; she was far older than me, which meant she'd given me a powerful tool to help Rachel succeed in her quest. I would be able to withstand sunlight in limited exposures.

The satellite phone in the Humvee rang as we settled in, and we stared at it as if it were a bomb.

"Oh for fuck's sake, it's just a phone." Rachel grabbed it and put it to her ear. The voice on the other side was all too clear, and his words were the bomb we'd feared.

"Ah, Rachel, lovely to see you've survived."

Hades. I knew it from her thoughts.

"Not like you were much help."

"I did my best. I even sent you a lovely gift made of silver. Did you get it?"

She tightened her grip on the phone, and I held my hand out. "Let me."

"Good luck, he's a slippery fucker."

He tsked on the other side of the line. I pressed the phone to my ear. "Hades."

"And who is this? Wait, let me guess...Lea, perhaps? The vampire gone rogue, killing her own kind in the hopes of redeeming an unredeemable soul?" He laughed, but it didn't bother me.

"And you would be Hades, the scientist Stravinsky wouldn't turn into a vampire?" It was a guess.

He sucked in a sharp breath. "Bitch."

I smiled. "Every day. What do you want?"

"You need help. And for a price, I can give it."

I motioned for Ivan to start the truck up and move forward. "I don't think we need your help."

"No? What about Stravinsky?"

I yawned into the phone, making sure that he heard it. "He and I came to an agreement."

"What?" He stuttered the one word.

"Yes, not that it's any of your business. But I do have something in mind for you, if you're willing to meet with me and Rachel."

Rachel tipped her head and I tried to convey the message of what I had in mind. Hades was a loose end—a man who would go to whomever he thought would help him acquire his goals. And like Victor, his goal was simple. Immortality.

"I assume you're close?" I yawned again.

"Very."

"The village?" I motioned for Ivan to slow the truck.

Hades was silent. "What are you offering?"

"Exactly what you want," I purred.

"The next village over." He gave us coordinates and I hung up the phone.

"What are we doing?" Rachel leaned forward and planted her hands on the dash. "The fucker led us on. He gave me just enough info to get me in and killed, and not much else. I'm pretty sure he doesn't have anything on Stravinsky now that the facility is gone."

"She's going to kill him, aren't you?" Antonio settled deeper into seat.

Rachel shook her head. "No, she's not."

I couldn't help but grin. There was a benefit to having Rachel in my head. No more back and forth about truth and lies. She grunted but didn't disagree.

"I intend to make him forget everything. To send him on a new path so we don't have to deal with him again. My guess is he was using us to show Stravinsky that he could hurt him in a bid to force the vampire's hand. It didn't work, and now he wants what I can give him," I said. "Loose ends kill people. I won't have Hades getting in our way or worse, siding with Stravinsky again."

It took us an hour to get there, and the sun was bright enough that I wanted nothing more than to curl up in the back of the truck. But we had to deal with Hades first.

The village was empty of people and several of the homes smoldered with a thick black smoke. Nothing moved—there weren't even any stray chickens pecking at the dirt.

"This isn't Stravinsky's doing, is it?" Ivan asked.

"No, this is the war," Rachel said, her voice soft. Ivan parked the truck and we climbed out. I let Ivan lead, Rachel and I followed—side by side—and Antonio brought up the rear.

Ivan didn't knock on the door, just shoved it open and grabbed Hades while the scientist screeched at the top of his lungs. Two werewolves leapt from the shadows of the room.

Ivan took one.

Rachel and I took the other. The fight was intense, brief, and over before it had really begun.

I gave Ivan a nod of thanks as he threw the two bodies outside. "I wasn't going to kill you, Hades." I stepped toward him. "But I think I've changed my mind."

I grabbed him and bit into his neck, draining him down. With it I saw his memories and thoughts. How the blood cells in the suicide pill had been derived from what Stravinsky had mistakenly believed was the last witch, and how Hades had discovered that Rachel was connected to the Sangre de la Bruja.

But mostly how he'd planned to use that information to capture Rachel and me. He'd planned to use me as a blood donor to change him, and Rachel as leverage…and a whore in a much more literal sense. I shivered and spat him out. "Fuck, that was nasty."

I grabbed his head and twisted it sharply to one side. The dirty thoughts he'd had about Rachel were enough to make me not want another single thought from him.

To my surprise, it was Antonio who asked the question. "What did you see?"

"You don't want to know." Rachel went green and I nodded.

Antonio shook his head. "This mind reading shit between you two is getting old, fast."

"Get over it," Rachel snapped.

As if that was going to calm him down.

I deliberately sent Rachel a thought. According to Hades's memories, the witch blood—broken down into its base elements—was what had powered the other compounds in the suicide pill. Without it, the pill wouldn't have done anything to a vampire. Magic had been the key factor in making it work.

Rachel nodded. "So that means Stravinsky has a witch working for him?"

I squinted one eye. "Or captive."

Antonio's jaw ticked. "Are you going to fill us in?"

"In the truck. Elena won't wait forever and that child's life is in the balance as well as our own," I said.

We piled back into the Humvee. Rachel snorted. "I feel like a teenager again, taking my dad's truck and cramming all my friends into it for a joyride."

Ivan glanced at her. "So…we're all friends now?"

She shrugged. "Yeah, sure. Whatever. Wolf."

He grinned at her. "Witch."

Antonio shrugged and mock-glared at me. "Vamp."

I snorted. "Wannabe."

He burst out laughing, as did Rachel and Ivan. The released tension felt good, and it was needed. Because I was about to tell them the story I knew of Sangre de la Bruja, which would add a whole new level of pressure to our group.

For good or for ill, we were tied together.

I only hoped all four of us would make it through alive.

AUTHORS NOTE

Thanks for reading "Replica". We truly hope you enjoyed the continuation of The Blood Borne Series. If you loved this book, one of the best things you can do is leave a review for it. Amazon and iBooks is where we sell the majority of our work, but feel free to spread the word on all retailers.

For more information on Shannon Mayer and purchase links to her other novels, please visit her website at www.shannonmayer.com.

For more information on Denise Grover Swank and purchase links to her other novels, please visit her website at www.denisegroverswank.com.

Enjoy!